LOUDER THAN SILENCE

A novel

By Peter Beere

Let me whisper in your ear. Don't you worry they can't hear.

You and Your Sister: This Mortal Coil

PART ONE

CHAPTER ONE

(i)

It began in June, on a Tuesday, at 2.45 in the afternoon. Jackie had just left *The Golden Lion* pub at the bottom of Queensbridge High Street. It wouldn't be fair to say he was drunk, but he wasn't quite sober either. He was at a level he would classify as normal.

The black SUV that hit him came from his left at reasonable speed, although it was slowing down in an attempt to avoid running into him. It singularly failed in that regard. The offside headlamp housing of the vehicle caught him just below his left hip. The impact fractured his femur in three places and partially wrenched his hip out of its socket.

Jackie was unaware of this. He was conscious that his legs were crumpling beneath him and that he was no longer moving forward. But he was inside a moment of startled confusion, where time itself appeared to be stunned.

That's all it was, a single moment. By the time the moment had completed its course he had been entirely upended and his upper body was slamming into the frame of the SUV's windscreen. This strut of metal succeeded in severely damaging Jackie's upper arm and fracturing three of his ribs. He slid from the bonnet, over the wing of the car, with a movement both clumsy and balletic.

For a surprisingly long time he was unaware of any pain, and when it began it arrived in escalating stages, as if exploring a possible route.

The occupant of the car exited it in a distraught state. Emily Marchant was 34, with a son who was good on the cello and a husband who wasn't, and she was completely unaccustomed to such drama.

She began to wail. She wailed at such a high pitch that no sound actually emerged from her mouth, though it was clear that she was trying to produce something. She dithered, in the way that confused people will, not knowing whether to advance or retreat, to stay still or disappear. She hoped that it all had not happened.

As did Jackie, who was now beginning to experience a considerable part of the pain that had been unleashed in his body. When Jackie began to wail, it was very audible. People a hundred metres away turned to see the cause of commotion. And, such being the attractive power of commotion, several began to approach.

Jackie's wail continued unabated for some time, doing nothing to assuage Emily's own silent anguish.

She began to turn from side to side, like the start of a strange and sinuous dance. Her fists were clenched, her sinews were tight, and her lightly tanned forearms were turned to the sky, which at that time of day was mostly blue with streaks of varying white.

After a time – it may have been forty seconds – Emily could sustain her choke-held silence no longer, and as her gaze finally settled upon Jackie her mouth emitted a tremulous cry.

'I'm so sorry,' she cried, as she crouched at his side. 'I'm so sorry, so sorry, so sorry.' Jackie paused for a moment to point at the pedestrian crossing he was on. Then he returned to his howling.

Eight people had phoned for an ambulance and with remarkable efficiency one appeared within three minutes. Which surprised everyone in the expanding throng.

Because of the way he had landed – against the front wheel of the car with his right leg vertical, resting against the wing – the paramedics had to request Emily to back her car up a little while they supported Jackie's leg.

It required several attempts for her to get the car started, and then she almost reversed over a Shih Tzu. Emily was having almost as bad a day as Jackie. When a paramedic tried examining Jackie's leg and he screamed like a banshee, Emily vomited up half a Bounty bar and fainted. Which caused a further distraction.

(ii)

'Okay Jackie, we're going to roll you onto your left side while we slide a board underneath you. I'm going to hold your head steady and before we roll you back I'm going to fit you with a collar and head support. Okay? Do you understand? I don't want you to move. I don't want you to do anything. Just let us do the work.'

'Okay. Wait!'

'What?'

'My left side's the injured one.'

'Yes. We need to preserve its integrity. We don't want you flopping about.'

'Right. Wait!' Jackie's dark eyes darted about, but whatever he was looking for he couldn't find. He was stuck, and that was the truth of it. 'Is it going to hurt?'

'It probably will. But we'll try to make it brief.'

The two paramedics rolled him before he could say any more, and the suddenness of the movement and the realisation that things were not entirely right within his body rendered Jackie devoid of any speech. The best he could do was gasp and hold his breath and marvel at the pretty colours in his head, which was where the pain somehow managed to reflect itself.

'That's good, Jackie. Just stay still.'

He felt movement at his back as a plastic board was manoeuvred into place. The paramedics carefully rolled him back. This time Jackie did give vent to some of the sound that had been building in his throat, and he yelled obscenities at the paramedics. To an extent that brought tears to his eyes.

'You're doing fine, Jackie, just lay still. We're getting ready to move you to the ambulance. Can you hear me all right? Do you understand what I'm saying?'

'I'm not deaf, you stupid bastard.'

'That's fine; I've been called a lot worse. Here we go – '

The spinal board was lifted onto a trolley, and straps were fastened around Jackie's upper chest, abdomen and lower legs.

'You're doing fine, Jackie. Nearly there.'

As he was wheeled towards the ambulance Jackie wondered whether he ought to wave to the crowd. But the thought was lost in the haste of the movement.

(iii)

In some ways the ambulance was worse than the street: the ambulance looked like it meant business. It was formidably equipped with a sense of purpose and arresting resources; sufficient to make an average man quake. Jackie would have preferred pastel drapes and muted uplighting. He cared little for the trappings around him.

His trousers and tee-shirt had been cut open. The younger of the paramedics had fitted a cannula into Jackie's right arm and was connecting a bag of Hartmann's solution, a fluid replacement. The older man was examining Jackie's leg.

It was plain it had been fractured but the paramedic didn't know how badly, nothing had penetrated the skin. But there was a great deal of internal bleeding. The thigh was purple and had ballooned to bizarre proportions. The purple stain was heading upwards, past the left hip which had clearly been dislocated. The paramedic couldn't see anything obvious showing on the chest, but assumed there was a good chance that ribs had been broken.

'We're going to have to put support around this leg, Jackie. We need to keep you immobile. Movement's your biggest enemy at the moment.'

The younger man rhythmically squeezed the Hartmann's bag, getting the fluid more quickly into Jackie's system to replace the leaking blood.

'This part's likely to hurt a bit, Jackie. But we need to do it.' The paramedic had a leg splint roughly in position. His colleague was going to help him fit it. Jackie screamed as they lifted his damaged leg slightly. 'It's all right, Jackie. We're nearly there.'

The younger paramedic produced a black laptop and began asking questions. He asked Jackie's age. 54. He asked about his next of kin. He said he had none. He asked if there was a friend they could contact. He said there were none. He asked if Jackie had an employer. No. He asked if he had a permanent address. Of course he did; he wasn't a vagrant. He was asked if he'd been drinking. No more than usual. How much was that? A bit. Jackie was asked if there was anything he was allergic to – anything he might react to. Running out of booze, thought Jackie.

By this time the older man had moved to the driving seat and the ambulance was heading for the trauma centre.

'We'll soon be there, Jackie. Stay awake.'

(iv)

At the trauma centre a team had already assembled and was waiting for him; as if they were throwing him a surprise birthday party.

The two paramedics wheeled Jackie straight into a resus room. They helped lift him and the spinal board onto a hospital trolley. They chatted for a few minutes with two nurses and a doctor before departing in moderately good spirits. Leaving Jackie on his back in terrible pain, and with an increasing amount of panic, staring fixedly at the lights on the ceiling. Even as, all around him, considerable activity was taking place, with the express purpose of making his life better.

There were doctors and junior doctors. Nurses and junior nurses. There was a tall thin anaesthetist with a lot of freckles and round glasses. Two radiographers were hovering in the wings with their hands on a portable x-ray machine. There was even a member of the hospital management team.

The manager was the most well groomed person in the room, and wore a look that suggested he knew what was happening. But only because he'd perfected it.

'You're in the way, Mister Harrison.'

'Sorry.'

There was an element of 'nobody knows what they're doing here' about the scene. Until one of the junior doctors took control and started issuing instructions. 'Put another Venflon in his other arm. Get another drip going. Get his clothes off. Do his blood. Look at the poor sod – he's going into shock. Somebody go and talk to him. Check his airway. You – do his BP and keep on monitoring. Where's the x-ray? Get that in. We need a full set from neck to knee. Somebody check there's a theatre free.'

A lot of blood was being lost inside Jackie's leg. This was a major concern. As was the state of his spine. Much had to be delayed for the spinal assessment. The radiographers glided to centre stage.

Yet again Jackie was rolled onto his side while x-ray plates were slid underneath him.

Everybody left the room. What looked like the face of a damaged flamingo was looming over him. Apparently this produced x-rays. Someone was still talking to him though he couldn't really hear the words. But he felt an affinity with the flamingo.

The device was moved and repeated. Moved and repeated.

Everyone seemed fairly happy with the result and to celebrate they rolled Jackie onto his side again. It was becoming an uncomfortable occurrence.

The x-ray team hurried off with their plates, and when he was rolled back onto his back – the irony of which struck him – Jackie vomited a little through the back of his throat. This caused a level of consternation and the liquid had to be siphoned out of his mouth.

The tall thin anaesthetist with the abundance of freckles and the round glasses hove into view, adjusting his glasses. He approached Jackie with a reassuring smile which was at least as much genuine as it was professional.

'Hello, Mister Conor. I'm Doctor Connaught. I'm going to administer you a painkiller which should help relieve a lot of your pain and discomfort.'

'I need a lot.'

'I shall give you as much as I reasonably can.'

(v)

He hadn't always been an accident victim.

Jackie had a fairly standard upbringing. Went through school, where he didn't excel at failure, success, or mediocrity. Simply it was a period of his life that he had to pass through, and was relieved when it came to an end. Not because he was bullied, shamed, or anything else, rather that he was mainly bored. He looked at a place beyond the brick walls, and hoped that when he got there things would be better. (Whether they were or not is still open for debate. He believes he hasn't got there yet.)

Eventually Jackie left school, got a job, got a girl, changed his job, changed his girl, lost his job, got another girl, got another job. By this time he was 21. He got another job.

For Jackie, getting a girl was the easy part; he took that for granted. It was getting a job that was difficult. By which is meant, getting a job that he found of any interest. Such work appeared to be thin on the ground.

So Jackie fell back on an old recourse; he started telling stories in his head. Stories about everything and everyone around him. Stories to reshape the world. Jotting them down. Little snatches of poetry on tiny scraps of paper. Fragments of what he called 'thoughts'.

Eventually, whilst working at a carpet warehouse (a job physically beyond him, but they liked his face) Jackie realised that he should be a writer. A proper honest-to-goodness professional writer, who would produce novels to transform the world. 'Good luck with that,' some people would have said. But Jackie was blessed with naivety.

So he began writing, because that was all there was to do. With a pile of paper, six pencils, and a portable Olivetti.

Amongst it all he found a girl. A girl who stayed around longer than most. A girl whom he eventually married.

The girl was called Laura.

And Jackie kept writing.

(vi)

'Mister Conor. We need you to wake up now. We're about to move you.'

'Move me where? Am I dead?'

'Not yet. You are being taken for a CT scan. The x-rays showed that you have three fractures of your left femur, and your hip is partially dislocated. We need to have a clearer picture before we go any further. Jenny and Safira here are going to take you. I'll be along shortly to look at the images. I'm Mister Culthorpe. I'm the consultant surgeon. How are you feeling?'

'Pretty grim.'

'In an odd way that's a good sign.'

Jackie was wheeled away. He hadn't been told yet that there were three fractured ribs in his chest. But there wasn't much that could be done about them; they would have to heal themselves.

The trolley clattered and rattled under bright overhead lighting.

The journey didn't take long.

Forty-five minutes had elapsed since he entered the hospital.

(vii)

Laura. She wasn't a muse but she did encourage him. 'You write your book, and I'll pay the bills.'

Laura was an accountant, and knew the importance of paying bills on time, but at the last minute. She also cooked, and introduced Jackie to foods he'd not tasted before. Such as lasagne. ('Not everything needs to have potatoes.') At the time of their marriage she was twenty-six years old; two years older than Jackie. Their courtship had lasted for seventeen months, with nothing particularly noteworthy to emblazon it.

Laura was tall, at almost two metres, but walked with an uncontrived gait. Her eyes were hazel, she bore a modicum of freckles, and her hair was brown; of a shade that some products refer to as 'medium'. The hair was styled, initially, into a thin fringe with chopped sides. It altered considerably over the years, in both structure and content.

That was how it went for several years. Jackie wrote, and Laura paid the bills.

Along the way Laura became pregnant and Jackie was blessed with a son, who they named Luke.

Luke, taking after his mother, was also tall, and because of his lankiness excelled at several sports. Though that was of little use to him as he had no interest in sport, other than supporting a major football team. The team he supported varied according to its level of success and the attractiveness of its kit.

Academically he was of moderate achievement.

Jackie remembered that, at one point, he had sat down with his son and asked him what he wanted to do with his life – what he would like to come out of it. Luke had responded that he wanted to 'Fuck off and never come back again.' And Jackie had nodded in agreement.

Jackie's parenting skills were of average.

(viii)

A bizarre and unsettling procedure took place as Jackie lay still on his trolley.

The head collar had been removed. A thin lilac gown had been draped loosely across him in a belated contribution to modesty. And he was being prepared for theatre.

As part of the preparation the surgical staff wanted to straighten out his leg as much as possible. This was achieved by the simple expedient of strapping a line to the bottom of his leg, passing it over a pulley at the foot of the trolley, and attaching a weight to the end of it. This caused things to happen. Mostly it caused Jackie to try to sit upright, in an instinctive reaction to the arrival of pressure. Although there was no direct physical pain, the sensation of movement beneath his skin was both obvious and deeply disturbing. If the room had been silent he might possibly have heard the scraping of bone upon bone.

A nurse was prepared for this reaction. The nurse, who was called Joseph and from Guatemala, pressed his hands to Jackie's abdomen and chest. 'It's all right, Mister Conor. Everything is fine. All is exactly as should be.'

Jackie gripped Joseph's left hand in a desperate plea for comfort, and to give himself something to hold to.

Someone else appeared with a stool which she positioned at the head of the trolley. 'I'm Caroline Steadworth. I'm a doctor on Mister Culthorpe's team. I'm going to run through a few things with you.'

Caroline Steadworth was a tall South African with stunning blonde looks and hair that probably cost more to prepare than Jackie spent on his booze in a month. She looked like she could swim the Atlantic Ocean and paddle her way back on a lilo.

'I don't know how much has been explained to you yet, but you have several fractures in your chest and your femur – which is the bone running through your thigh. We can't do much about your ribs, but because you are losing a great deal of blood we need to operate on your leg immediately.'

Jackie nodded, although he wasn't entirely focused on the conversation, and his attention was flicking between his new friend Joseph and the somewhat Amazonian transatlantic swimmer. Neither of whom were, at that moment, relieving his discomfort to any noticeable degree.

'What this entails is cutting through the upper part of your femur, and inserting an intra-medullary fixing – basically a long nail made from titanium – which will then be screwed into position. We will also put your dislocated hip back into place.'

Even through his anguish, certain aspects of this description sprang to Jackie's attention.

'Where are you putting this?'

'The nail? It will run down the centre of your femur.'

'And how will you get it there?'

'We'll tap it.'

It all sounded perfectly reasonable.

It was, in truth, a brutal procedure. Anyone who remained awake throughout the operation would sue the hospital for gross inhumanity. The femur would be cut through with a stainless steel saw. The titanium rod would be bashed in with a hammer. The hip joint would be forced in by the strongest person in the room. It was not a procedure to stay awake for.

'I'll just run through some of the possible outcomes, then I'll need you to sign a consent form.'

(ix)

Darkness comes rapidly with a general anaesthetic; so rapidly one can fail to appreciate it. Jackie would have welcomed the onset of oblivion with open arms, and prepared for its arrival with a smile. But there was no time for that. No sooner had Doctor Connaught, the anaesthetist, explained what he was about to do than Jackie was already gone. Darkness. Maybe beyond death. Darkness without any dreams. How long it lasted, Jackie had no idea (it was four and a half hours).

Then somebody beckoned him from it.

On that day, and for days evermore, Jackie had a vision of angels. Two of them, perfect, standing side by side. Leaning slightly towards each other as if unable to resist the attraction of their own radiance. They were dressed all in white, and bathed in a pool of ethereal light. They murmured such gentle things to him.

'Can you hear me, Jackie? How do you feel? We're just going to prop you up a bit higher – I need to get these tubes sorted out. I'm just going to lift your arm – '

And so they did. They sorted out tubes. Then blessedly, mercifully, they sent him back to sleep. Jackie had already decided, without any prompting, that sleep was the best place to be.

(x)

Laura was not the best wife in the world, but in no way could she be considered amongst the worst. Their relationship, basically, fell into the mid-zone; where there is sufficient love to bind two people together, whilst barely enough to keep them from drifting apart.

Looking back, Jackie blamed himself for many of the failings, most of which were minor and common to the situation. For a perfect marriage would surely result in annihilation: it would be a question of which perfect partner blew their brains out first.

For Jackie, too, there was a propensity for blaming himself. (This, he believed, stemmed from his relationship with his parents. But he never roused himself enough to probe that too deeply.)

Laying blame on himself was an easy option. And Jackie indulged it a lot. However, whilst he was doing this Jackie continued writing. And at some point, somewhere along the way, Jackie succeeded in his aim. Jackie wrote a book, of some fashion.

Amongst his list of life's failures that ranked high amongst them. But at least Jackie gave it a shot.

His first novel concerned three couples in a winter chalet, cut off by snow, with their supplies and relationships gradually dwindling. He liked to think of it as an adult 'Lord of the Flies' with added snow. But nobody else did.

The second was a fantasy concerning a god whose power emanated from five precious gems which where pillaged and scattered across the known world. It was the job of one man to retrieve the gems. But by the end no one cared if he did.

With his third novel Jackie sought to emulate Dostoyevsky, and wrote a tome of such weight and grandeur that his desk threatened to collapse underneath it. As did the spirits of all who attempted to read it. Including those of Jackie himself.

With his fourth book he got lucky. Strangely, it was a book about a duck. A rare and special breed of duck which belonged to someone who – blah blah blah. His original title was 'The Duck Got Fucked'. But the publishers changed it to 'Avilon', which they assured him was the mythical home of all ducks: it is the place they go to when they die. Jackie thought it was rubbish, but went along with it. As things turned out he was right, it was rubbish. But by then it was too late, the die had been cast. He was doomed to be semi-successful.

Whether this contributed to the eventual divergence of Jackie's marital path was a matter never brought up by either party. There were, obviously, other factors which, should he ever become self-absorbed enough, he might be inclined to consider.

It wouldn't be happening at this time as he was struggling with anaesthetic.

(xi)

'Jackie – '

'What?'

'We need you to sit up a little. You have to get something to eat.'

'Sausages.'

'No, it isn't sausages.'

'That's good. I hate fucking sausages.'

Two nurses helped raise his upper body and adjusted the frame of the bed and his pillows until he was more or less physically wedged in a position from which it was feasibly possible that he might be able to eat. Although Jackie wasn't so sure.

'Look – can you put your hands up here for me, Jackie? We've got the cutlery and – you just need a spoon. Pick up the spoon with this hand. Try to eat a little, and then we'll try to sort you out and get you into a better position.'

They tried to sort him out while he was trying to eat. He didn't even know what he was eating.

'What is this?'

'Mashed potato.'

'Has someone been sick on it?'

'I think that's mince.'

'I want to go back to sleep.'

But they wouldn't let him go back to sleep until they'd done painful things to him.

This wasn't the angelic performance of before.

These were the hard core nurses.

Jackie entered a whole new area of Hell, where the pain of before became the pain of the present, and the difference appeared minimal at best. Pain that had been 'general' became much more focused. There was a precision to its angles of attack.

He quickly came to realise that the more he battled against the pain, and the better he coped with it, the more people around began to bully him. They forced him to do things he didn't want to do. Things like sitting up. Coughing. Moving. Waking, when he wanted to be asleep.

He discovered that terrible things had been done to him. Such as the insertion of a tube which passed through his penis into his bladder, and allowed his urine to drain directly into a plastic pouch.

Jackie had never contemplated things like this. They were not a part of his life plan.

He had two Venflon cannulas, one in each wrist, and through these were administered Hartmann's solution, to replace lost fluids; antibiotics, to fight potential infections; and industrial grade painkillers to help with his pain.

One of the additions which Jackie thought was a good idea was self-administered morphine which could be delivered through the click of a button which he himself controlled.

It came as a bitter blow to him when he discovered that the morphine flow was rigidly restricted and that, after a time, it didn't matter how much frantic clicking he did the morphine monkey had gone back to its tree and wouldn't appear again for a while. He could receive additional painkillers in the form of paracetamol, codeine or tramadol; but they were never as exciting as the morphine.

At no point did anyone offer him a drink. Which he considered to be something of a failure.

The hospital staff followed their machiavellian path and cajoled, encouraged, bullied and persuaded Jackie to engage as much as he could with the world.

They made him aware of what had happened to him in the theatre – the parting of layers of muscle, the cutting through of the femur, the insertion of the nail, the insertion of ten titanium screws, the careful stitching together of the replaced layers of muscle with absorbable sutures, and the stapling of the original incision which ran the entire length of Jackie's left thigh, and involved the implanting of fifty-six metal staples, which gave the appearance of a raggedy zipper, spaced, as they were, quite apart.

The colours in Jackie's leg were obscene, ranging from gentle shades of ochre to blazing fireballs of crimson, with several areas of deep brown and purple.

Everything about the leg looked bad. So they didn't show it to him. His leg was kept undercover. There was a metal frame protecting it from the weight of bedding, and accidental damage. The weighted traction was still in place. From most perspectives it was still a leg.

(xii)

After three days the drips were removed, but the antibiotics continued for a week. The painkillers were fairly constant. Jackie discovered that the more he protested the more painkillers he could receive. The morphine was administered for two weeks. It was a shame when it stopped.

In the interim, though, other things were taking place. Keeping him awake, alert and mobile. Ensuring that he ate and making sure he excreted – which was a procedure he preferred not to dwell on.

All the time the pain kept grumbling and rumbling; never leaving, just shifting position. Sometimes burning, sometimes pulsing. Sometimes with stabbings like needles.

Once he was asked how much his leg hurt, on a scale of one to ten. Jackie replied that it was fifteen.

Healing can be as painful as the cure.

But it was all as nothing – it was mere baby steps – until the sixth day of recovery. Then Jackie was introduced to the greatest monster of them all. Jackie encountered physiotherapy.

It came unexpectedly. It came in disguise. It came in the guise of a beautiful woman.

Later he reconsidered and decided that the woman – who was thirty-four and had been named, by her parents, Jessica Roeburn – was not exactly beautiful, but she was certainly attractive. And that was what lured him in. As, no doubt, many others had been lured in before.

As far as Jackie could discern, the primary purpose of a physiotherapist is to locate the area of a body where pain is most severe, then make that area hurt even more. If Jackie gasped or grunted with any level of pain, the physiotherapist seemed pleased with her work.

Jessica came to him regularly to perform her brutal duties, and Jackie dreaded her arrival as a rabbit fears a snake. Yet he envied her capacity for cruelty.

Jessica Roeburn had once dreamed of becoming a ballerina. It was a vocation befitting of her station, and her parents had actively encouraged her in it. Alas it became clear, from a very early age, that her body had other ideas. Her thighs were better suited to crushing the ribcages of horses than performing delicate plies at the bar. So she turned to horses, possibly much to the horses' regret, and proved herself an adequate horsewoman. The attributes of her thighs, and the control she could exert over horses, would later become useful in her chosen career. A dominant woman, forcing men to do things, will probably always have an advantage. A physiotherapist pulls all the strings.

'This is a long term process, Jackie. You're not going to heal yourself rapidly, and it's very important, even though you hurt, to keep the rest of your body mobile and strong. Even in the wheelchair you have to keep exercising. There's a lot of your body you can still use.'

Jackie would grimace when she said such things. He would curse her a thousand times beneath his breath.

'Come on, Jackie – just one more. Just five more. See if you can do another five.'

Fuck off, he thought. Fuck off and leave me. Even as he attempted to lift a moderate weight; a weight which he considered too much.

In the physiotherapy gym, a utilitarian torture chamber for the modern age, Jessica attempted to shame him by directing him to other patients whose levels of damage far exceeded Jackie's own.

'John's really trying, Jackie. Have a go for me.'

It's not my fault he's lost his fucking legs. Stop trying to feed me with guilt. This thought as he manfully strove to complete press-ups in his wheelchair; dreading the day she made him move on to star jumps.

(xiv)

Back on the ward, Jackie was neither a popular nor unpopular patient. He didn't cause any problems. He took what they gave him and did what they told him. He thought that was the way to behave.

He was not so blind that he could not realise that he favoured attractive nurses best. He tracked their movements; he awaited their coming. It was always a disappointment when they altered their shifts or had some days off. Then he had to await the arrival of new nurses; many of whom may not like him.

Occasionally Jackie tried to make nurses laugh. Whether they laughed because he was humorous or because they were polite was difficult to say. Jackie thought it was probably professional, and vowed not to keep trying to be funny. But if he didn't say something he would have to say nothing. That little lone area of silence was a terrible place to be. So he kept embarrassing himself, for want of a better alternative.

One of his regular nurses was older than the others and also, by far, the most brutal.

Her name was Bernadette. She was from Ballymena (in Northern Ireland). She was a nun, and her home was a convent. Nursing was a practical vocation encouraged by her order: everybody had to do something.

Bernadette had an earnest, intense way about her, and if anyone was likely to accidentally lean upon his leg support or pat his fractured ribcage, it would be her.

On one occasion Jackie inadvertently muttered the word 'Jesus'.

Bernadette said, 'That's my husband.'

Jackie spent some time pondering whether she was the kind of wife that Jesus would want, but concluded that there was no way of deconstructing the divine mind.

He just hoped she was gentler in bed.

The other nurses didn't like Bernadette. Jackie could recognise this from their glares and glances and two-fingered gestures; but even this didn't make him warm towards her. Bernadette was destined to walk the lonely pathways of her cloisters, whilst battering startled patients with her elbows.

(xv)

One day, unexpectedly, Bernadette died. This was a shock to everyone. It seemed Bernadette had an embolism which appeared out of nowhere and ended up somewhere, and caused her to collapse in a stairwell at the end of her evening shift. Which would have been at roughly 10.00 pm.

Because of the strict and observant rules of her order, the burial would come to take place within the convent walls, and no one from outside was allowed to attend.

Bernadette came, and Bernadette went.

Little but bruised patients, bemused nurses, and a chap who worked in a sandwich shop two blocks away, ever took the time to remember her.

This event did not signal an end to Jackie's stay in the hospital; but it gave him a day to consider and reflect.

His reflections made him gloomy, but gave him no answers.

Life is a business with precious few answers.

(xvi)

'You're not progressing as well as we'd hoped for, Jackie.'

Which left him short of an answer for a time.

He had been in the hospital for twenty-four days. He had no idea how long he was supposed to be in there, nor how his progression was supposed to be progressing. Nobody, to this point, had thought to tell him.

But he recognised the importance of what was being said to him; and that he had to deliver a response.

'Are we talking about mental application here?'

'That will probably come into it.'

He was in his adapted wheelchair in the physiotherapy gymnasium, and two figures were standing in front of him. One was Jessica Roeburn, his assigned physiotherapist. The other was Jacob Rosenthal, the senior physiotherapist at the hospital.

Jacob Rosenthal was wearing a grey three-piece suit, paired with a sombre tie. Jessica Roeburn was in her customary apparel of white tunic, black trousers and non-slip shoes. Both had their arms folded across their chests. Jessica Roeburn's chest was much bigger than Jacob Rosenthal's. Indeed, Jessica's chest was substantial; Jackie had observed it before. It appeared to generate its own gravitational pull.

'You don't seem to be trying. That's the impression I get.'

Jackie pondered a while longer on Jessica's bosom.

Jacob Rosenthal's eyes narrowed behind his round spectacles.

'Are you finding the exercises difficult?'

'Not unduly. But they are devoid of any interesting content. It's hard to get animated when you're having to pull on a bungee. I do find it difficult to concentrate.'

'Would you like some music?'

'I'm not sure that would help. I think it's a problem with me.'

There was an audible sigh, which appeared out of both of them. The physiotherapists were working in harmony.

'I need a drink.'

'You don't need a drink.'

'I'm afraid I do. It's all right for you, you can have a drink any time you like. I'm stuck here with pain I've never known. And yes, there are a lot of people here a lot worse off than me, but that's the situation regardless. There's always going to be someone who's worse than me. I'm not responsible for the state of their injuries. I'm not responsible for them.'

A less than dramatic pause ensued. A pause of pondering and contemplation.

Jacob Rosenthal, the senior physiotherapist who would never achieve the title of Doctor, far less Mister, unfolded his arms and rubbed at his brow with a weary expression which suggested he had been here a thousand times before; though in reality it was much less.

He adjusted his spectacles. In the old days he would probably have lit a cigarette, but they had even taken that pleasure from him.

'Would you like to talk to someone, Jackie?'

'I'm fucking talking now. I'm sorry, I didn't mean to start swearing.'

'Jackie, I have to ask you a blunt question. Do you want to get better?'

Did he want to get better? Of course he wanted to get better; nobody wanted to be in pain.

The problem was – the problem was –

He didn't know what the problem was.

'Maybe there isn't a problem.'

Jackie was talking, sotto voce, to one of the regular night nurses with whom he had struck up a darkened hours friendship. Their friendship had developed organically through the failure of Jackie to get much sleep, largely as a result of the noises around him. Jackie had pointed out, on more than one occasion, that the world's problem with methane was not solely due to cows, it was in large part due to the men on his ward. If someone struck a match at the right moment, much of the world's methane problem could be obliterated in an instant.

Unusually for a patient/nurse relationship, they were sharing a glass of vodka. Felony Courtois, twenty-six, had brought half a bottle in one night. Jackie considered her a pretty good egg. They talked of this and that and that and this, but nothing of any great substance. He told her snippets of his life and she told him fragments of hers. Much of their talk, now that he'd been there for a while, was everyday hospital gossip: who was walking on thin ice, who was dating a doctor; who had been given their third final warning. The new IT system came in for a lot of criticism. You could die and it wouldn't even notice.

There was also the matter of the introduction, preparation, assimilation, indoctrination, continuation, dehumanisation, with the inexorable consequence of institutionalisation (of both patients and staff). Jackie had already considered writing an essay on this, with a view to becoming the new George Orwell.

They chewed the fat in the depths of the night, whilst sipping the forbidden nectar.

Later Jackie would come to view that nighttime friendship as an almost perfect relationship; platonic and interested, with no pressures or demands, and a limited future. The friendship would end as abruptly as it came. And memories were better than truth.

But one night, as she was about to leave to focus on her other duties. Slipping the vodka bottle into a pocket of her uniform. Felony turned to him with a sombre expression and said –

'Why don't you have any visitors, Jackie?'

CHAPTER TWO

What people could he contact?

Laura, his wife, who he'd hardly seen in two years. Mike, the landlord of *The Golden Lion*. Dawn, a barmaid at *The Golden Lion*. Jackie's son Luke (who hated him). Jane, a former editor who he had kept in touch with: but she lived three-hundred miles away. Molly, his agent, who he seemed to think had already passed away. Plus sundry diverse casual acquaintances who he knew rather by default: the postperson, shop assistants, a regular delivery driver, a woman who waved in the street.

Other friends, even the best amongst the best of them, had simply dropped by the wayside over the years.

Such was the way of Jackie's world.

CHAPTER THREE

'How the hell did you know I was here?'

'Is that the thanks I get?'

Mike, the landlord of *The Golden Lion* pub, pulled up a chair and sat down. A lugubrious man of ample proportions, he seemed quite at home in his surroundings.

'A nurse came in and told me,' he said. 'And I've brought you a bag of grapes.'

'You can take them away.'

'And a bottle of Scotch. It's under the grapes, wrapped up in kitchen towel. That's why it's such a big bag of grapes.'

'Thanks.'

'If I'm honest, the grapes were Dawn's idea.'

Mike leaned forward to put the grapes, and their whisky accompaniment, into Jackie's bedside cupboard. It took some time because he was a big man. He had to make the effort of consistently big men.

'How is Dawn?'

'Same as ever. Still doing her damn crosswords. She asks me the other day, 'Who was the first husband of Angelina Jolie? Three words.' I said Attila the Hun. She said it didn't fit. I wonder why I bother paying her the wages. She sends her love, by the way.'

'That's good.'

Dawn was *The Golden Lion*'s regular daytime barmaid. She was twenty-four, slightly overweight, had a fine personality and a head of bright ginger hair which made her slightly of the appearance of an angry marmoset, from the less attractive end of the spectrum. However, everybody liked her, despite her function at the pub remaining often unclear as she appeared to pass most of her time bending over crosswords.

'How are you doing, though?'

'I'm okay.'

Mike chewed on some grapes that he'd rescued from Jackie's bag.

'A woman came in the other day looking for you. She said she was your wife.'

'Was she an ugly broad?'

'She was very attractive.'

'That would be her. The bitch.'

That conversation faded away into the ether, and they stared into space for a while.

'How is it going? Are you in a lot of pain?'

'It hurts like hell, Mike, if I'm going to be honest. It makes me want to cry. And it fucking itches - itches like mad. And I can't even scratch it. It's not fully healed – it looks like a right mess. It looks like a flaming relief map.'

Mike nodded as he spat grape pips into the palm of his hand. 'Not so good then?'

'It's worse than that. Nothing they do does any good. They give me painkillers but they're never enough. Nothing they do is enough.'

Mike had been in hospital, too. He knew how it went. In the course of the last four years his gall bladder had been removed, half of his spleen, and one of his hips had been replaced.

Discomfort was the easy part: getting back to life was the problem.

'You kind of get used to it, in a way. But it's never that good. They keep – ' Mike chewed some more grapes, 'asking you to do things.'

'Tell me about it,' said Jackie.

'And you're not always ready for it. Their timetable, it's not the same as ours. They don't always know what's best.'

Mike wiped the pips from the grapes onto a leg of his trousers and somehow they miraculously clung to it.

Jackie nodded. When men get together there can be a lot of nodding. Particularly when there's nothing to do.

'Bloke died in here the other night.'

'Did he?'

'Yeah. Really old bloke. In that bed opposite, two beds up. He just – I don't know - he didn't do much, you know? He just lay there. Really old bloke – not much bigger than a sparrow. And he started coughing, in the night. Just coughing, really weakly like a – I don't know. A sick little bird or something. Really weak. And I was awake, you know, 'cause I couldn't sleep. And I didn't know what to do. Or whether I should do anything. Because he started flapping about with his arms, and I thought – should I call for someone or press my buzzer or something? It was like he was choking on his own spit. And I thought – I didn't know what to do. You want to help, but you don't know what to do. Do you know what I mean? You ever been like that?'

Mike nodded.

'So I was dithering and fussing, and two nurses appeared. There was a bloke, who was about thirty-five, and a younger nurse, who was maybe eighteen. That's what she looked like, but she was probably older. It was dark and my eyes aren't so good. And they walked really fast, but almost silently. And they got round the bed and they pulled the curtains round and the little overhead light went on and – pretty much everything went quiet. Just like that, everything went quiet. Like no one was moving or breathing.'

'You think the bloke died?'

'I know the bloke died. 'Cause a little while later the young nurse went away and came back with another nurse and a metal trolley, and ten minutes later he was gone. On the trolley. Just a little lump on a trolley.'

'It's kind of sad.'

'I guess it was. Little bloke just dying, on his own. Nobody there for him or nothing.'

They stared at the bed, which now had somebody else in it. A sad-looking man of twenty-eight, who had lost one of his legs. (To diabetes, Jackie thought, of all things.)

'Do you want a few grapes?'

'I don't eat fruit.'

'Is it all right if I have some more?'
'Help yourself.'

CHAPTER FOUR

Jackie decided to focus his attention on Jessica Roeburn, the physiotherapist. In many ways she was his ticket out of there. If he made her happy, she could release him. Even though she was his main figure of torment.

Jackie studied her, watched her, while she was at work; either with himself or somebody else.

Through her trousers he could see the outline of her legs. They were certainly substantial – she could prop up a bridge – but they weren't by any means unattractive. They were the kind of legs that could both vault a vaulting horse and crush it at the same time. He stared at them for a while because that was his nature. He was a novelist, and novelists watch.

Her upper body was generally consumed by her tunic, as was her bosom. Her arms (it being a short-sleeved tunic) were strong and well formed, and often bore a tinge of self-applied tan. Her head, it was, that most interested him. It was a large head, by the standards of anybody, which she did her best to conceal by pulling her hair back into a tight bunch. Sometimes he wasn't sure if it was a bunch or a short ponytail. It was held in place by several kirby grips and a purple scrunchy. Either she only had one scrunchy, or every scrunchy she had was purple. Her eyes were unremarkable, and of a colour he could seldom remember. Her nose was broad, with a certain regality; and her lips were full and well placed.

Physiotherapy is an intimate activity: very much a hands-on affair. It involves people being very close together, touching, leaning on, breathing on each other. It's very important that physiotherapists use breath fresheners.

There were signs on the walls of the therapy chamber declaiming in bold letters that a chaperone would be provided, if required. Or one of one's own choosing could be brought along. Jackie often wondered why a group of men, handled largely by women, would ever wish for the presence of somebody else.

She was a brutal therapist, there was no doubt about it: she did not pull any of her punches. Jackie sometimes looked at other patients, working with their designated partners, and was of the opinion that theirs were much kinder. It was his lot in life to be punished. 'Do you ever do massage, and such-like?'

'Often,' she said. 'It depends on the problem.'

'Do men ever get excited?'

'Not if I hurt them enough.'

With her efficient efficiency Jessica Roeburn continued to work and probe at his left leg, flexing it, pulling it, trying to get him to put pressure against her.

'What about women? Do they get excited?'

'Women get excited all the time.'

CHAPTER FIVE

Laura didn't. Laura was a very measured person, at least until the latter years when differences of opinion started to appear; most of them concerning her opinions.

For a long time Laura was a bastion of serenity; a swan in the maelstrom of the flock; a calmness in the face of the storm. The first time he met her she was the only sober person in the room.

He recalled that she had been ill and was forbidden alcohol. He had offered to drink hers for her, and she seemed to draw pleasure from watching him do it. He had always been a pleasant drunk. He considered that a point in his favour. Of course in those days drinking was more of a social thing.

It was only later that it became a commitment.

CHAPTER SIX

Jackie kept working as best he could at the exercises Jessica imposed on him.

Increasingly her bosom came to dominate him; it was in such close proximity to his face. It looked – 'strapping'. A large bosom barely contained by whatever mechanism she had contrived to keep a grip on it. He thought about Jessica's bosom in the night. He thought about it when he woke up in the morning. When he was eating his breakfast. He thought about it on the commode. He thought about it when there was a summer shower pressing raindrops against the windows of the ward. He thought about it to such a degree that even he couldn't stand it any more.

One day he said to her – 'When am I getting out of here?'

Six weeks. Six weeks until he could put any weight on his leg. It had been four and a half weeks. He would have to work harder; show more resolve, make more effort. He would have to pretend that the pain wasn't really a problem, and tolerate it with good grace. Six weeks until he could stand on his leg.

An indeterminate time after that.

CHAPTER SEVEN

He talked to Jessica about how things would be when he left the hospital.

'You'll probably have crutches initially. And then, all being well, you'll graduate to a walking stick. Then, hopefully, you'll be walking unaided.'

'Will I have a limp, do you think?'

'That's quite possible. It's one of the variables in these situations. Some people, for psychological reasons, maintain a limp even when all the discomfort has gone.'

I bet I have one, he thought. That's me all over. I'll be the one with a limp. 'It might become a self-fulfilling prophecy.'

'It will if you think about it.'

Jessica Roeburn punched and pummelled Jackie's lower body.

'Make some effort, Jackie.'

CHAPTER EIGHT

Seven weeks. He was on both feet, hobbling about the ward with the aid of crutches. This gave him no pride; he felt like a cripple, and a fraud. A cripple and a fraud combined. Not damaged enough to demand much attention, but too damaged to manage on his own. He was overlooked and in the way. One of those people who occupy beds.

He tried talking to some of the other patients, but his heart wasn't in it. He didn't give a fuck for their problems. Other people's problems, like other people's dreams, are never as interesting as they think. He was approaching the stage of his confinement where depression was threatening to kick in.

Jackie wasn't averse or immune to the convolutions of depression, but he didn't want to face them at the moment. He was having enough problems as it was. So he paced and paced on his crutches, up and down the ward, stopping at the window to stare out across the car park, the laundry and unidentified buildings behind. Across to trees and semi-rural land that appeared to go nowhere, and then there were low hills beyond. Then the sky, bright and open, filled with blue and slow-moving clouds. White as snow and grey as slush, doing what clouds always do.

It became clear to him quite quickly, during his pacing, that it was beginning to annoy other people. Whether it was the rattling of the crutches or his under-the-breath muttering; Jackie was getting on people's nerves.

'Jackie – we need to talk about what happens when you get out of here. We need to start making preparations.'

This was a change of emphasis that had been developing over the last few days.

People who weren't in standard medical outfits were coming to look at him and talk to him. They didn't poke him physically but they appeared to be appraising him. Their eyes stared at him for longer than he liked.

This was the social assessment team.

Despite the fact that they tried to smile and appear interested, Jackie wasn't sure whether he liked or trusted them.

He'd grown used to the people in outfits.

CHAPTER NINE

Today it was the turn of a young man from the occupational therapy department. Jackie had taken an instant dislike to him; partly because of his youth and partly because of the suit he was wearing. It was a black suit with widely-spaced thin pinstripes, and it looked as though it had come from a charity shop, having previously been rejected by several other charity shops. Jackie barely dared look at the man's shirt and tie.

'I understand from what you've said before that you live in a ground floor apartment?'

'That would be true.'

'So there are no stairs to climb?'

'Only if I create them. From boxes or whatever's lying around.'

The young man from the occupational therapy department typed rapidly onto his laptop.

'And what about the bathroom? Is it a shower or a bath? Can you walk into the shower?'

'When I'm drunk I can walk into anything. But I'd have to climb into the bath to get a shower.'

'So there are no grab rails?'

'There certainly aren't.'

'You don't seem to be taking this very seriously.'

'I'm just trying to lighten the mood.'

'The mood doesn't need any lightening.'

Jesus, somebody climbed up your ass today didn't they?

'We've noticed that a young woman comes in to visit you occasionally. Is she a relative?'

'No, she's a barmaid.'

'Is she the one who brings you the whisky?'

'I didn't know you knew about that.'

'You're not very subtle about it.'

CHAPTER TEN

Maybe the staff really were getting fed up with him. Perhaps they did want him out of there.

The pressure to get better, to improve faster, was increasing on a daily basis. It was a long time since someone had bathed him in bed. Now he had to fend for himself. And yet the pressure was a double-edged sword, for much of it was coming from within. Jackie wanted to get out of there, he needed to get out of there – he had a life to live which wasn't inside a hospital. His life was in *The Golden Lion*. He needed to get back to that. Perhaps he'd write another book.

A seed had been planted; a seed of doubt. People had been kind to him and taken care of him. It doesn't happen much as an adult, it's something one learns to grow out of. But it's very comforting. It's remarkably easy to embrace. Everyone wants love, even if it comes with a syringe and a thermometer.

His depression became a sadness. He thought about sulking but the sadness came more easily. The shock of the trauma and the subsequent (at times baffling) events were at last draining from his system, and nothing had yet come in to fill the void.

But one thing was clear. He needed to get out of there.

'I need to get out of here,' he said.

CHAPTER ELEVEN

So they took him home.

A team had been in to assess it. They had installed a raised toilet seat and rearranged the furniture. They had made everything convenient and easily to hand, and Jackie hated it from the moment he hobbled in.

It wasn't his home, it was somebody else's idea of how his home should be.

He said nothing, though. He smiled gamely and nodded, and appeared to give agreement to everything that had been done and all that was suggested by the two women who'd taken him home. He beamed approvingly at the provisions (which he had to pay for) that they had carried in with them. They were pleasant women who were trying their best and it was hard for him to dislike them. Their smiles were genuine and both of them treated him as if they'd known him for years and he was one step away from being part of their families.

But he wasn't.

The two women followed and encouraged Jackie all round the apartment until they were sure he could cope. They asked him if the adjusted toilet was all right and if he would like to try it. Jackie had never expected to be asked such a question in his life, and was embarrassed on a level he had rarely experienced (although the commode pushed it close). He mumbled that he would be fine and didn't need to try it out in front of them.

When the women left and the door closed behind them, leaving Jackie alone in his apartment, he felt a sense of gloom and abandonment that went far beyond terrible and passed from his chest, down through his damaged thigh, past his battered knee, all the way down to his metaphorical boots; and even then it didn't want to stop.

The first sigh he gave was the deepest sigh of his life: he sucked in all the air of the room and slowly let it out again. Then he didn't even seem to breathe for a while, as if the very act of breathing would disturb the silence of the room, and maybe the room wanted things to be quiet.

He thought that this might be a good day to start smoking again.

He eased himself from his armchair and, with the aid of his crutches, hobbled to the kitchen.

From the first low cupboard on the left he took a bottle of whisky and a bottle of ginger ale. He hobbled back to the lounge with them, which was no easy task with the accompaniment of the crutches as they appeared hell bent on making him become teetotal overnight. Never had he encountered such an obstacle in all his many years of drinking. It was something they'd not prepared him for at the physiotherapy gym.

He put the bottles on an artisan coffee table, let out a sigh almost as big as the first, then hobbled back to the kitchen to fetch a glass.

When he was finally settled into his chair with a full glass of whisky he said, 'Fucking hell,' and rubbed at his leg.

CHAPTER TWELVE

Carers came in twice a day to make sure he was up and moving and getting himself washed and fed and had everything he needed.

Would he like the TV moving closer? Were they his only underpants? They had a lot of comments to make. Jackie felt ninety years old.

He hadn't told them, but he wasn't going to bed, he was sleeping on the sofa. It was too painful to get up and go to the bedroom. Every morning he had to go in and muss the bed up before they arrived.

He was aware, or had the sense, that the carers who came in (two of them, both of them women, one in her thirties, one in her twenties) did not really like him. Which may have been because he was frequently drunk and stinking of whisky. He understood their position; he wouldn't like it either; even though he presented no danger. Eventually they arrived at a situation where he pretended he was better than he was, and they agreed to pretend that he was. It was hoped that this agreement would foreshorten the process. The understanding appeared to suit all parties. Indeed it was so successful that one of them, the younger one (her name was Georgia) started joining him for a drink sometimes.

Georgia was a cyclist. She had dreams of becoming a professional one day. The route to becoming a professional cyclist (Jackie didn't know this) was so beset with obstacles, pitfalls, jealousies and rivalries that it made the Boer War seem peaceful.

Jackie came to know the name of every woman in Georgia's cycling club, and every time one of their names came up he would say, 'Fuck her, what does she know?'

Georgia, generally, completely agreed with him; and eventually they dispensed with the caring entirely and just sat drinking vodka.

CHAPTER THIRTEEN

'What sort of books did you write, Jackie?'

'Er – mostly crap ones.' Jackie and Georgia were sat on the couch. His leg was propped up on the artisan coffee table. It was 7.00 pm and they were drunk. 'They were kind of thrillers, you know? Mysteries and thrillers. About people getting into bad situations. My best one was a book about a duck. A valuable duck. You can get a lot of mileage from a duck.'

'I don't like ducks. I've got a friend who was attacked by a seagull once. She thinks she must have been near its nest, but it flew down pecking her head. She had an ice cream as well. She ended up in hospital, she had to have stitches. It wasn't a duck, but they're pretty much the same. She could have been killed.'

'By a seagull?'

'These things happen, Jackie.' Jackie nodded. It was hard to argue. He had seen some peculiar things himself.

'She's still got a thing about seagulls.'

CHAPTER FOURTEEN

'Why did you stop writing if you like books so much? You could have kept writing a better one.'

It was the question that kept cropping up. Over the years, and here and there – in conversations, in a bar, in his head, in an email, in a phone call – why did he give up his writing? He'd heard it so often that he thought, if he had a pound for every time he'd heard it he wouldn't have to contemplate the question. He could lie under palm trees, fanned by dusky maidens, asking them to turn down the waves because the lapping was getting on his nerves. And drink himself to oblivion. With drinks that contained ice but no umbrellas.

He'd be a beach bum with an author's background. Oh yes, he'd get some respect then. He'd be Ernest Hemingway, Hunter S Thompson; drinking his way through the days like a gonzo wastrel. He could even picture the shirts he'd be wearing – oversized tee-shirts in Caribbean colours, patterned with parrots, pineapples and palm fronds. Wearing baggy khaki shorts and canvas sandals. He would watch the sun set from a padded wicker lounger and when it rose again he would still be there. And the music would still be playing in the background; that endless calypso music. The drone of cicadas. The laughing of the fishermen as they got ready to launch their boats.

'Jackie?'

'Yeah. It wasn't a conscious decision. It simply petered out. In fact I've never said I have stopped writing – I just haven't written for a while. I suppose it's a moot point where one attitude ends and another one begins, but I guess I'm still kind of a writer. Or I would be if I wrote another book.'

He leaned forward to pour the dregs of a vodka bottle into Georgia's glass, holding the bottle upright until it stopped dripping, then holding it a few seconds longer.

'We've only got Scotch left now.'

'I can drink whisky if I have to.'

Jackie put the empty vodka bottle down and returned to his own whisky bottle which, mercifully, was two-thirds full. There were more bottles in the kitchen, but that was several feet away.

'Anyway, what about you? Do you ever think all the drinking might be a hindrance to your cycling?'

'I have thought about it. I fell off the bike twice last week. Yesterday I rode into a tree.'

'It's very hard to pursue a dream.'

'Some days it's hard to ride a bike.'

They both drank to that.

CHAPTER FIFTEEN

At Georgia's insistence, Jackie contacted a firm of no-win-no-fee lawyers to pursue a personal injury claim against the driver of the car.

'I'm not that fussed,' he'd said.

'You've got to do it, Jackie. You might get a lot of money.'

So he did. He contacted a firm. He thought he'd contacted a firm; he wasn't entirely sure. There was a lot of blurring going on at that time.

A couple of weeks went by where nothing happened.

But one day a lawyer turned up at his door. Jackie, who was drunk at the time, had, by this point, completely forgotten the whole scenario. He wasn't sure why he needed a lawyer in the first place.

'Yes?' he said, blinking at the sunlight.

'I'm from the claims firm you contacted.'

That sentence completely bypassed Jackie, who was still trying to steady himself against the door frame.

'The er – '

'You spoke to Maria. You arranged an appointment.'

'Did I?'

Jackie stared for a time at nothing in particular, while he tried to get his thoughts in order. Then he said –

'You'd better come in then.'

Fuck.

Using one crutch, as opposed to his earlier two, Jackie led the way, in a fairly erratic fashion, into the lounge.

'Have a seat,' he said, gesturing vaguely in the direction of the sofa.

For himself, Jackie sat down on his usual armchair and lifted his leg to rest it on the artisan coffee table. He winced as he did so. He always winced. It was becoming a habit. He wondered, sometimes, if he was pre-empting it.

'I'm like the White Queen,' he said.

'Pardon?'

'The White Queen. In Alice in – oh never mind. Would you like a drink or something?'

'Do you have any minted water or herbal tea?'

'Er – '

Jackie blinked a few times.

'I have whisky or beer. Or water from the tap.'

'It's okay. I had a glass of tap water yesterday.'

The lawyer, who was twenty-eight and called himself Joseph, sat down on the sofa. He was dark haired, bespectacled, and wearing a grey suit which, by Jackie's assessment, didn't cost very much. Jackie became rather fixated on his suit.

Joseph put his laptop on the artisan coffee table and set his briefcase, which also looked cheap, on the floor beside him.

Jackie was beginning to have some doubts.

Joseph opened his laptop and began to type furiously.

'I need to take some personal details first.'

'Would you like a biscuit?'

'No thank you.'

Joseph, a man so intense that his face threatened to implode under the pressure of it, continued to type with genuine ferocity, pounding his mission onto the keypad. He typed for so long that Jackie's attention drifted away and he stared out of the window. He stared for a long time – looking at the birds and wondering if they ever got drunk. He supposed some of them might if they ate fermenting fruit in the autumn. It couldn't be easy, flying through the air if you were drunk. There was always the danger –

Joseph suddenly slammed his laptop shut, which just about frightened the crap out of Jackie. He opened his briefcase. He took out a folder and several forms which he spread out on the table next to Jackie's leg.

'As I understand it, you were utilising a pedestrian crossing at the bottom of Queensbridge High Street and an out of control vehicle recklessly crashed into you. In order to distract attention from the incident the driver of the vehicle feigned injury and threw herself to the ground, more or less adding insult to injury. And potentially diverting urgently needed medical provision away from yourself, and towards her. Is that a correct appraisal of the situation?'

'Er – '

'This woman put you at considerable risk of additional harm, having already careered into you in a blind and incomprehensible fashion. A woman with much on her mind and you in her way.'

'Er – '

'As I understand it she was driving a black SUV with bull bars on the front. Is that correct?'

'Er – '

'Bull bars? In an urban situation in a middle-England town on a sunny day in June. She was hardly at risk of hitting a buffalo.'

'I suppose not. Am I supposed to comment on this?'

'It doesn't matter. But she did hit you with a bull bar, or an area of the car close to it.'

'I don't think she meant to.'

The lawyer gave a shrug. 'That isn't a matter for us to decide.'

CHAPTER SIXTEEN

Jackie took a break.

The guy's suit was bothering him, and the direction of the conversation was not what he'd been anticipating, even if he'd remembered it was coming.

He went to the kitchen and leaned against the worktop that supported the toaster, the kettle and the microwave, and was clearly in need of a clean. Maybe he should get a cleaner in. That wasn't a bad idea. Perhaps he could claim for that as well.

He rubbed his forehead. A thumb and middle finger smoothed out his eyebrows.

Sometimes, he thought, it would be better not to drink so much.

He took a fresh bottle of whisky back to the lounge with him. Joseph appeared to have barely noticed his absence and was once again pounding on his laptop.

'Did you drink as much before you had the accident, Mister Conor?'

'Er. Possibly. Probably. It's hard to remember.'

'How would you describe your monthly income?'

'Minimal.'

'You're a respected and well known professional author. What would you say is the average monthly income of a professional author?'

'Erm – '

'Four thousand pounds?'

That would be a fucking miracle.

'Let's say five thousand pounds was your projected monthly income at the time of the accident. Factor in the stress and trauma of the actual carnage, and your subsequent inability to even be able to sit at your desk and work on your typewriter – '

Typewriter?

' – and I think you have quite a case building here, Mister Conor. Obviously there are no guarantees. The law operates in strange and mysterious ways. Even the law doesn't understand some of them. But I think you have a very strong case. Very strong indeed. I would be surprised if we couldn't get you something.'

Jackie nodded, and munched on a biscuit.

There was always something, with life.

CHAPTER SEVENTEEN

Not much happened for a while.

Jackie recovered, as best he could, and graduated to a walking stick.

He tried a couple of domestic cleaners but couldn't get along with them. They irritated him. So he dusted and cleaned in his own best fashion, which looked good enough to him. And he kept drinking. Kept getting his weekly grocery delivery. And he stared out of the window a lot. But he'd been doing that since long before his accident.

The year had progressed into winter. It was December and the streets were wet and it was getting to the time when he had to start going out again. The profits and future livelihood of *The Golden Lion* depended in large part upon his trade.

One sad aspect was that his friendship with Georgia had petered out: she had moved on to another caring job. She gave him a big bunch of flowers when she left, and he gave her a collection of bath oils. He figured a person probably gets pretty sweaty while cycling and she might like to freshen up.

One thing he didn't know yet was that (amazingly, from Jackie's point of view) Joseph's legal firm was going to obtain £178,964.20 for him.

Jackie would spend years trying to figure out what the twenty pence related to.

PART TWO

CHAPTER ONE

It was February. Jackie had been signed off by the hospital but was still having regular physiotherapy sessions with Jessica Roeburn. He had been offered hydrotherapy as an additional treatment, but thought that was mainly for horses so didn't bother turning up. Eventually they stopped offering it to him.

He was still using his walking stick, and his leg ached all the time. He was constantly rubbing at it, pressing on the scar. He didn't even notice he was doing it now.

Overall, he was back to normal.

As was his custom, he walked into *The Golden Lion* at a little after midday. As was also his custom he paused a few steps in and looked cautiously around, as if he thought he was likely to be bushwhacked. When he wasn't, he limped his way to the bar.

Dawn looked up from her celebrity crossword.

'Yo, Jack.'

'Dawn.'

Mike was polishing a glass with a tea towel. A special tea towel that he only used for polishing glass. And it always seemed to be the same glass.

He nodded as Jackie approached. The bar was quiet. It generally was at this time of day; things started to pick up a little later.

Mike put down the glass, draped the tea towel over a shoulder, and reached for a pump handle. 'The usual?'

'I don't have a usual.'

'What do you want then?'

Jackie studied the beers on offer. Those in bottles behind the bar, and those on draught right in front of him.

He took a step back so he could better survey them.

'I'll have a pint of that,' he said.

'You mean the one you usually have.'

'Piss off.'

While the beer was pouring, Jackie turned to check that his customary booth was unoccupied. It housed a scarred wooden table, opposing fairly comfortable banquettes with dark wood backs, and a window that looked out onto the partly pedestrianised lower aspect of the High Street.

Occasionally his booth would be occupied by other clientele, and Jackie would have to stand at the end of the table staring at them, with his glass of beer in his hand, until they got uncomfortable and moved.

Once or twice people had stubbornly refused to move and he'd had to sit down opposite them, resolutely staring until their discomfiture became so great that they not only left the booth but usually left the bar.

This behaviour irritated Mike no end.

'You've got to stop scaring people off, Jackie. This is my business.'

'Pff.' Jackie would shrug. 'You get more business out of me. I'm only being territorial. It's not my fault if they can't take it. I'm not actually threatening them.'

'For chrissake.'

On this day the booth was empty. Jackie took his pint of beer and walked across.

Two minutes later Mike came over with a glass of whisky and a small bottle of ginger ale. He put them on the table in front of Jackie. This was their usual ritual now that Jackie used a stick. Sometimes Mike didn't put the whisky on Jackie's tab. Jackie didn't know that.

'Thanks Mike.'

Jackie rubbed his leg. All the time it ached or itched, or something. A lot of the time he didn't even know what it was doing. But it was always doing something. It drove him nuts.

He sipped his beer. He was half-glad half-sad that he hadn't taken up smoking again, and wondered if it would be the same third time around. He wondered if he could afford to – cigarettes seemed to cost as much as a small mortgage these days. He'd have to look out his old friend who used to get him the smuggled tobacco. Although he had a feeling he'd died from cancer. Not lung cancer, something obscure. A rare type of cancer. Cancer of the toe, something like that. Cancer of the follicles. Cancer could get into places you couldn't think of. If you wanted to design a disease, cancer would be a good model.

He sipped some more of his beer, and stared from the window.

The day outside was dismal. Dreary rain that almost couldn't be bothered to be rain; it was merely moisture roaming about the air.

The spot where he'd suffered the accident was just out of sight, a little way up the High Street, to the left.

He hadn't been back to look at the spot. He supposed he'd have to some day.

He let his thoughts lead him; but they were idle and not going far.

He thought about Georgia, and what she had said. Maybe he should write another book. A book of adventure and drama, involving his duck. If he could find a way to resurrect the bird.

He could certainly do with the money. He'd been living off residual royalties and money received during the separation from Laura, when she'd kept the house and he'd moved to the apartment. He supposed, theoretically, there might be some kind of state benefit to claim; but he'd never made the effort to find out.

That ought to be done. He made a mental note of it. *See if I can get any benefit.* His bar expenses were huge.

Jackie finished his whisky, which never took long, and returned to the bar for another. Mike was serving a couple who were passing through town and interested in the food menu.

I wouldn't eat that, he thought. *I've seen the bloke who cooks it.*

Dawn served him, and didn't bother entering it on his tab. Dawn had a soft spot for Jackie.

'How's it going, Dawn?'

'Fff.' Dawn puffed her chubby cheeks out and pulled a face. 'It could be a lot better, Jack, I'll tell you that. That guy I thought I was going out with – effin Ryan – only turns out he's having an affair with his own mother.'

'His mother? Bloody hell.'

'Tell me about it. Turns out his mother left him and his dad, and his brother, and his sister – who's only his half-sister – I'm not even sure if she's that. Anyway. He was only eight.' She frowned. 'Or was it six? But she left them, you know, the whole family, and went to her cousin's in Scunthorpe. Which I *think* is up north. But apparently there'd been problems for years with his father, who drove a truck, and spent a lot of time away.'

Jackie leaned on his stick, drank the whisky, and Dawn poured him another.

'Anyway. His dad had to give up the trucks, and got a job local as a plumber. Or a painter. Something like that. Something that starts with a P. And he looked after the family. Yes, madam – '

Dawn moved a few steps to her left to serve a woman smartly dressed in a cheap black business suit, with blonde hair tightly pulled back and a fraught expression on her thirty-year old face.

Jackie looked over his shoulder. There were two forty-year men in virtually matching suits leaning towards each other across a round table at the far end of the bar, engaged in what was clearly a very intense and high level conversation, probably involving the future of the entire galaxy.

The woman had clearly been sent to fetch the drinks.

Jackie hesitated then at the bar; unsure whether to return to his booth or wait for Dawn to return to her post. It seemed impolite to leave.

He nodded at a pump and Mike poured him another beer.

'So she went away.' Dawn resumed talking as if she'd never stopped. 'And nobody heard much from her. She was just 'gone', you know. Didn't even send Christmas cards. And this was *after* all the business with the insurance.'

Jackie squinted. He must have missed that bit.

'And pretty much that was that. The woman had gone, and nobody heard from her. *But*, 'unbeknownst' to anybody – ' she fixed Jackie with direct eye contact and a knowing nod - 'she'd come back, and was living in one of those caravans upside the park.'

Jackie was becoming more intrigued by this encounter and found himself leaning against the bar.

'Hmm.' Dawn nodded, and still kept her gaze on Jackie's own, raising her eyebrows and widening her eyes. 'And you know what them caravans are like.'

Jackie didn't, but nodded anyway.

'Like chickens in a rabbit coop. The police are round there all the time. Anyway, Ryan bumped into her one night at *The Raving Lantern*, when he was out with his mates. And they started dancing and having a bit of a laugh. Course he didn't know who she was at the time, he just thought he'd got lucky with some sex crazed milf who was out on the lash and gagging for it. And the next thing you know they've started going out together. Although when I say 'going out' they were mostly staying in that caravan. It's not hard to spot, it's the green one on the left. Yes, sir – '

Jackie was in danger of losing his booth at this rate. He'd left his coat on the seat as a marker, but people couldn't be trusted. A good slot in a booth in a bar that's filling up is an open invitation to skulduggery.

Fortunately Dawn returned quickly, and resumed without a breath. Although Jackie was a little distracted now because of the potential threat to his seat.

'Now I don't know if she knew who he was when they met at the *Lantern*, but they got to find out soon enough, and instead of doing something about it they just carried on, bold as brass. I think it's depraved if you ask me; she's old enough to be his mother. Well she is his mother. And he was supposed to be going out with me.'

Jackie nodded in a sympathetic way, and sipped his beer.

'How's college?'

'Effin rubbish. I don't know why I bother.'

Jackie took his glass back to his booth and resumed his desultory surveillance of the High Street.

This is my life, he thought.

CHAPTER TWO

Jackie had very strong painkillers. He had a virtually open prescription for them – anything he wanted he could get. He found they worked best if he swallowed them with whisky.

Staff at the hospital, whom he had spoken to; and his GP; were keen to reduce the amount he was taking. But Jackie wasn't. He liked the painkillers. He took a lot more than he should. He tried to pace them. But he still took a lot.

Ibuprofen, paracetamol, tramadol; he was on them all. Leapfrogging drugs to keep incipient agony at bay. He was terrified that if he stopped taking the drugs terrible pain would ensue; and he didn't want pain. He didn't want more pain. He had enough pain as it was.

Someone, he thought it was his GP, had suggested a 'wellness clinic', where he could join in group therapy sessions. It might help to talk to others in a similar position, people with persistent pain.

That didn't fly. He didn't actually recoil but it was plain from the expression on his face that Jackie didn't consider himself to be a wellness kind of person. He didn't like groups, teams, crowds or gatherings. He didn't care for social events, or matters involving people he didn't know or like. By and large he didn't like many people, so that rather restricted his options. Laura had told him that he couldn't go through life calling other people 'a bunch of bastards', but he hadn't yet come up with a better phrase.

He measured his dislike of other people by the amount of politeness he directed at them. Sometimes he was so polite it made his sphincter clench. He had been known to inadvertently break wind, such was the ferocity of his clenching. So Jackie stuck with his pills, and juggled them about. He was juggling them now, on a Thursday lunchtime, back at his place in the booth.

He was pleased to note that the weather had improved. Light showers had been forecast. Light showers with some sunny spells. A high of ten degrees.

It didn't feel that warm. Jackie was cold. He was often cold. He thought it might be connected to his injury; his body felt less resilient.

He had lost weight. One of the things about drinking was that you didn't necessarily need food all the time; you could fill yourself up with fluid. But his weight had been more or less stable for years; it was only recently that it had taken a hit.

He had never been a big man. Sixty-five kilos had been his weight for most of his adult life. It had crept up a little in his late forties, and in his fifties had climbed up to eighty. It was slipping back now, though. The alcohol diet could only take you so far in life. Maybe it was time to eat some more.

Jackie toyed with another whisky glass, drained it, and was about to get up to go for another when he realised there was a woman standing at the end of the table. Very serious, very grave. She must have glided up like a sylph while he was absorbed in his whisky.

'Can I help you?' he said.

The woman was on the tall side of short. She was wearing a blue raincoat, black trousers, black patent leather court shoes with a modest heel, and she carried a leather shoulder bag which was also blue. Her hair was cropped short and straight, and of a shade of brown known mainly as 'brown'.

Her eyes were dark, her face was pale and her lips were glossed with red. Blue earrings dangled at the sides of her neck. She was pretty, in a little girl way, although she was probably in her early thirties.

'Hello?'

'Yes, I'm sorry,' she said, looking flustered and fidgeting, flapping her hands around her bag. 'I didn't want to disturb you, but I wondered how you are doing. I'm Emily Marchant. I'm the woman who drove into you.'

After a pause that Jackie, in his authorial pose, might have described as dramatic, he said, 'Oh.'

He started to rise. Out of politeness. For a woman. The way his mother had raised him.

But she said, 'No, don't get up. It's just – I wasn't sure if I should come. A lot of people advised against it. But I wanted to check you are all right.'

Jackie blinked. He wasn't quite sure of the protocol of the situation, but basic politeness kicked in.

'I'm fine, yes. Thank you for asking. I'm, you know, getting about. Back on my feet. Still not dancing on pianos but, overall, pretty good. I guess. Except for the pianos.'

She smiled. 'That's good.'

'Yes.' Jackie smiled himself, vaguely. Still at sea. He still didn't know what was going on. 'Would you, er – how are you? Are you okay?'

'Yes I'm fine. It wasn't – ' she fidgeted again with her bag. 'It wasn't me who got hurt was it? I'm so sorry.'

He realised, in that moment, that her eyes were glistening, and she blinked as she looked away from him. Doing what Jackie did; looking out of the window at the High Street of the town. But she wasn't really looking at it the way he did. Emily Marchant was looking right through it. If she bit her lower lip Jackie would burst into tears himself.

'Why don't you sit down for a minute, Mrs Marchant. Your hands are shaking. You look cold.'

'It's just nerves,' she said.

'I know. Have a seat anyway. I'll er – would you like a drink or something? Bottle of gin? Cup of coffee?'

'I only have half an hour. But a small glass of white wine would be nice.'

'Okay.'

Jackie rose to his feet as Emily slid her legs beneath the table and seated herself on the padded bench opposite. Her nervousness was palpable. She had broken the pact that exists between the motorist and the victim; between the idea and the real world. It was a big step to take; even her legs were trembling. She wondered, in so many ways, how wrong she might be.

Jackie hobbled to the bar with his whisky glass.

'Large glass of white wine,' he said.

'Who's that?' said Mike. 'Your daughter?'

'No, I don't have a daughter. That's the woman who ran into me.'

'Blimey.'

They stared across the bar to where Emily Marchant was sliding the strap of her bag from her shoulder. She put the bag next to her. Then she picked it up and put it on her lap. Then she put it back on the seat again.

'She's quite active,' said Mike. 'Quick, like a chipmunk. It's a pity she didn't pay for the drinks, though.'

Jackie took the white wine and hobbled his way back on his stick. Mike followed him with a large glass of whisky.

Emily Marchant had moved her bag again. This time it was on the other side of her.

'This is very kind of you,' she said as she took the wine glass. 'I wasn't sure what to expect.'

Jackie quietly grunted. He hadn't even had a chance to expect. If he'd known she was coming he probably wouldn't have been there. He'd have gone to *The Raving Lantern* and looked for Oedipean Ryan and his mother.

Or maybe he wouldn't. He would have been here, waiting in his usual seat, drinking his usual whisky and sipping his usual beer. Because he would have had a need to know. The curiosity and itch to know would have been extreme.

'How did you know where to find me?' he said.

'I work at an estate agency up the road. Often I take an early lunch, and two or three times I've seen you coming in here.'

'I don't remember you. I don't recognise you.'

She smiled faintly, not looking at him. The glass turned in her hands and she took a small sip from it. A full bottle would do her no favours right now. 'No. But you were in a very bad state at the time. I don't imagine looking at me was a major concern.'

'I think I spoke to you.'

'Yes, we both said something. Then events took over. You were swamped by people and I foolishly collapsed. It wasn't one of my finest moments. Everything went wrong. It was like a comedy of errors without any humour. Everything leading to – this.' She nodded at Jackie's walking stick – a simple old-fashioned beechwood affair that he'd picked up in a junk shop. The stick supplied by the hospital had been metal and devoid of all style. 'When I saw you with that I felt so awful. It was as if I'd turned you into a cripple.'

Jackie picked up the stick and ran his hands over it. The curved top was worn smooth by God-knew how many years of use. The wood probably dated from the eighteenth century. Hewn from a sapling, that was supporting him now.

'It's not so bad,' he said. 'It's kind of a status symbol. And it has a sword inside in case I'm ever attacked.'

'But the pain. You must be in pain.'

'Well.' He shrugged. 'You get used to it. And they give me lots of drugs.'

Emily looked away. She didn't think you would get used to it.

Her eyes were sparkling again. She sniffed, then wiped the back of a hand under her nose. She took a proper gulp of the wine and finished half of it. She stared doggedly from the window, as if maybe there were some answers out there. But there never were. Jackie had found that out. You could stare as much as you liked, but it was still there and you were still here. Life never goes away. It just carries on.

She looked down at the table.

'I haven't driven again since the accident. Because I fear it might happen again. I keep looking back and I still don't know how I hit you. I can't conjure it up in my memory. It was a – one moment you're there, doing things in the real world, and then you're somewhere else. And it's all chaos and bedlam, and people yelling and running and – you know you've hit somebody. It dawns on you – the realisation. You've run into someone, and you might have killed them.'

She took a deep breath. So did Jackie. Maybe oxygen would help. He'd finished his whisky, so he needed something.

He looked across to Mike, but Mike was serving someone else. Even Dawn was busy. There probably wasn't enough whisky to help him anyway.

'Mrs Marchant – ' He reached across the table to put a hand on her trembling arm. 'You mustn't dwell on it too much. It's just something that happened. That's what accidents are. It could have been me who ran into you.'

Emily gave a tight smile.

'Except it wasn't.'

She pulled herself together.

'I'd better get back.' They rose together and, unsure of what to do in the moment, found themselves exchanging handshakes.

'Thank you for seeing me, and being so gracious.'

She walked daintily and delicately from the bar.

Jackie remained standing for a while, then looked across *The Golden Lion* to Mike.

He gave a shrug, then went to get another drink.

CHAPTER THREE

There had been a few outpatient appointments to check his progress, but they had petered out after a while. He was on his own, except for the less than tender ministrations of Jessica Roeburn, who continued to inflict her particular brand of punishment on him. Punishment for something he hadn't even done.

'It's getting better,' she said whilst working on his back. 'But you're still too tense – you're all knotted up. You need to get more exercise, Jackie, or you're going to end up with even worse posture than you already have.'

'What posture? What's wrong with my posture?'

'When you walk you twist to one side. You walk laterally, like a crab.'

'No I don't.'

'Yes you do. It's going to become permanent if you don't make some effort. You slump too much.'

Exercise. 'Walking.' He was always being told to walk more. He walked to the bar most days of the week; one would hope that would be sufficient. Apparently not. He was supposed to walk to the park. Feed the ducks. Walk to the shops. Run a marathon. Feed the bloody ducks. He'd seen those ducks: if they didn't get fed they were likely to attack you. The swans could bring a man down.

'Perhaps I could get an exercise bike?'

'Do you think you'd use it?'

Probably not. Perhaps he could think himself fit.

'How long do you think I'll need this physio?'

'Until such time as we both agree that it's no longer necessary.'

'When do you think that will be?'

'You tell me.'

CHAPTER FOUR

He walked to the shops with the aid of his stick. It was now mid-March, and the unusually mild and unseasonal weather continued to gather pace. In the planted flowerbeds along the High Street crocuses had already come and gone. Tulips were blooming so aggressively it seemed they were trying to muscle out their neighbours. Somebody claimed to have seen a swallow. But as they had, in a previous year, claimed to have spotted a unicorn, nobody paid much attention.

Jackie was sitting outside a café at the lower end of the High Street. He had a coffee on the table in front of him, and an unopened book in which he planned to write notes for his upcoming novel. Which he hadn't thought of yet. The book was quite fancy, with an elasticated closing strap and space for a pen, or a pencil. He hadn't decided which yet. Sometimes the debate was half of the excitement. He was thinking maybe –

'Hello mate! How you doing?'

Jackie looked up. There was a chap on crutches in front of him. A curly-haired chap with pallid blue eyes and a grin that could fit in a wardrobe.

Jackie had no idea who he was. He'd never seen him before.

'It's me – Chris. We did the physiotherapy together!'

'Oh yeah – of course.' (Jackie had no idea. The bloke was a total stranger.) He half rose and extended his hand. 'How you doing mate?'

'I'm good. Great. How are you doing?'

Chris manoeuvred himself into position on a chair next to Jackie and rested his crutches against the window of the coffee shop. He adjusted his artificial legs.

'Yeah I'm good. Fucking A. You sure you're doing okay? You look good.'

'Yeah, I'm fine.'

Jackie was desperately trying to recover any memories at all of the cheerful chap sitting next to him. There had been many people about, and he'd had no interest in any of them.

He made a wild stab.

'How's your wife?'

Chris rolled his eyes. He turned to adjust his crutches on the window, then turned again to readjust one of his legs.

Chris had been unlucky. He had diabetes. Diabetes can affect the circulatory system, and occasionally, rarely, it can lead to the loss of a leg. Chris was so unlucky he'd lost both of his legs. He was thirty-four years old.

'She wasn't my wife, she was my partner. We'd been together for nine years. But after this – ' he looked down at his legs, 'she fucked off with another bloke who just happened to have both legs. Bitch couldn't run away fast enough.'

They both burst out laughing.

'And I couldn't catch her – not with this pair!'

They laughed a while longer, and it was genuine. It added an extra brightness to the day.

'Why don't I get you a drink, Chris? What do you want – coffee latte? Or should we go to a bar?'

'I'm not supposed to be having alcohol. So fuck it, let's go to a bar.'

They didn't go to *The Golden Lion*, they went to *The Grapes*: Chris on his crutches and Jackie with his stick. It didn't take as long as you'd think.

It was a dingier pub than *The Golden Lion*. Old school. Dark wood everywhere. A dart board, pool table, and a landlord who looked like he bit the heads off chickens. He had made a positive gesture and put bowls of Bombay mix on the bar. The dust was visible.

He jerked his head in the universal gesture of 'what do you want?'. Even as he stood there, with his hands on the bar, his tattoos seemed to be multiplying.

'What do you fancy, Chris?'

'Pint of anything. As long as it's lager. I'll go and get us a table.'

Jackie surveyed the whiskies.

'What's the house whisky?'

The barman looked at him as if Jackie was insulting his intelligence.

'It's the whisky of the house. What do you think?'

'Okay. I'll have two glasses of that. And a pint of that and a pint of that.'

He took the glasses to the table in relays.

Chris was inordinately pleased. He was beaming as if this was the best place he'd ever been to in his life. Maybe he was just happy to be out.

'Cheers mate.'

'Cheers.'

They supped the tops from their respective glasses, then put the glasses on the table. Jackie adjusted one of the table mats. He felt self-conscious that he wasn't more severely injured. Chris was shaming him with his leglessness.

'Do you want any crisps or anything?'

'No I'm fine mate.'

Jackie nodded. 'Good.'

After a few moments he said it again.

'Good.'

They stared for a time at the particular feature each of them had picked out. Jackie was looking at a wall lamp; Chris was staring at a print of a fox hunt – hounds streaming ahead of a pack of men on horseback.

Eventually Jackie broke the silence.

'It's all a bastard, isn't it?'

'You said it mate.'

They took long draughts from their glasses, and for the second time in the space of three weeks Jackie was sitting with someone whose eyes were glistening, and who could do anything in the world but look at him.

They drank in silence for a time, and when the glasses were empty Jackie, without asking, picked them up and went for two more. He threw in two packets of nuts.

'The thing is,' said Chris, 'you don't just lose the things you've lost, you lose the rest as well. Not all of it, obviously, you've still got your stuff; but you still lose a lot of what's left. Like this, for instance, going to a pub. Struggling to carry a pint. Do you know how embarrassing it is to have to ask someone to carry it for you? You end up staying at home. And when you're there it's fucking ridiculous. You don't know whether to leave your legs on or take them off. If somebody calls unexpectedly you're stuffed.'

He opened a packet of dry roasted peanuts and tipped a few into his palm.

'I can't get used to it. When I take the legs off I'm so bloody short. I'm only half a man.'

'That isn't true,' said Jackie. 'The man is in here – ' he tapped his heart. 'And up here.' He tapped his head.

'That's because you've got both your legs. If I took mine off now I'd fall over.' They both gave a low laugh. 'I get so down sometimes. Do you get down?'

'Sometimes,' said Jackie.

'I suppose everyone does.' Chris drained half of his glass and ate the remainder of the nuts. His sadness was not being concealed. 'It's the complete and utter change in your life, you know? One day you can walk, and the next day you can't. One day you can kick a football, and the next day you're taking off your legs. I don't even know whether to stand them up or lay them on the floor. It's not the kind of thing you expect. Getting around now, I'm so conscious of it. I'm self-conscious all the time. People looking at me, sympathising. In some ways that's the worst – I don't want to be the guy who gets sympathy. I just want to be me – Chris McKenna. I don't want to be the guy with no legs.'

After a pause Jackie said, 'Go and get the fucking drinks in then.'

Chris laughed. 'Sex though – that's another thing isn't it? How's that going to work out for me? It's not going to be 'should I take my socks off?' it's going to be 'should I leave my legs on?' For the woman, if I ever meet one, it will be like making love with scrap metal.'

'You're a nice bloke, Chris, I'm pretty sure you'll meet a woman. Your legs will just be part of the occasion. Some people have hairy backs.' Jackie drained his whisky and got ready to go to the bar for more. 'You need some professional advice, Chris – counselling.'

'I get plenty of that. Always from people with two legs.'

They stayed in *The Grapes* until six o' clock. Jackie wasn't sure how Chris got home.

CHAPTER FIVE

It was getting hard work, bumping into people with problems. Jackie began to long for the old days when his biggest concern was tripping up and falling over.

On a sunny morning he actually followed someone's advice and took half a loaf of bread to the park to feed the ducks. The ducks were astonishingly grateful and flung themselves into the eating process with great gusto. The swans were surprisingly polite and well mannered, which was unusual. He took that as a sign that maybe things were looking up; although he didn't like the way they looked at him when the bread ran out.

There was blossom on some of the trees. Daffodils were still gleaming in their massed ranks; a silent orchestra of blaring trumpeters. On the grass and in the trees squirrels were squaring up for a fight as the sap rose and rivals faced off. There was going to be a bloodbath if they weren't careful. He wished he'd brought some nuts now, and made a mental note. Nuts and bread. It was a simple life when you stripped away the rubbish and clutter. Bread and nuts and the world was happy. Bread and nuts and a few daffodils. He headed towards the bar.

'Hey, Jack. Who sang the song 'Like a virgin'?'

'Jimmy Hendrix.'

'It doesn't fit. It's only one word.'

'I don't really know many virgins.'

Dawn shrugged. 'It doesn't matter. What do you want – the usual?'

Jackie nodded. 'Where's Mike?'

'He's in the kitchen. There's a problem with the cook. He hit his head or something. Don't eat the mince.' Jackie took his beer to the table and Dawn followed with the whisky. She ran a cloth over the surface as there were some crumbs on it. *The ducks could have had them*, he thought. He thought she fussed him a bit, like a mother. She would make a good mother, he thought.

Out of the window, his gaze always wandered. A woman with a push chair and a child sitting up in it. She seemed to pass by every other day. The child didn't get any bigger. He was beginning to wonder whether it was actually real; maybe it was a doll or an inflatable. *Inflatable babies*. What would they think of next?

Other people were bustling with a brighter spring in their step. People like sunshine. It makes them feel good. Like marmots they come out to play. There had been talk of pedestrianising the whole of the High Street. That would be a good thing. More people walking; pavement cafes. It would be cosmopolitan, continental. He could picture himself eating a baguette. A baguette and a coffee. A fancy coffee that no one had ever heard of. That came with a little biscuit.

Slowly emerging from his reverie he became aware of a dark presence looming at his left-hand side. It was brooding and bristling; he could sense that without looking. It was daring him to look at it; willing him with its eyes. He had learned long ago that resistance was futile. An insane wolverine was easier to ignore.

'Hello Laura,' he said.

'What the hell is this, Jackie? Why didn't you tell me what happened?'

He shifted in his seat as if he was being told off.

'I didn't like to make a fuss.'

'Make a fuss? You were run over by a flaming car, Jackie!'

'It sounds more dramatic than it was.'

'Jesus.'

Laura shook her head. In fact she seemed to shake her entire upper body, like a horse clearing its lungs.

'You're a fucking idiot. What do you want to drink?'

'Mike will know.'

Laura put her bag on the seat and went to the bar. When she returned she was carrying a tray bearing a pint of beer, two glasses of whisky, a small bottle of ginger ale and a glass of red wine.

She was a handsome woman; there was no denying that. Age had done Laura many favours. Her hair was better – her face seemed to have relaxed into itself. Her eyes still burned with fire.

'I can't fucking believe you didn't let me know. I would have come in.'

'I know.' Jackie lifted his beer from the tray and took a few long steadying sips. 'That's why I didn't contact you. I didn't want any visitors. It was embarrassing enough as it was.'

'It wasn't your fault was it?'

'No, not entirely. Well, not at all really. I was on the pedestrian crossing.'

'Shit.'

She unfastened her coat – a lightweight trenchcoat in navy – and shrugged it off onto the seat behind her. She was now wearing a jade and black top with three necklaces of varying sorts dangling across it.

'I could have been a widow,' she said.

'Only a partial widow. We have been separated for two and a half years.'

'Doesn't mean we stop caring.' She sipped her wine and shook her head again. 'You're a fucking idiot.'

They drank in silence. He watched her 'quietly', pretending not to watch her at all. But he was studying her face and those familiar expressions. Every line, he had seen it appear. He thought he was responsible for some of them.

For her part, Laura was staring at the pub carpet, still occasionally shaking her head. She had been genuinely rocked when she heard of Jackie's accident. Her hands were trembling slightly as she drank. She didn't know whether to be angry or relieved. She wanted to be angry with him.

'How's Luke?'

'Fine. He still doesn't want to talk to you.'

'He never does.'

'That's not true. You never let him talk to you.' Laura finished her wine and put the glass on the tray. 'You know his girlfriend's pregnant.'

'Melanie? Melanie's pregnant?'

'Her name's Alison.'

CHAPTER SIX

After his encounter with Laura, Jackie went for a walk up the High Street. It was on an incline and when you got to the top, if you looked back, you could see down to the river. There would be white sail boats on it in the summer. The ferry would start to run. Gulls would dot the surface – so white they looked as though they'd been through a washing machine.

He paused to peer through the window of a bookshop.

He used to write them. At one time his books would have been in there. They'd have been at the front, in the window, to promote 'the local author'.

They weren't now. There was a wicker basket with fluffy yellow chickens and chocolate eggs in it. The year was approaching Easter.

He sat on a bench. It was hard work going uphill; it took a toll on his leg. He rubbed at it quite vigorously, almost painfully. Distracting himself from thoughts he didn't know he was having.

He looked around, searching for the closest coffee shop. He might even eat out this evening; a sad attempt to avoid going home. Being on your own is one thing; feeling alone is another.

He went to a new coffee shop that had only opened in the last few months and modelled itself on the word 'spartan'.

'Jesus Christ,' he said as he walked in. *Where's the fucking furniture?* There were things hanging on the walls that looked like shirts ripped from the backs of refugees.

He ordered a moderate coffee and the barista brought it to where he stood/leaned/slumped against a table made from a slab of slate atop an upturned crate. Jackie asked if he could have extra sugar.

After a minute he took it outside and sat on a plastic chair. Even though the day was starting to cool a little now as the sun began to dip.

A pregnant girlfriend. Pregnant girlfriend.

That was something unexpected.

That would mean Jackie becoming a grandfather.

Shit. He felt barely old enough to tie his own shoelaces, how could he be a grandfather? Granddad. Gramps. Pops. Some other stupid name. He'd kill himself if the child called him Pops.

You had to do things with a grandchild. You'd have to take it to the park, to a fair. He wasn't going to take the kid anywhere near those swans. And he wasn't going to put it on anything that whizzed through the air at high speed.

Maybe he wouldn't even see it. His son didn't like him. They hadn't spoken for two years. They didn't even speak then they just yelled a lot. Jackie used words he didn't know he knew.

He finished his coffee. He probably needed another drink. He would have to go to in a bar at the top end of town.

He heaved himself out of the chair and leaned on his stick. Started heading towards a bistro bar calling itself *Gloriana*.

The place didn't sell proper whisky; he had to settle for a bourbon and coke. Which was okay.

The beer wasn't: the beer was fizzy and came in a ridiculous half-sized glass which was fashioned in the shape of a bulb. A hyacinth bulb.

If I'd wanted a fucking plant I'd have bloody ordered one.

The bourbon went down easy, though. As did the two that followed.

A bloody grandchild. Laura would be a grandmother. She'd love that. All that pent-up maternal frustration because Jackie had refused to countenance a second child. He had very rational reasons which he couldn't remember now, to do with the state of the planet and distribution of love.

Mind you, it was probably as well that they didn't have another child. He'd just have two children now who didn't want to talk to him.

Jackie didn't like the *Gloriana*, and wandered out into the High Street. He was swaying slightly now as his stick appeared to have become less rigid.

It was five o' clock.

He could get an Italian meal at the place that sold Italian food. Or –

Something else.

He ended up going home with a bottle of bourbon and a shredded beef curry.

CHAPTER SEVEN

Saturday was a bad day. He didn't feel well. Too much coke, he decided; bourbon was not his natural drink. God invented limitations for a reason. You should stay within your parameters.

He took a shower. He wondered how Chris managed in a shower. Maybe he could only take baths now. Maybe he needed someone to help him. Jackie should have got his number really; he was a nice enough chap. They'd simply parted in the street with a long friendly handshake and no promises at all. He didn't even know where he lived – he had no idea. Somewhere over 'that way' beyond the cinema complex. He remembered that much.

God, he needed a shave. He looked at himself in a mirror, while supporting himself against the sink. Guys who were still fighting wars in jungles had a better appearance than that. He ran a hand through his grey-streaked hair. It wasn't as spiky as it used to be. At one time he'd been a bristling porcupine; now he looked like a flattened hedgehog.

He went to the kitchen. Get some breakfast. Toast, cereal, or – toast. The crappy bread in the fridge that had been there for a while. It looked okay though, apart from the fluff. He could cut that off.

He should get somebody in to tidy the place.

He sighed. He'd already tried that.

He put the kettle on.

There was a tap at the front door. He looked at the clock on the wall. It was 11.00 am. Who the hell called at 11.00 am? Who the hell called on him at any time? This wasn't going to be good news.

He hobbled to the door with his stick. He was pretty dishevelled. But at least he had his trousers and shirt on. And one of his socks.

The door always stuck. That was another thing he meant to get round to. But there were always more pressing matters: like doing nothing. He put one hand on the frame, kicked the door at the bottom, and yanked it open with his other hand.

'Mrs Marchant.'

'Yes.' She smiled awkwardly. Which was a better smile than Jackie was producing. He was staring blankly.

'What are you doing here?'

She looked away. She was wearing a chunky quilted jacket and boot-cut jeans. Her shoes were somewhere between dainty and clunky. They probably cost more than his rent.

'I don't really know,' she said. 'You're probably wondering how I even know where you live.'

Crossed my mind.

'The truth is I followed you home one day. Not for any sinister reason. Just to see where you lived. And – how you manage.'

Christ.

He couldn't leave her standing on the doorstep.

'Would you like to come in?' he said.

'Thank you.'

She walked in with a definite daintiness. She wasn't a woman used to the rough side of life. Her clunky shoes were a statement that she was trying to live up to. One day she hoped to grow into them.

'I was making a cup of tea. Would you like one?'

'Yes, please. That would be very nice.'

'Right. Erm – take a seat.'

Jackie leaned against a worktop while the kettle boiled afresh. What the hell's going on now? he thought. I lead a very quiet life – where's all this shit coming from? I don't know anybody, and now I know fucking everyone. It's fucking ridiculous.

He took a mug of tea in to her. And a glass of vodka for himself.

She didn't take sugar. Obviously. And she didn't want a biscuit: which was useful because he didn't have any.

Emily Marchant was sitting on the edge of the sofa, looking round the room.

'It's very tidy,' she said, as if that was a miracle. 'Do you own it?'

'No, it's rented.'

'Ah. We're renting too, we haven't mortgaged yet. Even though I could get a cheap mortgage through work. Somehow it seems so 'permanent'.'

Jackie sipped his vodka. Vodka was one of the few spirits he could drink neat; and it seemed to clean his teeth.

'Mrs Marchant – '

'Why don't you call me Emily?'

'Emily – ' He raised his gaze to meet hers. 'Why are you here?'

'Well Robert's taken Jason to football. He plays for an under-9 side, and is very good on the wing. He's very quick. He's quite a slight child and I think he runs fast to keep out of trouble. He also plays the cello. Not at the same time, of course.'

'That's not why you're here, Emily. Why are you here?'

She took a deep breath; so enormous it seemed too big for her lungs. She looked down at her hands. Then at Jackie's glass.

'Can I have a glass of vodka?' she asked.

'Yes, of course.' Jackie made to get up.

'It's okay, I'll get it.'

'Vodka's on the worktop. Glasses are in the cupboard above. Mixers are scattered around anywhere.'

She came back in with a bottle, a glass, and no sign of any mixers.

'Cleans your teeth,' she said.

'I've noticed that.'

She filled the two glasses and they drank in silence for a time. It wasn't a comfortable silence, but it was a silence.

Emily ran her fingers across her face then through her short hair. 'It's silly really. I don't even know, to be honest, why I'm here. I think it's guilt. I can't let it go – the damage I've done to you. It haunts me more, it doesn't haunt me less. Once I met you, in *The Golden Lion*, the guilt and pain hurts me more. To think you can do so much damage to a person – to have that effect.' She looked up from the table and straight into his eyes. 'I could have killed you.'

Jackie stared at her. He understood her difficulty; he knew it in every corner of his body. She'd made a mistake. Or he'd made a mistake. And her life was more affected than his.

Of course he was older; you get used to shit. You come to expect it. But she was much younger; she shouldn't be having anguish like this. She had a young family; everything should be going well for her. He was taking life from her every bit as much as his damaged leg was taking life from him.

'Emily – '

'Would you like to go for a walk some time?' she said. 'The ferry will start running soon. We could go to the coast.'

CHAPTER EIGHT

He figured the only thing to do, with regard to Luke, was to start trying to repair some fences. And preferably do it while he wasn't staggering about in a drunken haze.

He went on a Sunday, at lunchtime, figuring they would probably be in then. He wasn't greatly drunk, but he had stopped at the *Hunter's Moon* to fortify himself. That took a while, so it was a late lunch by the time he arrived. They weren't expecting him.

It was Luke's girlfriend who opened the door. Alison.

Good God, she was pregnant. He'd never seen anyone so big. It looked like she was going to give birth to a fridge.

'I'm Jackie,' he said. 'Luke's dad.' He offered her a bunch of flowers that he'd spent a long time picking out. He thought they were good flowers. So did Alison. She sparkled as she took them.

'I'm so pleased to meet you,' she said. And she actually hugged him, despite the fridge that was bulging between them. 'Come in, come in. The flowers are beautiful.'

He preceded her along the hallway of a terraced house that smelled so much of air freshener it threatened to make his eyes bleed. He went into the lounge. It was better furnished than his place and decidedly homelier. He could see his grandchild living here.

'Where's Luke?' he said.

'He's out back working on the car. Something to do with an overheating alternator? Does that make sense? Something like that. Cars are cars, aren't they? They get you there, you wear them out, and you get another one. Would you like a drink?'

'Erm – '

'We've got tea or coffee. Or – Horlicks.'

'I've brought a hip flask, if that's all right.'

'Of course. Do you need a glass?'

'No, I can manage.'

Alison lowered herself into an armchair while Jackie took a seat opposite. It looked so uncomfortable for her he winced.

'Luke said you liked a drink. To be honest, I thought you'd look like some wild-eyed monster – like one of those aggressive beggars that you see.'

'It's a Sunday,' said Jackie. 'I smarten up.'

She laughed. She laughed well. It was a laugh you couldn't find fault with; honest and clear and innocent. The kind of laugh that the world could do with more of.

'Shall I fetch him?'

'No, it's okay. We can just sit here and talk. He probably doesn't want to see me anyway.'

Alison pulled a face. 'He's just stupid sometimes. As stupid as you are, from what I hear.'

'Is that from my wife?'

'And from Luke. And from the man on the corner. And the man at the bus stop.'

It was Jackie's turn to laugh. He took a swig from his hip flask.

'I wouldn't disbelieve any of them.'

'You seem all right to me. You have to go by impressions, don't you?'

'You do.'

'And you seem all right to me.'

Alison shifted in her seat, trying to find a bit of comfort. That seemed like a tall order; everywhere she moved the bulging child moved with her. And it often objected to the moves she made.

'I'll be glad when this is over,' she said. 'Seemed like a good idea at the time.'

Jackie said, 'What did you do before you got pregnant?'

'Had sex.'

He laughed again. 'No, I mean what did you do for a job, for a living?'

'I was a government cartographer. I used to draw maps of things that were already mapped, but might need mapping again. Things change, you know. Contours, coastlines. Everything alters. I used to put in power lines and such. For the military. Places of interest. They wouldn't make very good tourist maps.'

'Are you still under contract?'

'You're always under contract. It's like having a government pimp.'

'I never knew this.'

'Who would? It's just a job when you sign on. It still is, if I go back to it. I get a lot of time off for having a baby. If I keep having babies they'll never catch me. It's nothing too high level anyway; it's mostly pylons. You wouldn't believe how many pylons there are in the country. They use wind farms to try to disguise them.'

'Is that true?'

'No, I just said it for effect.'

They grinned across the space between them.

Jackie thought he should go before Luke came in and spoiled the mood.

'You're going to need a car seat,' he said. 'For the baby. I could get you one.'

'You'd better,' she said.

CHAPTER NINE

So he still hadn't seen his son. He didn't even know what had gone wrong between them. Well he did. It was the separation from Laura, and the problem with drinking.

Mike, too, had a son that he had problems with. Mike's son was a bastard. Jackie had met him once. He'd frightened the crap out of him. He had, apparently, been a troublesome child as a child. Had had run-ins with teachers, to the extent that he beat them up. Had been expelled from two separate schools. Had joined the Navy and been ejected after six weeks. And now made a living as a bouncer. Although he preferred the term 'security'.

If anyone was going to bite the head off a chicken it was going to be Mike's son Felix.

Sometimes Jackie thought he and Mike should be in therapy.

'Yo, Mike.'

'Jackie.'

Mike started pulling a pint while Jackie stared around an empty bar.

'Where the hell is everyone?'

'Spring fete. Everyone fucks off to dance with flowers and wave fucking bells. Even Dawn's gone.'

'I thought that was next week.'

At least there was no danger of his booth being occupied.

Jackie took his beer and limped across to his table. There were definite signs of bunting outside; he could see it strung across the High Street.

Two minutes later Mike joined him with a bottle of whisky and two glasses. He squeezed himself into the seat opposite and poured out two large measures.

'Cheers,' he said.

'Cheers.'

They clinked their glasses.

After they'd supped a bit Jackie said, 'You've got kids, haven't you Mike?'

'Yeah. The lad you've met, and there's two girls as well. One's a midwife over in Wappingthorpe, and the other one's out in Australia.'

'Do you think they like us?'

'Our kids? I don't know. The boy doesn't like anyone, so he doesn't count. He'd fucking pick a fight with himself. The girls are all right; they seem to like me. I'm going to Australia next year.'

'Have they got kids?'

'Stacey has. The one in Australia. Two little boys. Arran and Vincent.' He reached for his wallet and produced a photograph. Jackie nodded as if it meant something.

'You met them yet?'

'No, that's why I'm going. The trouble is fitting it all in.'

Somehow their glasses had become empty, and Mike topped them up.

'I'm going to be a grandfather,' said Jackie.

'You'll be a good one, if you don't kill yourself. It's a one way trip, Jackie.'

'I know.'

CHAPTER TEN

What if he did write another book? Stuff the duck; that was never going to happen. What if he thought of something new, something genius, something no one had ever thought of before? What if he wrote THE BOOK? That wouldn't happen. No one writes THE BOOK. The best he could hope for was to come up with something that he could maybe write, and hope that somebody thought it was good enough to publish. Some bastard he hadn't met yet. Yeah, I could do that, he thought. Maybe. Write a book for my grandchild; leave a legacy. A book about – Christ knows. It wouldn't be about a happy family. Having said that, he liked Alison. He thought maybe he liked her better than his son; who he still hadn't seen for two years. Alison looked like she'd make a good mother. His son, he thought, was an idiot.

'Hello Dad.'

Jesus Christ. His son had never been in *The Lion*; what was he doing here now? 'Luke.' Jackie stood up and shook his hand. His son's grip was stronger than it used to be; he thought that was a good sign. 'You're looking well. Impending fatherhood suits you. Why don't you have a seat?'

'Okay.'

Luke angled his body into the booth and loosened the zipper of his jacket. He was a tall man, very straight in the body, with pale brown slightly curly hair and somewhat pallid blue eyes.

He bore a vaguely unshaven look but his stubble was pale and unremarkable In many ways he looked what he was. A quantity surveyor. He was twenty-two.

When he spoke his voice was soft. 'Mum said you'd been in a major accident. You don't look too bad.'

'It's mostly on the inside. I bounced like a baby and softened the blow. You got time for a drink, son?'

'Sure.'

Jackie went to stand up, but when he saw his father reaching for his stick Luke jumped up and said, 'I'll get them. Usual?'

'Anything's usual.'

Here was a problem, Jackie thought while Luke was at the bar. How to keep being nice. How to keep things being nice. They were so prone to opposite directions.

It had started off quite normally in Luke's early teens, but as the years and weights grew up so did the distance between them. It was easier to shout than simply talk; and he couldn't even remember half the things that made them shout.

Luke returned with the drinks. Like his mother, he was carrying them on a tray. Maybe Jackie was drinking too much.

'The guy at the bar wouldn't take any money.'

'He'll put it on my tab.'

They shuffled the drinks around and Luke took the tray back. By which time Jackie had drunk one of the whiskies.

Luke slid himself into his seat and took his glass of lager.

'Your partner, Alison – for some reason I thought her name was Melanie; I don't know why.'

'That was my last girlfriend.'

'Oh. Yeah. Anyway, Alison is a really lovely woman. I can see why you like her, and you're a very lucky man. Though God knows what she sees in you.'

Luke sipped at the lager. 'That's what I keep thinking.'

'That's what I used to think about your mother. What the hell does she see in me?'

Jackie sipped at the second of his whiskies, and followed it with a beer.

'She's hell of a big though, Alison, isn't she? I mean the baby's still two months away but she looks fucking massive, doesn't she? I don't remember your mum being that size with you, and you were a big child.'

'Mum wouldn't. She'd be too fastidious.'

'Yeah.'

They both laughed. First time that had happened in years.

'I'm proud of you, you know. Being a father and all. Getting a home, making a family. It's kind of what life's all about. But it's easy to forget it.'

'Yeah.' Luke looked away; the magnet of the High Street was always irresistible. 'It's all life, isn't it?'

They drank in silence for a while. It wasn't a bad silence, though; Jackie had sat through a lot worse. Often in his own company.

Maybe his son didn't hate him as much as he thought. As long as he didn't say anything out of order that might continue for a while.

'Do you know what you're going to call it?' he said.

'Dominic, if it's a boy. Astrid if it's a girl.'

Jackie nodded. 'Good names. Astrid sounds like a Norse goddess. She'll be strong.'

Luke kept staring from the window, and supped of his lager. It was two-thirds gone, and Jackie suspected he wouldn't be having a second.

Luke turned back to his father and looked at him with what appeared to be genuine concern.

'How are you getting on, Dad, with your injuries and everything? Your stick.'

'Bit of a pain, you know. But I'm getting used to it. I've got a scar like you wouldn't believe.'

Luke winced. 'The flowers were nice.'

'Yeah. I spent a while looking for them.'

'They were nice. Alison loved them.'

'I'm thinking of writing another book,' said Jackie.

'That would be great, Dad, it really would.'

'Yeah.' Jackie drained his second whisky and ginger.

'I really liked the duck.'

'Everybody liked the fucking duck.'

CHAPTER ELEVEN

'I'm going to be a grandfather.'

Emily turned to him with a smile that startled him. Nobody smiled that much. Not at Jackie. Nobody smiled that much in the same street as Jackie. It was almost – 'uplifting'.'

'That's wonderful news, Jackie, it really is.'

'Yeah. I guess.'

'Oh come on, it is. Don't be such a moody.' She dug him in the ribs and he had to allow a rueful smile.

'That was my cracked ribs, you know.'

'Oh gosh, I'm sorry.' She put both hands on his arm and squeezed so hard she almost hurt it. 'I'm so sorry.'

He laughed. 'It's all right. They don't hurt any more.'

She dug his ribs again, then sat back in her seat.

They were sitting outside a café half way up the High Street. Drinking lattes, with occasional shots from one of Jackie's hip flasks. The sun was shining. It seemed to do that a lot lately. This was a peculiar year.

He told her about his time with Alison, and his meeting with Luke. 'All through the encounter I kept thinking he would say, 'Alison says why don't you come round for a meal sometime?' But he never did.' Jackie sighed, then swirled the dregs of his coffee. 'I guess we're not as advanced as I thought.'

'It's early days, Jackie.'

'Yep. Early days.' He pondered that in his head. He knew it was early days. At least they'd made a breakthrough. They hadn't shouted at each other or thrown a punch.

That had been a bad day.

He swirled the dregs of his coffee again and said, 'I'm sick of this fucking coffee – should we go to a bar?'

They went to *The Grapes*; the place he'd been to with Chris. It wasn't very busy and the landlord was as cheerful as before. Jackie thought it would be a long time before he struck up a relationship with him. He might not have been the killer that he actually looked, but Jackie thought that he probably was.

'A white wine, beer and two whiskies please.'

'That bloke was in here again; the one you were with. The one on crutches. He didn't look very happy. I think he was crying; I couldn't swear to it.'

'Jesus.' Jackie was entirely flummoxed by this. Partly because of the news about Chris, and partly because the landlord had remembered him.

He was counting out his money as the landlord placed down the drinks.

'Thanks. Would you like one?'

'I fucking live here. I'm never short.'

Jackie took the glasses across to the table in shifts. Emily had chosen one that wasn't near a window, but was in a fairly gloomy corner. They had differing views on tables.

'Are you all right?' she said.

'Yeah, it's just something the bloke behind the bar said. About someone I came in with once; someone from the hospital. It's nothing important, it's just a bit of news, you know.'

He lifted his beer and took a few sips. 'Long life and health, Mrs Marchant.'

'You too, Mister Conor.'

CHAPTER TWELVE

The next day, he spent a lot of time lying down. He didn't feel well. He wasn't sure whether it was a malaise of the mind or a malaise of the body. Either way it left him feeling down. Physically, morally, emotionally and spiritually, Jackie was feeling down.

It took him until ten o'clock to get out of bed, and that wasn't a pretty affair. He immediately fell over and hit his head on a chair.

'Fucking hell!'

God, that hurt. He sat in a miserable heap on the floor and rubbed at his head with the palm of a hand, and that made it marginally better.

'Shit.'

He crawled to the kitchen on his hands on knees.

He drank coffee, vodka, whisky and tea whilst sat on a stool at the rickety table, which overlooked the rickety rear yard. It was supposed to be a communal yard – a 'communal courtyard' – which everyone contributed to. But he couldn't see where the money went. There was a bit of grass, a few plants, a couple of wooden tables and chairs and a barbecue pit.

As far as he knew people seldom went out there; and if they did they were stupid.

A family went out sometimes; a family who lived further along in the block of six apartments of which Jackie's formed a corner. They were nice. He thought they were Iraqi or Syrian, something like that. The two children were very happy and ran around squealing. Even Jackie couldn't object to that. A couple of times they'd waved to him through the window; and Jackie had raised a glass and smiled.

They weren't out there now, though. Nothing was out there, apart from a couple of plastic balls that the Iraqi children had played with, but were now just resting by the rear gate.

Food.

He couldn't be bothered having food, he'd get that later. What he was going to do today was housework: the place was a tip, it smelt like an animal farm, he was going to do something about it. Every bit of cleaning material he had was going to be called into play. He was going to clean the fuck out of the fucker.

He had a lie down first.

At 12.15 he got up and threw himself into the work with a certain degree of gusto. He still couldn't walk unaided, which was a problem and annoyance for him. He had to help himself along by means of the furniture or his stick. That drove him mad. There was a loss of dignity even when he was on his own. God forbid that anyone should ever see him, crawling around on the floor of his own home.

But he did it. He cleaned everything, manfully; 'heroically' in his own mind.

He cleaned the bathroom; the bedroom. He changed the sheets that hadn't been changed for four weeks; because when you live on your own these things don't matter so much.

He cleaned the lounge. He opened the windows to let some fresh air in, and a bee flew in. 'Oh for fuck's sake.' He had to catch it in a glass to release it.

He cleaned the kitchen, which was the worst. It seemed like every second piece of muck in the house had ended up in the kitchen. And he had to get down on his knees a lot, which was bad, very bad. Getting up was even worse. If he'd had a gun he might have shot himself.

But he did it.

At seven o'clock he sat down at the end of the kitchen table with a fresh bottle of Scotch, a bottle of ginger ale, and a glass that sparkled so much it dazzled.

At eight o'clock, with half the whisky gone, he wandered through to the lounge and slumped on the sofa.

He was still there at nine o'clock the next morning.

CHAPTER THIRTEEN

Jessica Roeburn was still trying to get him to work his leg and exercise his other muscles. She was adamant in her admonishments that he clearly wasn't working hard enough, and she wondered if he had made any effort at all.

She had altered her hairstyle since the last time he was there, and appeared to have changed her perfume.

The hair he wasn't sure about. The perfume he approved of; occasionally in the past she had smelt a little of sweat.

'Do you know Chris?' he said. 'The bloke without any legs?'

'Not really,' she said. 'He's not one of mine.'

'Do you think you could get a message to him?'

'About what?'

'Just to give him my phone number. If he wants to get in touch.'

'It's not a gay thing is it?'

'No, I just met him once and he seemed a bit down. I thought maybe I could invite him for a beer or something. Try to cheer him up.'

'I'll see what I can do.' She turned away and slapped some massage oil onto her palms. It wasn't done in a very erotic manner.

'Do you fancy going for a drink sometime?'

'Maybe next year,' she said.

CHAPTER FOURTEEN

Emily Marchant was more dishevelled than usual. Since she was never dishevelled it was quite a departure, although the contours of her hair, which appeared to be heading in several different directions at once, in some ways made her more attractive.

'Oh what a day,' she said, as she slumped down at a coffee shop table next to him. 'Up and down, round about, in his master's chamber. Blooming sick children. They're something you really don't want to know about. I only got into work this morning and immediately got a phone call from his school to say that he's got a nose bleed and would I come and collect him. For a nose bleed! So I went and got him, took him home, his nose stopped bleeding so I took him back again. God. Never get a sensitive child.'

'Why aren't you in work now?'

'Oh – stuff them.' Emily gesticulated wildly with a hand. 'I'm on part time hours anyway, and that wasn't my choice. Stuff them.'

Jackie pondered his coffee for a while, and stirred it slowly in both directions. He knew about sick children. They were always sick. Luke was sick at every opportunity, even when there was nothing wrong with him. He hoped Luke wouldn't pass that on to his child.

'Would you like a bun? A Danish whirl or whatever they're called.'

Emily laughed, and shook her head. 'No, I don't want a bun. I need to relax, take my mind off things. Tell me something funny.'

Tell her something funny. That was easy. Why didn't she ask him to perform some minor surgery?

'Erm – '

Jesus.

'How funny does it have to be, on a scale of one to ten?'

'Eleven.'

Fucking hell. He racked his brain.

'A personal thing?'

'I don't care. As long as it's funny.'

'Right. There was a – no, that's no good.' He rubbed his face between his hands, and pondered as if his life depended on it. 'One time I was – no I wasn't, that was someone else. I was – ' He sighed. *Fucking hell.*

Emily stared at him with something approaching a sparkle in her eyes; which he would have noticed if he hadn't been so intense.

'I'm waiting, Jackie.'

'I'm fucking trying! Jesus.'

She touched his arm to put him out of his misery. 'That's good enough, Jackie. You've made me laugh.' She went to fetch a coffee, and came back with two Danish pastries. She worried that he didn't eat enough. She didn't know that he hated Danish pastries with a vengeance, and would have used them for target practice if he had a mini bow and arrow.

'Thanks,' he said, and smiled.

'Do you have your hip flask?' He passed one to her. He always carried two. One contained vodka, the other held whisky. He would have liked another one that contained dark rum, but he thought three was too many. He didn't want to look like a drunk.

Emily didn't bother pouring the vodka into her coffee, she sipped it straight from the flask. This was a moment that saddened him. He didn't think Emily was a natural drinker; not in the way that he was. He didn't want her following him down this path. It looked good in the early stages. It was tempting and easy, and God knows it tasted good. But you ended up not changing your bedding for weeks, and finding stuff on the floor that you couldn't identify. He went back to his own coffee; staring at the remaining froth. He didn't even really like the stuff.

'Is everything okay for you, Emily? At home and such. Is everything all right?'

Emily stared at her own coffee, and stirred it with the biscuit she'd been given. She didn't eat the biscuit, she just used it to stir the coffee.

She shrugged, looked up, looked away, looked back. She was a strikingly pretty woman, even when she was anguished and upset. On a good day she might look gorgeous. This wasn't the day; but she still looked, probably, better than average. To such an extent that Jackie had to look away. He was getting too old for this kind of stuff.

'Oh yes. Jason's nose bleeds and Robert works late. But I understand that's very much how life is!' She snorted. It was partly a laugh and partly a snort. She stared at a point on the table that Jackie couldn't see. Whichever point it was it was pretty intense; she couldn't take her eyes off it.

'There's a lot of good things in life, Emily. There are a lot of good things in your life. Your son sounds exceptional.'

She nodded. 'Oh yes. He's something of a prodigy with the cello. He's up to grade eight already.'

Jackie nodded. That sounded good. It had to be good or she wouldn't have said it.

'I hate the damn thing. It sounds like the body of a dying cat being dragged across the body of another dying cat.' She drained her coffee. It didn't look like she enjoyed it. 'I wish he played the flute.'

Jackie looked at his hands. Somewhere down there, inside his body, should be words that would help Emily over her moment, and take some of the angst from her life.

Jackie was good with words; he'd written entire books of them. But he was damned if he could think of any now. Even the stupid ones stubbornly eluded him: clichés wouldn't roll off his tongue.

It was Emily who changed it. She took a deep breath through her nose, sniffed, then shook herself like a damp cat. It was almost a shudder that passed through her.

'This is stupid,' she said. 'I didn't come here to make you miserable.'

She sniffed again, looked up and down the High Street, all the people walking here, strolling there, looking like people who'd never had a problem in their lives, even if on the inside they hurt like billyo and wondered where it was all going.

She gave a final sniff.

'Stuff this. Should we go to *The Grapes*?'

CHAPTER FIFTEEN

Laura came into the bar on a Wednesday. She was wearing a navy blue version of a reefer jacket, jeans, boots, an orange tee-shirt, and had her hair pulled back in a plastic tortoiseshell grip. She dispensed with formalities and went straight to the bar, said hello to Mike, got a glass of red wine, two glasses of whisky, and said to Mike, 'Put it on his tab.'

Jackie looked up as she approached his booth. Jesus Christ, his life had never been so busy.

'You look well,' he said.

She put down the glasses, plopped onto the seat opposite, shook her hair as if she'd forgotten she'd tied it back, and dropped her bag on the padding next to her.

'Thanks. I'm trying out a new style.'

'Well it's working. You look good.'

'I wish I could say the same for you. Do you ever get a shave?'

'It's my new style. I call it rockabilly.'

'It looks more like rockatwat.'

She took a swig of wine, tasted it a little in her mouth, then took another one.

'Who was that woman I saw you with the other day?'

'What day? What woman?'

'Outside that coffee place with the ridiculous refugee shirts on the walls.'

'That was Emily. She's the woman who ran over me.'

Laura blinked. She paused for a while then blinked again. Almost unconsciously she drank one of his glasses of whisky.

'Oh.'

'She came in here one day and we got talking and – that's it really. We just talk sometimes.'

Laura blinked again. 'And this seems entirely normal to you?'

'I don't know.' Jackie shrugged, and reached for the glass she'd just drained. He was a bit nonplussed to find the glass empty. He must be drinking faster than he thought.

'Let me repeat the question. Do you think this is normal?'

This time he simply shrugged his eyebrows. 'There's nothing going on between us, if that's what you think.'

'Didn't look like that. Do you see the way she looks at you?'

'She looks like that at everybody.'

'Maybe. But not everybody's you.'

Laura drained her glass, waved to Mike, and he started pouring her another. 'I should buy the damn bottle.' She left the table to collect her drink, and came back with an additional two whiskies.

'You drink far too much you know. It's going to kill you. It probably is killing you. I'm looking at you dying right now.'

Jackie shrugged again. It was becoming his default position. She was right, of course. Everybody knew she was right. He knew she was right when she first said it six years ago. He could almost remember the occasion.

'The trouble is I like it so much.'

She smiled sadly at him. 'I know, babe. I know you do.'

They drank quietly for a while; possibly sharing memories that they didn't quite remember. Possibly making new ones – it was always hard to tell with a marriage. Especially a marriage that had gone wrong.

At least they could still talk.

'What you did, with the flowers and going round, that was a nice thing, Jackie. That was okay.'

'Yeah.' He cradled his glass. 'It was good to see him, in a way. She's a nice woman. I might take flowers again.'

'Do you think we should do something, for the birth? Do people do things?'

'I don't know; you're the woman.'

'Don't get sexist with me.'

She gestured across to Mike, indicating that she was going to pay for some of the drinks.

'Think about it. And watch yourself with that woman.'

CHAPTER SIXTEEN

'The ferry runs again next week. They make a big day of it – lay on drinks and everything. I'll get us tickets, if you like. You have to book in advance.'

Jackie smiled. Emily had a way of making him smile, even with her problems.

'Okay,' he said. 'Get some tickets. Maybe you'd like to take your son?'

'He's at camp,' she said.

He went back to his drinking after Emily left.

The Golden Lion was quiet. After a time Mike walked across with a bottle of whisky and two clean glasses. He eased himself onto the bench. 'She's a strange one.'

'She's all right. She's just a bit lost I think.'

'Aren't we all?' Mike poured the whisky and raised his glass. 'To our enduring health.'

Jackie laughed as he raised his own glass. 'Have we got any health? I don't think we could make a fit body between us.'

'Speak for yourself. I'm a fucking god.'

They drank peaceably for a while, revelling in the quietness of the bar and the laziness of the day. Sunlight didn't stream through the windows, but at least it limped in in its fashion. The only thing disturbing the silence was Dawn's occasional tutting and clucking as she pored over her latest crossword.

'Your wife's an interesting woman.'

'Yeah. You can bloody have her. Even when we're separated I can't get away from her.'

'I had a wife like that.'

'Yeah?'

That completely puzzled Jackie. He realised how little he really knew of Mike; and possibly the rest of the world. One can find many answers in the bottom of a bottle. But not all of the answers are there.

'She wasn't the mother of my children; she was another one, earlier. Veronica. Called herself Ronnie. I met her at a bikers' convention in Huddersfield. Way back – must be in the late eighties. I was on a Honda which I'd borrowed from a mate. She rolled up with a candy floss.' Mike smiled, casting his mind back through the decades, licking his lips at the memory. 'I still remember that candy floss. I can smell it now.'

Jackie smiled with him. He could picture that candy floss, too. He hadn't had one for years. He'd always marvelled at the way it was made.

'What happened?' he said.

'A few years later she pissed off with a bloke with a Harley. Kept coming back, though.'

He poured more whiskies.

'Years later she kept coming back to slap me about. Said I'd ruined her life. Ruined *her* life? She took all the fucking furniture. That's when I came down south. Came down here. Ended up in Queensbridge.'

'It's not a bad town.'

'No; I like it. Peaceful.'

Mike stood up as a group of people entered, and Dawn was too busy to notice them.

'I don't know why I fucking bother with her.'

Mike shook his head as he trudged back with the whisky bottle.

CHAPTER SEVENTEEN

It was Dawn who served him on the Thursday of the following week. It was another good day: the temperature was climbing and spring was well and truly in the air. One could almost be glad to be alive.

'Oh hi, Jack. Come down here – ' She gestured with her head to the quiet end of the bar, and led him down for a chat. 'You won't believe what's happened now. Effin Ryan. He only thinks he's gone and got his mother up the duff. I said to him, she's only after your money.' She glanced away and shook her head. 'I don't know why I said that, he hasn't got any. Anyway. What do you think?'

'Erm. Can I get a drink?'

'Yes of course.' They went back to the pumps. 'What do you think, though?'

'Well. It's Oedipus all over again.'

'Oedipus? Is that like Bagpuss?'

'Yes. It was a series about a cat who had a thing about his mother.'

'Sick.'

Dawn pulled a beer; nodded to acknowledge another customer, and shouted to Mike who was in the back, dealing with the cook, who was new, and only understood German.

'You're looking very smart today, Jack. Very handsome.'

'Thanks.' Jackie looked down at himself. He had on smart brown shoes that were almost clean. Stone-coloured chinos with an elasticated waist. A beige and white shirt that was hanging loose; and a tan sports jacket that he'd had to buy especially for the occasion.

'You got something on?'

'Yeah. Two o'clock, I'm walking down to the ferry – I'm going to its annual launch.'

'Yeah?' Dawn smiled brightly as she passed him two glasses of whisky. 'It's really good. I did it once. Threw up over a seagull.'

'Brilliant.'

He limped to his table with his drinks, and rested his stick at an angle. He'd invested in a new one. This was much snazzier: lightweight carbon decorated with purple swirls and indigo racing stripes. He could move at the speed of light with it. He loved the handle, which was a chrome goose. And the tip, which was battered chrome with a goose motif.

He sipped his drinks, one after another; and Dawn snuck across with a couple more.

It would be fair to say he wasn't looking forward to the afternoon trip. He would feel out of place and incredibly conscious that he would be there with Emily Marchant. He didn't know why she kept doing it; spending time with him in public. Queensbridge wasn't a big town, people would notice. She seemed oblivious to that. Or maybe she wanted to encourage it. Who the hell knew? Jackie didn't.

For Jackie the question would have been simple. He kept meeting Emily because he was lonely.

He decided to ease back a bit on his drinking; he'd be staggering before he got on the boat. He didn't want to be the first of the season to fall over the handrail. That always got in the local paper.

It wasn't a big river trip. He'd never done it, but he knew how it was.

The ferry didn't go far: two miles downstream to the small town of Littleburn: two miles back against the flow. On certain days it bypassed Littleburn and carried on for another four miles to the coast.

Women would wear fancy frocks and men would wear bow ties and boaters. Damned if he was going to do that. Last time he wore a fancy frock he tripped over it.

He had another drink. Sod it.

He was supposed to be meeting Emily at the landing stage. Despite all his internal protestations he was looking forward to that, seeing Emily again. Seeing her in a pretty dress. Smiling at him, waving. Young enough to be his daughter.

He shook himself. *Fucking idiot.*

Fucking idiot.

Dawn brought him another beer.

He looked at his watch. It was twenty past one.

He'd set off for the quay in ten minutes.

CHAPTER EIGHTEEN

She was there, just as he'd pictured. She was wearing a calf-length summer dress of pristine white with a purple iris motif, and a loosely tied belt of the same material. She had on a white broad-brimmed hat with a thin purple band.

'I'm going to wear something to go with your stick,' she had said. She was as pleased as Punch. Her smile could have cracked the heart of a statue. She kissed his cheek and linked his arm.

Shit, there were a lot of people there. It was quite an event for Queensbridge, which didn't have much to celebrate. They didn't make a huge amount of fuss about the killing of several Cavaliers in 1642. 'Have you got your hip flasks?'

'Not today.'

'That's my boy,' she said.

She led him to the edge of the quay, where there was a chain of linked iron hoops to prevent people from falling in prematurely.

'You look very nice.'

'So do you,' he said. On the list of the many understatements he had understated in his life, that one would have to be near the top. He didn't want to tell her how good she looked because that would take the whole afternoon and they'd never get anything done.

The river rippled. On the far bank, trees were massed in their early year colours, leaves fleshing out with the brilliant greens of spring. There was a small jetty opposite, backed by a lane going up into the low hills of the 'other side'. Cottages flanked it, doing nothing in particular. It wasn't clear, from this distance, whether anybody lived in them. Pastures extended beyond them, dotted with sheep and bisected by walls. A tractor or somesuch was slowly advancing.

Emily smiled as she peered straight down towards the water. 'Look at the ducks,' she said. 'Look at the colours they wear. You couldn't invent or create that.' Jackie nodded. They were beautiful creatures. Ducks always appeared to have a purpose to their lives. They were always going somewhere or other, even if it was only in circles. He wondered what they dreamed of at night.

As a klaxon blared, people began to ascend a ramp to board the vessel.

The boat itself wasn't as fancy as the event suggested. It wasn't a big ferry and, although the owner had tried to keep it in trim, years on the water had affected it. The paint wasn't as bright as it once would have been, and the deck had a strangely adhesive feel to it. It could accommodate sixty passengers. Crew-wise there was only the captain and a 'hand'. The hand was young and changed every year. On this occasion he was a handsome young local wearing a white steward's jacket and smart black trousers. There were also two professionals, hired for the day; a young slender woman and a young slim man. They were offering drinks from behind a makeshift bamboo bar. The drinks were priced at the higher end of the market.

The ferry pulled away with surprisingly little fuss. An increase in the engine noise and the merest of judders and shudders. But the crowd got excited; the people on board. All of a sudden there was a huge surge towards the bar.

Being grown-ups, and completely averse to the whims of the mass and the press of the crowd, Jackie and Emily hung back, leaning over the side rail. Possibly on the port side; maybe on the other. They watched the outskirts of Queensbridge slip quietly by, and noticed how picturesque it looked. It was a fine town to find oneself drifting past. 'Have you done this before?'

'Yes, I came once with Mathew. It wasn't long after Jason was born. We left him with Mathew's mother.'

As the ferry drew out into the centre of the river the air grew cooler. Emily wrapped a white shawl around herself and Jackie fastened his jacket. He caught the eye of the steward and despatched him for a couple of drinks. He hoped that a heavy tip would make him come back again, but the young man waved it away. 'I've read your stories, Mister Conor. I loved that duck. Best duck ever.'

'What is this duck of yours?' said Emily.

'The book I wrote. 'Avilon'. Everybody liked the damn duck. It wasn't even the best thing in it. You should have met the frog.'

'The frog?'

'I just made that up; there wasn't a frog in it. It was just about the duck, and the people who fought over it for their own nefarious purposes. It flew away in the end.'

Even without being asked the young steward brought fresh drinks. Emily thought there were benefits to knowing Jackie.

CHAPTER NINETEEN

After two hours the ferry pulled in to a small jetty at Littleburn. Everybody spilled off the boat and straight into the *Swan's Nest*, a waterside pub that briefly hosted the annual launch party.

Wooden tables in abundance. Seats, tablecloths, flowers, things on sticks that waved about, and copious amounts of finger food and alcohol. Jugs of water with sprigs of mint. Early Pimms for those of a mood.

They had sixty minutes to expend there. They chatted to a few people who were as happy as Larry and giggling like fools. They tossed crumbs of food to the doves and ducks that had been waiting all year for this, and were strutting around the freshly mown lawn like exiled courtiers reliving the glory of Versailles.

They wandered back to the river, and leaned on the fence at the foot of the garden Another four feet and they would fall in. Emily was drinking a glass of white wine and Jackie had the largest glass of neat vodka she had ever seen. In proximity to a naked flame it would be a fire hazard.

'Do I make you nervous, Jackie? Do you feel uncomfortable around me?'

'On the contrary,' he said; and he took a swig of vodka so strong it almost stripped the enamel from his teeth. 'That's the problem; I'm far too comfortable with you.'

Emily gazed at him with a look that was somewhere between serious and sad. She had taken off her floppy hat and her hair was shining and ruffling in a breeze. She even had the sun behind her.

'Why is that a problem?'

Jackie exhaled long and slowly. He'd got himself into this situation; and she had asked the question. He had to do something about answering it. He wished he'd brought his hip flasks now.

He took another sip from what truly was a large glass of vodka. But some days it was never large enough.

'I – ' he started; then stopped. That wasn't the right answer. It wasn't the way to go. He took her glass of wine from her and took a sip of that as well.

He blinked at the water. He knew what he was getting into when he came here. He couldn't even blame it on naivety.

He said, 'I can't afford to like you so much. It's morally wrong. Ethically wrong. You're young and talented and smart and beautiful. You have your life ahead of you, and a family to share it with. For goodness' sake Emily, you have a young son. You can't be throwing that away for a fling with me. Look at the state of me; I can barely bloody walk. And I'm old enough to be your son's grandfather.'

Emily nodded. It was a perfectly reasonable and sensible explanation.

'What if it isn't a fling?' she said.

Shit. Jackie drained his vodka and limped to the bar for another.

'Just keep pouring,' he said. 'And throw that fucking ice out.'

CHAPTER TWENTY

Two days later, in the bar, Mike had a faintly quizzical look on his face. 'Jackie,' he said, as Jackie hobbled forward, having performed his usual bushwhacking routine.

'What? What are you looking at me like that for?'

'Nice one, Jacks,' said Dawn, nodding at him 'knowingly', giving him a tender look.

'What the hell's going on?' he said, looking from one to the other.

Dawn gave another knowing look and nodded approvingly. She almost gave him a wink.

What the hell?

Mike passed him the beer and slid two glasses of Scotch towards him.

'You seen the paper today?'

'What paper? I don't read the papers.'

Mike pushed a copy of the weekly *Queensbridge Gazette* across the bar. The paper had only come out that morning. Its front page celebrated the launch of the summer ferry; lauded its long and noble history, dating back to the days when people didn't even have boats and got about by sitting on logs and paddling with their hands. There was a half-page picture of people on the deck. Two of them looked familiar. 'That isn't me,' he said.

'The stick's a bit of a giveaway.'

He should have thrown the fucking stick in the river.

'So what's this then?' said Mike. 'Local celebrity makes good?'

'I've always been a local celebrity. The locals just never realised it.'

Jackie took his drinks to the table in relays. His leg wasn't getting any better. All the time it hurt and ached. He thought maybe the surgeons had missed something. Left a pair of scissors inside. Somebody's empty lunch packet.

He sighed and drank and tried not to think about the front page of the newspaper. But it was the only thing to think about. He knew this wasn't good news; although he wasn't entirely sure why. Partly it was because her husband might see it. A lot of people she knew might see it. And that wouldn't be a good thing – for her. It wouldn't affect him, but –

It wouldn't be a good thing for Emily.

And also – it was one thing to have a private friendship; a private relationship. But to have people at the bar talking about it. Mike and Dawn. This wasn't a good thing. He didn't want Emily having bad things said about her. He wasn't so bothered for himself, nobody gave a fuck about him. It was just –

After twenty minutes Laura walked into *The Golden Lion*.

Oh Christ; he knew this was coming.

She didn't even bother going to the bar, she simply indicated to Mike and he nodded and started getting the drinks together.

She sat down and threw her bag on the seat. This day she was still wearing the reefer jacket, but she had an 'I hate God' tee-shirt on underneath it. She hadn't bothered with the tortoiseshell grip, and her hair was tumbling about her face. She looked good. The hurried, frustrated, slightly flushed look suited her.

She put a copy of the *Gazette* on the table.

'What's this about then?'

'It isn't me.'

'The fucking stick isn't yours?' She snorted. 'At least get rid of the fucking stick, Jackie.'

Dawn came over with the drinks on a tray. Mike thought it prudent to stay out of the way.

'I'll end up a fucking alcoholic myself at this rate.' Laura drained half the red wine and even before she'd signalled to Mike, Dawn was on her way back with another. 'What's this all about, Jackie? This is so wrong on every level. This is the woman who ran over you. She's young enough to be your daughter. She's got a bloody child.'

Jackie nodded at all of this. She was right on every point so far. He just couldn't entirely see what it had to do with her. He wasn't shaking the world. 'Why does this bother you so much? What's so wrong about it?'

'Wrong? *Wrong?* I'll tell you what's wrong. Your son's having a baby, your life's going to pot, and you're fannying about with some tart.'

That was sufficient incentive to take a long draught from his beer, and swallow a whisky.

'I don't think she actually qualifies as a tart.'

'A tart's governed by her behaviour. Not by anything else.'

Jesus. Something had got up Laura's ass. And it certainly wasn't Jackie: that had never happened.

'You can't see what's happening, can you? She's manipulating you for – whatever reason she's got in mind. Answer me honestly. Are you having an affair with that woman?'

'No.'

'I don't believe you.'

Laura finished her drink, sat a while longer, said nothing more, then left.

Mike came across to clear the empty glasses.

'That was an interesting conversation,' he said.

CHAPTER TWENTY-ONE

They were sitting on grass on a low hillside overlooking the town, the river and the countryside beyond. Emily had driven him there in a Porsche; which was a crappy idea because he could hardly get in or out of it.

'You're driving again,' he said.

'Yes. Meeting you somehow gave me the confidence. Although I'm still not very confident; particularly in that bloody car.' She looked at it, gleaming in the sunlight; parked on a patch of dirt which gloried in the title of a car park. 'That's why we hit the hedge.'

Jackie stared at the car, too.

'The Porsche was a mistake, wasn't it?' she said. 'I thought it would be amusing, but I forgot about – '

'Me being a cripple.'

'Something like that.'

She laughed, and turned to the picnic basket she'd brought. There was nothing in it but a bottle of vodka, a bottle of whisky, and some lemon-ginger biscuits.

'I don't want us getting fat.'

They had to drink from the bottles as she'd forgotten the glasses.

It wasn't the first time, and it wouldn't be the last.

'This isn't really something we can do, Emily. We can't keep doing it.'

'What isn't?'

'Whatever we're doing. It isn't – it's not going to work.'

'We haven't even touched each other yet, Jackie. Can't we just sit and enjoy the view?'

'Yeah, I guess,' he said. 'That would be all right.'

And then she kissed him.

CHAPTER TWENTY-TWO

He couldn't –

It was addictive. She was addictive. Her clothes, her hair, her smell, her humour. Everything about her was something he shouldn't be getting involved with. She even had a son; a little boy. He was only seven. Good on the bloody cello.

Christ. This had 'everything that's wrong' written all over it. Her husband. He said to her once, 'What does your husband do?'

'Computers, phones – items like that. He's an agent, a liaison, for a group of low level tech companies. He changes his car about three times a year. I think he changes it when it needs refuelling.' At least he wasn't a body-builder who was likely to come round and kill him. 'He goes to the gym a lot.'

Oh fucking hell.

'What was the deal with the duck?' she said.

He snapped out of his reverie.

They were at a waterside bar a couple of miles from Queensbridge. She'd driven him there in a Range Rover Evoque. It was white with black leather interior. Jackie had never had a car better than a Fiat in his life. He didn't even like the Fiats, it was just – that was the first car he'd got.

'It wasn't the duck per se,' he said. 'It was its colouration. Particularly on its wing feathers. It was kind of – like a shade of turquoise that was so rare it was almost unique. And the pigment, the colour, was highly prized – particularly in some of the oriental countries; and a couple of countries in eastern Europe. The Romanies liked it. It was thought it would give you protection from the gods, or your enemies, or time itself. Stop you getting older, preserve your children. Of course you couldn't kill the duck because then the supply of feathers would cease. So you had to 'milk' the feathers, and try to breed the duck. Which, because the genetic mutation that produced the colouration also had an effect on its fertility, wasn't as easy as you'd hope.'

He swirled his drink in his glass. He was drinking more vodka than usual. He didn't know why this was; except some of the authors he liked appeared to like vodka, and put it in many of their books. Mind you, a lot of the authors he admired had got by on whisky and bourbon; so it was a tricky one. Maybe it was better to keep all your options open.

'Was it a male or a female?'

'A male.'

Emily was wearing another summer dress. A frock. This one was yellow and white; irises, or something, climbing up her body from her calves to her arms. Over her thighs, across her belly. Everything about her was –

'Do you want another drink?' he said. Then he added, 'You shouldn't be drinking so much when you're driving.'

'We could get taxis,' she said. 'I can afford them. But I like the driving – driving you. It's the most private place we get in the world – driving through the lanes. Driving through the coppices, driving past the quarries.'

She picked at the remains of a salad as Jackie went for fresh drinks. Somehow even staff in strange places seemed to know what he wanted before he reached the bar.

'I never thought I'd like it again,' she said, as he put a glass of white wine in front of her. 'The driving. To be honest, I never liked it much before the accident. But I like it with you. It gets me away. It gets you away. Do you not think that? Being in the car?'

'I don't know. I – '

He just wanted to wrap his arms around her and kiss her so hard that his lips might bleed. But he couldn't do that. All the time he kept fighting it. Laura was right; it was wrong on so many levels. She was young, he was old. She was innocent, and he was a fraud. Everything about her was at the prettiest end of the spectrum from him.

'Do you think we should have sex?' she said.

CHAPTER TWENTY-THREE

'He punched me once.'

'Who's that?' said Mike.

'Luke, my son. We had an argument about his mother, and I said something and he said something, and I didn't like what he said. So I slapped him. And he punched me, kind of as a reflex I suppose. Wasn't a big punch. Didn't hurt or anything. But it shocked both of us. It stopped, you know – the world stopped for a minute. Just paused, and everything altered. And it never got back again, back to what it was. We'd crossed an unknown barrier.'

Mike stared at the table. Stared at his hands. Mike had hands big enough to strangle a camel.

He looked up and across the bar to where Dawn was serving.

'I'd be bloody lost without her, you know. If she didn't have parents I'd adopt her. Do you know what she said this morning? 'Who won this year's Oscar for best director?' I said Frederico Fellatio. She said it didn't fit.' He shook his head. 'You couldn't fucking buy that.'

They drank whisky for a time; and ate pork scratchings and nuts that were out of date. They looked out of the window. The window was the best place in the world as far as Jackie was concerned; and Mike was getting into it too.

Dawn brought them some more nuts.

She'd had her hair altered; possibly in an attempt to leave Ryan behind. She looked older; better for it. She looked more mature. She'd probably get the next job she went for.

'I'm fucking up, Mike. I'm getting into trouble.'

'With that woman?'

'Yep.'

Mike nodded. Ruminated. Chewed on a strange mixture of pork scratchings and peanuts.

'I'd get into trouble with her,' he said.

'Aye.'

'What you have to ask yourself Jackie is – what are you getting out of it – and is it worth it. Is it good for her? Is it good for you?'

'I don't flaming know,' Jackie said. 'If I flaming knew I wouldn't be talking to you about it.'

'I'm assuming you like her, and it's not just – '

'Of course I fucking like her. I can't get her out of my mind – can't stop thinking about her. She's driving me nuts.' Mike nodded. Ruminated some more. He brushed salt from his hands and wiped them on his trousers. He finished a whisky, picked up the bottle.

'You're in trouble mate.'

CHAPTER TWENTY-FOUR

He met Luke, at Luke's request, at a place down at the quay. In Italy it would be called a trattoria; in Queensbridge it was simply a café.

He was offering lunch. Luke, that was. Jackie settled for a pizza. 'Mum's going purple.'

'Over the baby?'

'That and this woman you're dating.'

Jackie shrugged, and sipped at his Peroni. 'We're not dating; we just meet as friends.'

'That's what you all say you older people, don't you?'

'When the hell did you get so smart?'

Luke shrugged. So did Jackie. They stared out across the water. Sunlight was reflecting off it. Seagulls were sitting on it. Little white sailing boats were bobbing on it. It was an idyllic spring day on an idyllic small town to live in.

Two rowing teams were having a practice session on the downstream run. It looked like it wasn't meant to be a race, but the crew that was trailing didn't seem to recognise that; they were rowing hell for leather to catch up. Their oars were rotating like the vanes of crazed windmills. If they rowed any harder they would lift the boat into the air.

But still they trailed. Sometimes it's not about effort, it's about style.

Jackie sipped his Peroni, and wished that someone would bring him another one.

'So. Don't keep me in suspense. How's Alison doing? Is everything going well, to plan, all the rest of that stuff? It's all on course? It's all set?'

Luke gave a snort like a small horse and finished off his own beer.

'God. You don't want to get pregnant, Dad.'

I certainly don't.

'I don't know how women stand it. If it isn't pain it's pain, or discomfort or something. All the time. Getting up stairs is like tackling a mountain. Everything looks *painful*, you know?' He grimaced and winced and flapped a hand at his face. 'Everything looks hard.'

'Have you packed your bags yet, for the rush to the hospital?'

'I haven't. Alison has. Her mother has. And Mum has. We've got about eight bags lined up. By the time we decide which one to take the baby will be going to school.' He waved his hand at a waiter and indicated for two more beers. 'Do you want anything else?' he said.

'If they've got whisky I'll take that.'

The drinks arrived with the food. The place didn't serve Scotch so Jackie was back to Jack Daniels. He figured he could live with that at a push; although the cola was flat and did the drink no favours. He asked for a second one before the waiter left.

His pizza was large, utilitarian, and very pizza-like. He wasn't sure what some of the things on it were.

'They're Egyptian capers,' said Luke.

'Fucking hell.'

But he did not glance at Luke's heaped plate with any hint of envy. Luke's meal was mostly greens and purples, with more lettuce leaves than Jackie had seen in one place before. The sliced cherry tomatoes appeared like little beacons of hope amidst the beginnings of a swamp.

Hiding amongst it, almost guiltily, was a pallid fillet of veal.

'You losing weight?'

'I'm trying to. We're supposed to be living more healthily. Got to keep myself alive for the baby.'

'I was thinking of taking up smoking again.'

'You probably need it,' said Luke.

Jackie waved for another Jack Daniels and realised that he would be paying for this meal. It didn't bother him at all; he was getting to like his son.

He picked up a slice of pizza between his fingers, and chewed on it in a knowledgeable way.

'I thought I might go round to see Alison again, if that's all right.'

'Yes of course, she'd like that. You should go when Mum's there, see how she fusses. Or go when Alison's mum's there, and watch some real fussing.'

'Mothers, hey?'

'Yeah.' Luke cut into his veal and chewed it vigorously. 'They're nearly as bad as fathers.'

Jackie couldn't argue with that. Fathers and sons. Someone should write a book about that. D H Lawrence; he'd probably be good at it.

'This woman you're seeing – '

'Emily.'

'Mum's really concerned about her. She thinks she's after something.'

'We're just friends. We don't do anything but mostly talk. I don't know why your mother has a problem.'

Luke shoved the lettuce around on his plate. 'Jealousy I guess. Emily's a younger woman.'

Jackie shrugged. 'Maybe.' He picked up the menu and studied the desserts. 'What did you say this place is called?'

'*Nostra Pastrami*.'

I shan't be coming here again.

CHAPTER TWENTY-FIVE

He was lying on a hillside with Emily. They seemed to spend a lot of time in meadows: in meadows, on meadows, looking at meadows, driving past meadows. They inhaled a lot of meadows.

The grass was tall, and Emily was chewing on a long stem of it. She had on a silver top. It was satin, or something. Baggy, like a tee-shirt; but not a tee-shirt. Below that she was wearing distressed blue jeans that were so distressed they must have suffered real heartache. She'd taken off her shoes, and her feet were bare.

'My family is going completely mad,' said Jackie. 'My son is turning out okay, but my wife has become persistently hysterical. I don't know whether she's going to implode or explode; but she looks to be on her way to something. You'd think, being separated, you wouldn't see so much of each other. I see more of her now than when we were married. She's even taking over *The Lion*. She's got a better relationship with Mike than I have.'

'She'll be worried,' said Emily. 'You have the birth of a grandchild imminent and –' She took the stem of grass from her teeth, stared at it quizzically, then tossed it aside. 'And that's a big thing.' She rolled onto her side, and propped herself on an elbow. She looked down at him gravely. She had the sun artfully behind her again. Sometimes he wondered if she arranged that deliberately. 'Tomorrow Robert will be away at a conference in Bristol. Why don't you come to my house? I'll pick you up. There's plenty to drink in the cabinet.'

Too soon, too soon. I could never make love in your house. Jackie felt panic rising in him like an onrushing heart attack. He didn't know why he was so scared.

Emily gave the slightest of shrugs. Even that made her satin shirt shimmer. There was no eye contact here. She was looking down at the grass.

I couldn't even be there. Another man's territory. I couldn't make love in your house. I don't even have to ask myself; I know I won't be able to.

'We don't have to make love. We can just sit and talk. I'll show you the garden.'

What would be the point of me going?

'Maybe you could come to my place again?' he said.

'Or we could go to a hotel.'

Jesus. A hotel. In the middle of the day. This situation was getting all kinds of serious.

'Okay,' he said. 'But maybe not tomorrow. Maybe we could leave it 'til next week.'

CHAPTER TWENTY-SIX

Laura came to the bar the next day and didn't even bother waving to Mike; he just prepared the drinks in the manner of an eager puppy. 'I hear you saw Luke the other day.'

'I did.' Jackie finished his whisky and pushed the glasses aside to make room for the new arrivals. 'We went for lunch. It was okay.' Laura put her bag down. Today she was wearing a baggy-sleeved something-or-other in orange and black. It appeared to have a mix of tiger stripes and leopard pawprints. There were combat trousers beneath, in a deep shade of khaki. And she wore boots that would frighten a paratrooper. Her hair was tied back. Her make-up was remarkably good, as if she'd been to 'a place'. And she was chewing a piece of gum. Which didn't last long. She took it from her mouth and stuck it under the table.

'Mike has to clean this you know.'

'Tff. It's only a little bit. What did he say?'

'Who?'

'Luke. Did he say that I'm being too fussy? I'm clucking?'

'No. He said Alison's mother is a lot worse.'

'Thank God for that,' said Laura. She practically snatched the glass of wine from Mike's hand when he arrived with it. 'It's not like I'm a bitch, is it?'

'No.'

Laura agreed with that, and nodded while she drank. She wasn't quite herself today. It was hard to put a finger on why, but Jackie did the traditional man-thing of assuming it all related to female hormones.

He sipped his beer while he looked out of the window, There was the woman with the push-chair again – the baby that never seemed to grow. This time it looked as though the baby was upside down.

'Are you seeing what's-her-name later?'

'Emily,' said Jackie. 'No. It's not a regular thing. She has family, commitments, a job. Usual kind of stuff. We only meet up on odd occasions, and it's only to talk.'

'She's definitely after you,' said Laura. 'And do you know what? I genuinely can't see why.'

'Thanks for that.'

'The thing is, Jack – ' (She only called him Jack when she was drunk. She must have been drinking before she arrived.) 'Even though we're separated we've never talked of divorce. I always assumed we'd kind of stay married, even if we're not together.'

'I haven't talked about divorce,' said Jackie. 'I don't want a divorce. I don't want to get married to Emily. And that's not the agenda anyway; it's not that kind of friendship.'

'What kind is it then? Lust and booze? Is that what attracts her – your stench of alcohol?'

'I think you're being unfair.'

Laura lowered her head. She traced a pattern on the table with a fingertip. No one else would have been able to see what the pattern was. 'You're right. I'm sorry.' She finished her wine, but this time she didn't seem to want another. 'Do you ever wish we could take up smoking again?'

'No,' Jackie said. 'I never think of it.'

CHAPTER TWENTY-SEVEN

Jessica Roeburn had made the effort, or contribution, to get in touch with Chris McKenna and pass on Jackie's number. For his part, Chris responded and phoned Jackie at home. They agreed to meet at a bar near the quay. In the summer this was becoming the new destination. Fresh air and water sounds. It had to be healthy, thought Jackie. Fresh air, water, and the life enhancing qualities of alcohol.

'How's it going mate?'

'Good, good.' Chris manipulated his crutches and manhandled his legs and got into position at a ranch-style table, with his back to the water. His face was flushed but he was looking happy. 'I'm good mate. How are you?'

'I'm okay. Still got my stick but I'm pretty much used to it now. I'd probably miss it if it wasn't there.'

'I know what you mean.' Chris adjusted himself at the table. The adjustment was always the hardest part; finding a position in which life was comfortable. He was panting when he finished.

'Shall I get us a drink?'

'Yeah.'

Jackie came back with a tall jug of it. A waitress trotted behind with glasses.

'Cheers mate.'

'Cheers.'

They smiled and drank and enjoyed the ambience. A quayside tavern on a good day in summer is one of the better places to be in the world. It was hard for other people to even annoy them, such was the quality of the day.

'You're looking well,' said Chris.

'I am. I've passed through puberty now and apparently it's all uphill from here.'

Chris laughed, and raised his glass as if he was checking it for impurities. The sun shone through it as if it was a glass of amber jewellery. It didn't take much to make men happy.

'I'm making progress,' Chris said, 'of sorts. I was put in touch with a dating app for – people like me.' He looked at his legs, and his crutches were clearly prominent in his mind. 'It's supposed to be fairly discrete and that, you know? It's not cheap. It's not for weirdos.'

'That's good, Chris, it genuinely is. You need to get out more – meet some chicks.'

'Yeah.' Chris grinned as best he could. 'The trouble is – I don't know if I'll fancy them. It sounds ridiculous but – cripples and that sort? I don't think I could ever fancy a cripple.'

Jackie could see that. He understood it. You might get weaker but you don't want to lose what you had. 'Do you want anything to eat?' he said. 'I'm going for more beer.'

'No, I'm fine mate.'

Jackie went for another jug. It felt heavier than the first one. He must be getting older. He heard someone laughing and looked back. But they weren't laughing at him; it was children playing with a ball. He smiled and sat down. He poured out the beer and rearranged the glasses. 'They're probably as scared as you are,' he said. 'It might even be worse for a woman; I don't know.'

'I think they adjust to things better,' said Chris. 'They cope more easily than men, don't they?'

'Possibly. I don't know. Have you been in touch with any?'

'I've looked at a few. I've probably looked at most of them. They all look very nice. You know. In their pictures. You just wonder what's going on down below.'

'Same as you then.'

'Yeah.' Chris shrugged his eyebrows. 'You'd think you'd get over your inhibitions, wouldn't you? Sometimes they only get worse.'

CHAPTER TWENTY-EIGHT

Chris McKenna died. Suddenly and out of nowhere. It was nothing dramatic: no lonely suicide by drowning in the shimmering waters of the Queensbridge river. He caught a chest infection and died. The infection worked fast: Chris got sick, and two days later he was gone. He hardly knew what hit him. He died with his legs off, and he died alone. With an unopened packet of antibiotics.

This was more of a shock to Jackie than he anticipated.

He went to the funeral, and Emily went with him. She wore a smart dark suit. Jackie had put on the best suit he had, which didn't entirely fit him now. Only the belt was holding up the trousers; most of the buttons were unfastened.

The funeral was at the town's crematorium. There was hardly anybody there. Music played for about twenty minutes. Nobody spoke. Nobody delivered a tribute or eulogy. Eight people sat on separate benches, and when it was over they walked away.

Jackie stood on the gravel outside the entrance, holding hands with Emily and looking at the greenery which crematoria wrap around themselves.

'That was absolute crap,' he said. 'Poor bastard. Let's go and find ourselves a long drink.'

CHAPTER TWENTY-NINE

One day the inevitable happened. Emily's husband came to the bar. He walked in, tall, handsome, well built, gorgeous. Jackie always knew he would be. He had on a light grey business suit, a thin-striped pale blue shirt, and a red tie that he'd pulled down a little so that he could undo the top button. This was a day for casual.

He walked over to the bar, smiled at Mike, and looked around the place. His gaze settled on Jackie and he walked across. Even his walking was elegant.

He reached the table and looked down at Jackie.

'I'm Robert Marchant,' he said. 'Emily's husband.'

'Oh.' Jackie stood up and offered his hand and, for some reason, clumsily, they shook. 'Erm – ' Jackie indicated the seat opposite and Robert Marchant sat down. He didn't adjust the crease of his trousers, which was a plus point for Jackie. 'Can I get you a drink?'

'Do they have any herbal tea?'

'I wouldn't think so. I can ask.'

'Maybe I'll have a – ' the man stared around *The Lion* as if searching for inspiration. 'A mineral water.'

Jackie looked across to the bar, made a wimpy gesture with his hand, and Mike seemed to know what he meant. Dawn brought the drink over. She seemed a little coy and overawed by the man's suit. 'I put a cocktail stick in,' she said. 'With a cherry.'

'Thanks.' Robert continued to look around the place. Didn't look at Jackie. Gazed out of the window. 'It's a nice place,' he said. 'Is this where you come with my wife?'

Jackie didn't answer that. That kind of answer could only lead to trouble, and Jackie was in enough trouble already. He looked across to the bar, where Mike was studiously looking away. Dawn came over with two whiskies. She still seemed overawed by Robert Marchant and almost curtsied. She smiled at Jackie and raised her eyebrows. *Fucking hell*, he thought.

'You're not what I was expecting,' said Robert Marchant as he put his glass down. 'I suppose I was expecting someone younger.'

'Every day I wake up hoping to be a little younger, but it never happens.'

'And yet, for some reason, my wife is obsessed with you.'

Jackie exhaled so long and hard at the table he would have blown out a candle if there'd been one. He fiddled with his glass. 'I don't think she's obsessed with me,' he said. 'I think – for whatever reason – and this isn't a criticism of you and your family – Emily has found a lonely place, and she's found herself living with it. In many ways I'm a safe option. I'm old, I'm not vigorous, I'm a working alcoholic, and we're at opposite ends of the spectrum. You and I, I mean, not Emily. I'm the antithesis of what you represent. And she doesn't love you any the less for it.' He took a long swig of whisky, then started on the second glass. 'If it's any comfort, my wife feels the same.'

'You're married?'

'I am. Separated. Been apart for a couple of years, but we'll probably stay married for ever. The woman won't let me go.'

Against all his instincts and all his desires, Robert came out with a little laugh. 'How long have you been married?'

'Twenty-eight years. If you come in here often enough you'll meet her. She'll walk in, dominate the place, boss you about a bit then leave.'

Robert Marchant smiled. 'Why did you separate?'

Jackie looked down at his glass. 'I'm drinking it.'

CHAPTER THIRTY

He met Robert Marchant again two days later, at the bar at the quay that he'd been to with Chris. It was sort of nostalgic, but not enough to matter. This time Robert Marchant was drinking beer.

'We've never had sex, if that's what you're worried about. We talk about it, but we never get around to it. It's not that kind of relationship.'

Robert Marchant stared at a line of small orange buoys, floating on a rope beyond the edge of the quay. It wasn't obvious what they were for. Something to do with rowing boats he suspected. 'We don't have sex much either. We used to but – ' He shrugged. 'I suppose that's normal. It gets in the way. Everything. Life. Tiredness. A child. Work. You forget all the things that it was about.'

Jackie was staring at the buoys, too. He was actually thinking about Chinese cormorants at the time. Often cormorants appeared on the river. He didn't know what they ate. Salmon maybe, if there were any in the water. Sharks. Whatever there was.

'Everyone goes through periods,' said Jackie. 'It doesn't mean you stop loving. But I'll tell you your problem – you don't drink enough.'

Robert laughed and raised his glass. 'How's that working out for you?'

'It's not as bad as you'd think,' said Jackie. 'Some days it's not so good, obviously. The days you fall over, they're a bit of a write-off. But you don't get sick, you don't get hangovers, you learn to adjust to the pace. These days I'm thinking of starting another book.'

'You write books?'

'I used to. I used to do a lot of things. They've all kind of gone by the board.'

They spent an amiable hour drinking beer and watching the water; chewing the fat like a pair of strange friends with nothing in common and everything between them.

Robert told Jackie about his business, and it sounded as boring as hell. But then, he supposed, writing probably didn't sound much better. It was hard to glamourise a keyboard and an empty screen.

After the hour was up Robert left and Jackie stayed on, staring out at the water, looking for signs of sharks and pondering the mysteries of life.

There were too many to truly contemplate.

CHAPTER THIRTY-ONE

Jackie received some money; plenty of money; from the insurance settlement. They had never talked about this before, but now he told her the amount.

'£178,964.20.'

'We could go away on that.'

'Shangri-la?' he said.

'If it's not too far.'

They were in *The Grapes*. The landlord was so familiar with him now he actually grunted when Jackie approached.

'You're too good for this place,' he said. 'That bird definitely is.'

'I know. She's quite something, isn't she?'

The landlord looked across at Emily, who was fussing with her dress as she sat down at her favourite gloomy table.

'She is that.'

He suddenly extended his hand. 'I'm John,' he said.

'Jackie.'

Jackie took the drinks to the table. 'You've got a new conquest,' he said. 'John, the landlord. I don't know why he fancies you rather than me.'

Emily's face lit up with a smile, and she wiggled her fingers in the direction of John who turned away and began fiddling with some glasses.

'He's a nice man.'

'He looks like a fucking killer.'

They talked; of this and that, their days and nights. Emily was thinking of changing her job, the estate agency work had run its course. She wasn't sure what she could do. Some kind of secretarial work maybe. She was an intelligent woman and sharp as a whip, but she'd never had great ambition. She didn't know why and Jackie couldn't explain it. He couldn't explain why he'd given up writing. They were both in a phase of life.

At one point she puffed out her cheeks and looked like a girl of eleven years old. He imagined she was swinging her legs under the table.

'Robert told me he'd been to see you.'

'Twice,' said Jackie. 'He came to *The Lion*, and we met a couple of days later at the quay.'

She puffed her cheeks again. 'How was he?'

'Very civilised,' said Jackie. 'Better than I would have been. He was a difficult man to dislike.'

Emily nodded. 'He would be. He's very professional.' Then she said, 'I have a strange confession to make, Jackie. When I've talked about making love and suchlike – I wanted to see the scars.'

'Pardon me?'

'I wanted to see the damage I've inflicted. And maybe having sex would be a way to do that.'

Jackie stared at her for a long time. Again he understood it, without properly understanding what it was he understood. It would be a strange world that didn't have such strangeness in it.

He cleared his throat. Then he went to the bar for more drinks. He was loading up on whisky. He drank three of them when he got back to the table, and he cleared his throat again.

'I can show you,' he said. 'If you want.'

Emily drained her glass of wine. 'I do,' she said.

CHAPTER THIRTY-TWO

Two days later they were in Jackie's apartment.

It was a Thursday. The weather was fine. The wind was from the east, but wasn't as cold as it might have been. The temperature outside was eighteen degrees. It was warmer than that in Jackie's apartment. It was two o'clock in the afternoon.

In potentially awkward situations it is often better to pretend everything is normal, and carry on. As his mother often said to him, it doesn't matter where you want to be, you are where you are because you're there.

So they had a drink. Then Jackie took off his shoes, his socks and trousers, and stood in front of her.

His scar had long since healed but was still an ugly affair: a long ridge of pale skin running from his hip to his knee. There were still faint remnants of some of the staples that had been used to seal it.

Emily pushed her hair back, and knelt in front of him. She was wearing a pale blue smock-style dress, and her hair was darker than usual. It looked as though she had washed it and it wasn't yet fully dry.

She studied the scar for some time. Then she leaned forward and almost touched it with her fingertips. She ran them down the length of it, less than a centimetre away. He could feel her exhalations on it – breath as hot as the tongue of a dragon.

'It looks so angry and sad,' she said. 'I am so sorry, Jackie.'

She leaned further forward and kissed the scar gently.

'I am truly so so sorry.'

CHAPTER THIRTY-THREE

On the Friday, in the bar, Mike said, 'I'm going to Australia a bit earlier than I planned. My girl out there – Stacey – her husband's dumped her, walked out like a cunt. Got two fucking kids and one of them's sick. So I'm going out there to see what I can do. Someone from the brewery will come in to run things while I'm away. Make sure he doesn't bully Dawn. That part's up to you.'

Jackie nodded. 'I'll kill the fucker.'

'The bloke coming in will cost more for the fortnight than this place takes. Mind you Dawn keeps giving half of my flaming profits to you. Does she ever put anything in the till?'

'We didn't know you noticed.'

'Like I'm a fucking idiot.'

Jackie sat in his booth, let Mike pour more whisky, and gently rubbed at his thigh. It didn't hurt as much as it used to. Maybe dragon's breath was good for it. He looked out of the window. The woman with the push-chair wasn't there. He hadn't seen her for a week. He hoped nothing had happened to the baby. Maybe it had deflated.

Mike looked tired. He pressed his face into his strangler's hands and rubbed it so hard it turned puce. He ran them through his hair. His dark hair wasn't as thick and lush as once it had been, but it was still enough to be proud of. Needed a wash, though. And he had dandruff. 'Fuck, Jackie,' he said. 'Nothing ever goes to plan any more, does it?' He stared from the window. 'I think I might get married again.'

'Who to?'

'I don't know. I'll find someone.'

CHAPTER THIRTY-FOUR

Laura became ill. Jackie thought it was probably stress related, though he wasn't sure which strain of stress it was. Because her sister, who would usually keep an eye on her at such a time, was away in Lanzarote, Jackie had to step in and make sure she was all right. Getting something to eat and not wasting away. He hadn't been in his old home for two years, but it looked the same. Apart from the fact that she'd altered everything. He didn't realise there was that much paint in the world. 'Fuck me. Did you do every wall?'

'Shut up,' she said. 'I was removing every trace of you. Did you bring anything?'

'Obviously.' He opened a supermarket bag. 'Soup. Roasted chicken breast. Baby biscuits. A bar of chocolate. A strawberry protein drink. Tablets. A newspaper. Half a bottle of brandy. And a picture of the King.'

'What the hell's that for?'

'He's on a joke get well card.'

He sat down alongside her. She was lying on an ox-blood leather Chesterfield, wrapped in a tartan blanket, looking pale, sweaty, miserable and unwell.

'You okay, kid? You want a drink? Cup of tea?'

She nodded and sniffed. 'I'm dying.'

'I know you are. It's written all over you. But try to do it quietly.'

He went to the kitchen and clattered his way through the familiar cupboards. 'Where's the freaking tea?'

'In the tin marked tea.'

'Oh – so it is. Do you want any sugar in it? I can put some brandy in - might do you some good. Like a hot toddy.'

He brought the tea, sat down next to her, and took a swig from the brandy bottle.

'That's not going to last long.'

'I've got another one in my pocket.'

They stopped talking. The room fell quiet, with a silence that was only emphasised by the ticking of a clock.

This had been their home for many years. Everything had happened here. Sex. Rows. Christmas parties with friends.

Books had been written. Papers had been marked. A child had even been born in a room upstairs. 'Luke's room', as it came to be known He was a noisy bastard.

Everything that a marriage is, has been, and is likely to become, was contained within those walls.

They both seemed aware of it. He held her hand and rubbed his thumb over the back of it. She squeezed, and put her other hand on top of it. 'Life, hey?'

'Yeah.'

'How do I look?'

'One to ten? A twelve.'

'Shit.' Her head flopped back on a cushion and she gave an exasperated sigh. 'The baby's due any day now. I can't go and see it if I'm ill.'

'I'll go. I'll draw you a picture. I'll sketch it.'

'I've seen your fucking pictures. Oh Jackie – ' She sighed again. 'I feel so bloody ill.'

'It's only a passing thing,' he said, as he stroked her brow. 'You'll be better in a few days.' He touched her gently for a little time longer, then he reached for his stick and stood up. 'I'll let you get some rest. Do you want the TV on?'

She shook her head.

She gave him a final look as he reached the door. 'She's got a child, Jackie,' she said.

'I know.'

CHAPTER THIRTY-FIVE

'Robert wants to move away. He wants us to relocate to Gloucester.'

'Oh.'

'Oh.'

'Is this because of us?'

'It's not because he's in love with Gloucester. What are we going to do, Jackie?'

I don't know.

He knew this was coming. Somehow he'd always known it was coming. The good things never last for ever.

You hope and pray and wish and dream, but all the time, in the background, real life is waiting to butt in. It wants to snatch away the things you've got and give you something else. Things that maybe you don't want as much. Not the things that once you didn't even know you wanted.

They stared across the estuary. They didn't normally travel so far, but the day was so fine they'd pushed caution to the wind and Emily had driven through the winding country lanes at a speed that frightened Jackie as much as the horses.

They found a new place to stop. *The Oyster Bay*. It didn't have a garden but was possessed of a huge paved area with a few small trees and cordylines in tubs. Mostly it had tables that overlooked the sea. And the smell of the ocean was in the air.

'We could use your money and go away ourselves.'

That was a forlorn effort. They both knew it wasn't going to happen. Emily had a child. Emily would always have a child. Home is for ever the place where the child is.

'Fucking Gloucester,' he said.

'Yes. It's 120 miles. I looked on a map.'

120 miles was a long, long way. To hobble on a stick, limping along the verges. He'd need to buy an extra stick.

Jackie gave the sigh of his life. He was already starting to hurt inside. There was a pain in his solar plexus.

It was where the air was being sucked from his lungs.

'I love you,' he said.

'I love you too.'

It was the first time they'd ever said it.

A young waitress brought food, but they weren't really hungry. They'd ordered it out of habit.

She came back two minutes later with fresh drinks, which was considerably more interesting to Jackie.

He took Emily's hand while he gazed across a beautifully calm and silver sea. A home for fish and gulls and gannets and fishing boats. A home for storms and squalls and terrible whirlpools.

'It is a big sea,' he said. 'A big, big sea.'

He sighed deep and long, and Emily squeezed his hand.

'We'll sail on it one day,' she said.

CHAPTER THIRTY-SIX

It happened soon. Far too soon. So fast that they couldn't prepare for it.

One day she was in Queensbridge: the next she was moving into a house in the leafy outskirts of Gloucester. Robert Marchant wasn't taking any chances. A fresh start. A fresh break. He never doubted that his wife loved him, but there was a bond that had to be broken. One of those bonds no one ever sees coming.

They had the briefest of phone calls, and that was it. Emily was gone.

It was time for a permanent break. There was nothing he could do. Nothing she could do. It happened like a blitz; it was there, it existed, and then it was gone. You couldn't try to hang on to it because that would only extend it. Pain couldn't be allowed to find its own refuge.

Jackie walked to the corner. He walked to the bar. Knowing that as solace even whisky could not be a saviour.

CHAPTER THIRTY-SEVEN

He didn't even have Mike at the bar to talk to. The temporary guy was a man called Reebok, who Jackie hated before he'd even laid eyes on him. And he was pretty sure he charged more for the drinks than Mike.

Fucker.

The pain he felt inside was terrible. It was something he'd never known before. The loss that had appeared instantly, like a void in his stomach, refused to go away.

Dawn said, 'Are you all right, Jack?'

'Yeah. I'm just – missing a friend.'

'Is it that lady?'

'It is.'

'She seemed very nice. I can't even give you an extra drink. This man from the brewery's like a vulture or something following me. I think he's after me.'

'Give me your phone. I'll put my number on it. If he ever starts to bother you, any time at all, send me a text and I'll come and kill him.'

'Thanks Jack.' She looked over at the bar. 'I'd better go, he's watching me now.'

Out of the window. The endless view out of the window. If there hadn't been a window Jackie would never have come to *The Golden Lion*. If he hadn't come to the bar he would never have left it to cross the road at the pedestrian crossing. And Emily would never have run into him.

He couldn't even remember where he was going that day. Bookshop maybe. The Polish supermarket. Perhaps he was just stretching his legs in the warmth of a summer day.

Maybe he was going to feed the ducks. Maybe he was going to throw bricks at the swans. He'd always had problems with the swans. They hunted in packs and tracked him down. You couldn't throw enough bread at swans.

The guy from the brewery wandered over to collect his empty glasses.

'You all right, mate?'

Fuck off.

'Yes I'm fine,' said Jackie.

CHAPTER THIRTY-EIGHT

The following day Alison went into labour. 6.45 in the morning. Thankfully nobody phoned Jackie at that time to let him know. He was still trying to pull his underpants on at 11.15.

'Yes, what?'

'It's me Dad.' It was Luke's voice. 'He's here. The baby's here.'

'Of course he is, I knew that. I'm on my way. Don't let him go anywhere.'

He put the phone down. *What the fuck?* Where the hell were his trousers?

In the kitchen. He'd left them in the kitchen.

Crap. They had curry on them. Never mind, he'd get another pair. He had other trousers.

He took a swig from a bottle of vodka.

Fuck.

Where was his fucking bedroom?

CHAPTER THIRTY-NINE

He got to the hospital at 12.15. He was going to remember that for ever; because at 12.17 he was holding a newborn baby in his arms.

In his darkest moments; in the deepest recesses of his problem with alcohol; Jackie was always going to remember that.

A newborn baby. In his arms. Tiny and unique. Completely irreplaceable. There would never be another such Dominic in the world.

'He's great,' he said, crying. 'He's so beautiful. And so fucking ugly! Where in the hell did you get him?'

They took pictures; lots of pictures. Even Jackie took pictures, and he didn't have a phone. Oh yes he did – someone had taken it off him.

'Show these to Mum.'

Of all the people who should have been there, Laura was still sick in bed. On the sofa.

'I'll take them,' he said. 'As soon as I'm out of here. I'll take them right round. Fucking hell, Luke – you created a miracle!'

'I know. Who fucking knew?'

Then they both started crying.

CHAPTER FORTY

Jackie went straight round to Laura's to show her the pictures on his phone. He took a bag of Quavers, a bottle of champagne, a bunch of flowers, a punnet of peaches, a bottle of vodka, an assortment of biscuits, easily digestible pieces of 'something', and a bottle of Scotch.

'This is him,' he said. 'That's his head.'

'I can see it's his head. God. Have you ever seen anything more beautiful?'

'No. Not in this lifetime.'

There was even a video clip on the phone which Luke had transferred, which showed the baby at his best, screaming his head off.

'Jesus.' Laura sat up, coughing. She still looked terrible. In some ways she looked worse; she hadn't washed her hair for a week.

'We did it, Jackie. We got a grandson.'

'Yeah. I told you we weren't complete rubbish.'

They watched the video clip over and over again. Laura spoke to Luke on the phone. She spoke to Alison. She spoke to Alison's mother. She even spoke to a nurse.

'It's wonderful,' she said. 'The most wonderful thing ever.'

'Yeah.' Jackie was looking at the pictures on his phone, and his eyes were sparkling.

'You all right, Jack?'

'Yep.' He wiped his face on the sleeve of his jacket. 'Emily's gone.'

'Oh.'

Laura paused, in the excitement of the baby. She put his phone down, and held his hand. She wasn't quite sure what to say.

'She just went like that, suddenly, from the blue. And it pains me to say, but she took a lot of me with her.'

Laura stroked his hair. She didn't like the woman, but she loved Jackie. Nobody wants to see someone in pain.

'I'm so sorry,' she said.

'Yeah.' Jackie sniffed, and heaved in a breath to stiffen his shoulders. 'At least we've got Dominic.'

'Try not to cry,' she said.

'I'm trying. But I can't seem to help it.'

THE PRESENT DAY

CHAPTER ONE

A week after the birth of Dominic, Jackie received a letter.

He knew who it was from the moment it arrived: the quality of the paper, the colour of it; he thought he could even detect the scent of her on the envelope.

It was so treasureable he didn't even open it. He walked around with it in his pocket for two days.

The Golden Lion was doing its damnedest, in the absence of Mike and with the efforts of Dawn, to enter the modern age. There were tables outside, and chairs. There were two box plants in stainless steel containers; but they seemed more designed for someone to trip over than to add anything useful to the ambience.

However, Jackie was game. So he sat outside. And he took the letter out of his pocket. And he stared at it.

'You want anything, Jack?'

'The usual. And throw in a coffee as well.'

He fingered the envelope. He turned it in his hands. It was a good size for turning. It felt good and it smelt good. The colour of it would be described as 'champagne'.

Light clouds scudded across the sky and partially obliterated the sun. Which would make it easier to read. The letter. If he wanted to. If he opened it.'

'Here you go, Jack.'

'Thanks babe.'

He sighed. He tapped the letter on the table. Opening it could release so many things: demons, angels, dragons, butterflies. Any one of them would have the power to crush him for ever, or give him some hope.

Even whisky didn't have the answer to this. Tapping the envelope on the table seemed his best option. Tapping the envelope, watching the High Street, contemplating all that was real and all that was something else. Everything somewhere or nothing.

He sighed, and reached for his beer. He'd start with that, then move on to the whisky.

Shit. He wished he still smoked.

He tapped the letter some more. Looked at both sides of the envelope. He wouldn't get anywhere if he didn't open it.

A shadow fell across the table, and he looked up.

She was standing there, in a yellow dress, with the sunlight behind her, as she always managed.

She shrugged, and put her bag on a chair.

'You got it then,' said Emily.

CHAPTER TWO

He read the letter later, in his bedroom.

The room was gloomy. A small table lamp was on, but its glow didn't extend very far. He had to lean across the bed to read it. He still wasn't sure; but the scent of her perfume was coming off it. He couldn't inhale it for ever. He had to read it.

So he did.

My darling Jackie,

I cannot begin to explain my sorrow at the abruptness of my departure from Queensbridge. I do not know where it began, nor how it ended up at the point at which it did. I was caught up in commotion and detail and so many moments that were beyond my control.

I have never been a strong woman, and those events completely swept me up and swept by me.

It has not been a grand period in my life.

In the positive world, Robert appears very happy and Jason is settling into his new school with what appears to be affirmative gusto.

I have an interview next week for an administrative role with a firm of solicitors, but I would rather simply stare at the sky.

I miss you so much the pain cannot be mentioned. I do not know where pain begins nor where it ends. I do not know if it ever has an end.

Part of me, the sensible part of me, says that of course this will pass. Emotions are ever temporary things, they come and go like gusts of the wind. They thrive, they blossom, they falter. Obviously we shall carry on in our own separate ways, with the memory of what we didn't quite do but almost did!

I cannot wish you, with any more fervour, the desire I have for you to have a happy life and progress and write your books and be the greatest grandfather this world has ever known

I love you so much Jackie. And this will be the end

I send you so much affection and love

Your friend and confidante and one time almost lover

Emily. From the very depths of my heart.

XX

Jackie put the letter down and reached for the glass of whisky on the bedside table.

Emily was lying across his feet.

'So what do we do then?'

CHAPTER THREE

'Hello Mike. How did it go?'

'Fff. Don't even ask. You ever flown to Australia? It takes about four fucking weeks. And when you get there it's so fucking hot you can't breathe. And that fucking bastard the brewery put in – takings are so far down I might as well give it up now. You're the only friend I've got and you're milking me.'

He reached under the counter.

'Here. Australian whisky. 98% proof. Knock your teeth out with that.' He put such a bottle on the bartop that even Jackie blanched at it.

'Are you sure that's drinkable?'

'Of course it is. They use it to kill kangaroos.'

Jackie picked up the bottle, and could almost feel heat coming from it.

'What did you get Dawn?'

'A boomerang.'

They took a bottle of whisky to Jackie's booth and celebrated the safe return of – Mike's return. It took them a while to celebrate that, with all the drinking and toasting and pretending they didn't like each other quite as much as they did. And looking out of the window. And drinking some more, and eating peanuts.

Even the best of times come to an end, though.

Jackie shuffled on his seat, and cradled his whisky glass between his palms.

'I've got a problem, Mike.'

'It's not that woman is it?'

'It might be. We might have – '

Jackie looked away; out of the window. There was that woman again, with the push-chair. But it didn't look as though there was a baby in it. It looked like there was food in it. Like she'd come from the food bank.

'I might have had sex last night.'

'Jesus Christ.' Mike drank a large measure of whisky then poured himself another. 'This is your problem? Having sex with a beautiful woman?'

Jackie exhaled and looked around, looking vaguely like a fish out of water. A fish that would probably survive if you threw it back in.

'It wasn't 'real' sex, you know? It was – '

'Pretend sex?'

'No. It was better than pretend sex, it was more than that. It was – I think I need Viagra, Mike.'

'Well don't look at me, I haven't got any. Go and see your doctor.'

'It's embarrassing. I don't want to go, and you know – embarrass myself.'

'Fucking hell.' Mike shook his head, poured another measure of whisky, then screwed the cap back on the bottle. 'And I thought it was bad in Australia.'

CHAPTER FOUR

It was guilt, he understood that. It wasn't guilt for anyone on his own side; but she had a child and a husband. That was a different level of activity altogether. He had never been unfaithful in his own marriage, but now he was participating in the unfaithfulness of another. All his rules. All his morals. All his highfalutin attitudes about the behaviour of others. Where was that going to end? He was risking ripping a marriage apart, and potentially leaving a child without its mother.

Obviously Emily had a say in this too; but he had to think of it from his own side. If he had to sacrifice her child and her husband, was he willing to do it?

He thought about it for possibly ninety seconds.

The answer was yes. And it was always and for ever going to be yes.

Yes and yes and yes and yes. There was never going to be any doubt.

He could see that there might be problems along the way. He could see there were things that might go wrong. But God, when he looked at her – it was like looking into the eyes of life itself.

It was a sight he couldn't look away from.

CHAPTER FIVE

'You are not seriously thinking of moving in with that woman?'

He blinked across the room at her. He liked her better when she was sick. He was sorry he'd brought her the champagne now.

'Why not?' he said.

'Because she's fucking 32, Jackie. And you're what – 55 going on 80. You can hardly bloody walk. If you want to get a fucking nurse get one – don't pick on some woman who's dazzled by the fact that you used to be an author.'

'I still am an author.'

'Yeah right.'

Oof. This was reminiscent of the arguments they had in the past. In the past it was whisky: now it was Emily.

He hadn't even seen her for two weeks: they were still talking, it was just an idea. They had no place to go. They couldn't spend their days drifting from one pub to another and staring at oceans and meadows.

You couldn't hold hands for ever.

'Life isn't an endless summer, you know.'

I was just thinking that myself, he thought. But God – when you were in summer, while you were enjoying it – why would you want to look for the winter? Winter would come soon enough in its own time. Why couldn't you enjoy the sun?

'What are you going to do – go and live on a beach somewhere with her? Live the life of the Caribbean author? Dancing and talking and laughing and singing until the middle of the night? You're not Ernest Hemingway. It's a dream, Jackie, a dream. And she's not going to help you live it.'

Maybe she couldn't help him live it. But maybe he could live it with her. Maybe, between them, he and Emily could find a life that kept the dream alive.

It didn't always have to die.

Otherwise, what was the point of it all?

'What are you looking at me for?'

'Nothing,' he said. 'I just don't think it always has to die.'

'You never did,' she said. 'And then you sat and watched it die. You're an idiot, Jackie. A constant idiot.'

CHAPTER SIX

Jackie didn't think that was entirely fair. He viewed himself as more of an occasional idiot; but so was everybody. Nobody was perfect; nobody played by the rules. If everybody played by the rules life wouldn't get anywhere: it would be an existential version of painting by numbers. You might get a pretty picture but it was never going to be your own. He thought that bitterly as he limped away from Laura's house. He should have said it. He wished he could go back and say it now, but it was too late. Sometimes it is really difficult to get the timing right.

He headed for *The Lion*. At least there was some sanity there. You knew where you were with booze and barmaids. It would be a very rare day when one of them let you down.

He paused three steps in and checked for bushwhackers. Again, none of them appeared. Thank God. He was still faintly terrified that one day one would.

Fucking bushwhackers. That was the thing with them: you never knew where they were going to come from or when.

Why the hell they would be hiding out in *The Golden Lion* was hard to know; but it was best not to take any chances.

Bloody bushwhackers.

When he approached the bar Dawn was unusually animated and jumping and down on the spot.

'I won a hundred pounds, Jack.'

'What?'

'In a crossword competition. I won a hundred pounds.'

'Fucking hell Dawn, that's brilliant.'

'I know. I've never won anything before. I feel so smart, Jack. I feel brilliant. I've never had anything like that before. I don't know what to do with it.'

'Dawn, you're the most brilliant person I know. Whatever you do with it is going to be ace.'

'Thanks Jackie.' She beamed like her face would burst. 'It's good isn't it?'

'It's great.'

He took his drinks to his table. He was having a good run of luck with his table; nobody had sat at it for a while. Mike thought that was because Jackie had secretly scent-marked the booth, and kept sniffing when Jackie wasn't around.

A presence loomed, and sat itself down. Right on the seat opposite Jackie. He kind of knew who it was without even looking: but he had to look anyway.

'Robert,' he said.

The man was again dressed impeccably. It looked like he'd stepped out of a fashion advert. But fashion adverts seldom looked that good. Even Jackie was tempted to fancy him.

'I know that you and my wife are still involved. I know that she's thinking of moving out and living with you. This is not going to happen, Mister Conor; you cannot spoil another person's life. My son, and myself, we need her.'

Mike brought more drinks over. He didn't bring anything for Robert. He gave Jackie a look. Jackie couldn't interpret it: it looked faintly ominous. He lowered his head as he walked away. That looked even more ominous. Jackie was struggling to keep up with the ominosity.

'Robert – I don't know what you're talking about. Emily has said nothing of this to me.'

'Bullshit. You're not even good enough for her – on any level. Do you think you're good enough for her? Look at you – you're a damn cripple. Do you think you're good enough for a woman like Emily?'

Jackie stood up, swung his arm across the table, and punched Robert Marchant on the side of his face.

'Bloody hell!' That was Jackie. He didn't realise punching somebody hurt so much. 'You broke my fucking hand!'

'Get him Jack!' Dawn shouted encouragement from behind the bar.

'Bloody hell.' Mike came striding from behind the bar with a tea towel over his shoulder.

'He broke my bloody hand!'

'Yeah, with his jaw. Sit down the pair of you. I'm not having this in my bar – do you understand? Not even you Jackie – I'll throw you out the door myself. I can have you banned from every pub in town. Grow up both of you. It's not a bloody schoolyard.'

They watched Mike walk away with a grandiose swagger and a modest expression. He hadn't looked finer in years.

'Bloody hurt that,' said Jackie, rubbing at his hand.

'Well never mind my face.'

'Yeah, but you're tougher than me. You go to gyms.'

'I don't go to a gym.'

'You look like you do. I've never seen anyone so fit. Do you want a drink?'

'No, I'd better get back.'

Robert walked away shaking his head.

Jackie sat in his booth shaking his.

CHAPTER SEVEN

'He's right,' she said. 'I am thinking of moving out.'

They were lying on their backs in a meadow. Emily was chewing a blade of grass. He was holding her hand. The sky was one shade away from Wedgewood and the clouds were two steps away from cauliflowers. The buzzing of bees, other insects and God knew what was a chorus in the air; and butterflies were fluttering with wild abandon. Which seemed to be the only flight they knew.

'He said I can't have any money. He said I can't have anything. I can't see Jason. I can't go home. He said I've made my bed and I have to lie in it.'

Jackie squinted against the sun. When he was with her it was hard to take his eyes off her; she swallowed his attention like a pool.

'He can't stop you seeing Jason.'

'I know,' she said. 'He doesn't mean that part. I have my own money anyway. Not a lot, but enough. From my father's estate. Between us we'll have money, but what do we do with it, where do we go? We can't buy the world.'

She blinked at the distance. Nothing ahead but trees and shadows and fields and cattle; a low hill rising towards the sky.

Sheep as well, she noticed. Sometimes mingling with the cattle. Maybe they'd broken through a gap in a wall. Walls get tired and could fall down; although generally they remain as walls. Maybe something climbed over it or crashed into it. A drunken cow or a belligerent ram. A particularly insane butterfly.

'What did you do when you and Laura separated?'

'Got blind drunk and kept on going. Not with life so much, but certainly with the booze. What is it they say? The answers to life may not lie in the bottom of a bottle, but it takes a fool not to look.'

'Playtime's over isn't it?' she said, after a pause.

'Yes. Yes and no. It's a different game. Or a different version of the game. People will come to accept us: they just need time to adjust.'

'I shan't move in right away. I'll stay in a hotel.'

'That makes sense,' he said.

'It doesn't mean you can't visit me every day.'

CHAPTER EIGHT

Laura sat down. She looked better now she was over her illness; although her cheeks were still thin. Her hair was loose, and she was wearing a 'God Hates You All' tee-shirt. Obviously she was feeling in a good mood.

'I hear you're starting fights now,' she said as she put her bag down.

'I didn't start a fight. He provoked me.'

She shook her head so her hair was even looser. She waved to Mike and he started scampering about getting drinks together.

'Did you win?'

'Hard to say. I hurt my hand and he looked okay.'

The drinks arrived with Mike hopping about like a schoolboy. What the hell was it with him?

'He's got a thing for you,' said Jackie.

'Of course he has.' Laura delved into her bag and eventually came out with a lipstick which she applied with the aid of a small mirror. It didn't seem to make a lot of difference but Jackie detected the smell of peaches. Maybe she was eating the stuff. 'There's a party at Luke's house to celebrate the baby. I don't know why, it's just something they're doing. Cakes and presents and baby stuff. A sort of reverse baby shower, to make up for the fact that Alison didn't have one. You're not going to bring her are you?'

'No.'

'That's good. There's a place for things and a place that isn't for things.' She put the lipstick back in her bag and said, 'You're serious about this though, aren't you? You're going through with it.'

Jackie nodded. 'Yes,' he said.

'I can't endorse you in it. I can't support it. Well I shall support you, obviously; but I don't agree with it.'

'I know,' he said. 'I understand all that.'

'It's going to be hard, you know. She's got a child. You're a lot older. I don't care how much you think you love her, it's not going to be easy.'

She finished her wine and gave a wave to Mike. It had just been a flying visit.

As she rose and fixed her bag on her shoulder she seemed struck by a sudden thought.

'She's not pregnant is she?'

'Of course not. Don't be ridiculous.'

'Good. Because that would be bad, Jackie. Very very bad. Don't forget the baby party.'

CHAPTER NINE

He took Dawn to the party. Dawn was as thrilled as if she'd won another competition. 'I love babies,' she said.

'I know you do.'

Being uncertain what to take, Jackie had put £200 in an envelope. Dawn took a blue bonnet and blue bootees. Dawn was very thorough with babies.

There were a lot of people there that Jackie didn't know. The majority of them were people that he had no desire to know. Alcohol was in short supply and he was relieved that he'd taken his hip flasks.

Dawn branched off to talk to younger people; but she came up to him at one point to say, in a soft voice, 'I've got a bottle in my bag if you need it. It looks like water but it's vodka.'

He found himself talking to Alison's mother for much of the evening. She wasn't as bad as the reputation she'd received from Luke and his mother. In fact Jackie liked her. Even if she was in a twin-set.

'Is your husband not here?' he asked. 'Is he – 'around'?'

'He's dead,' she said. 'Cervical cancer. No not cervical cancer – what's the one men get?'

'Prostate.'

'Yes, prostate cancer. Eight years ago. He wasn't very old. Don't go to the toilet more than you have to.'

They wandered across to a table and started eating pink cake. Pink cake. What the hell was that about? 'Are you the one who's dating the younger woman?'

'I guess so,' he said; wondering what was wrong with the cake.

'It's vegan' she said. 'They don't put proper ingredients in.'

A young man in a black outfit that made him look skeletal served them coffees from a catering thermos. He produced warm milk that they could put in it. Or cream; he had that was well.

They found themselves seats by a window, where they could look across the dining room to the star of the show who was being cosseted and cuddled by a succession of women, while smiling men looked on wishing that they could do the same. 'He's beautiful isn't he?' said Alison's mother. 'They've done us proud.'

'They certainly have. He looks smart and intelligent and wise. I think he's going to be a star. Look at him playing that crowd like a maestro.'

'And only 21 days old.'

'He'll rule the world by 30.' They drifted apart after a time, with smiles and a handshake. What was her name again? He struggled to remember. Frances, that was it.

He found himself alone then for much of the time; and spent most of it staring out at the garden. There were patio doors that opened onto it, but everybody stayed indoors. It wasn't a bad evening, but it was a little cool. Only the smokers ventured outside. All of them smiled at Jackie as they passed: he was the old guy in the room. The guy with a stick and a much younger lover. He wasn't sure if they envied or pitied him.

Luke approached with two glasses of beer.

Thank God for that.

'It's going ahead then?'

'Yes.'

'Am I ever going to meet her?'

'Any time you want.'

They sipped the beers. They looked at the garden. Jackie wanted a cigarette so much his guts and his anus were aching.

'She's not so bad about it you know.'

'Who?'

'Mum. She thought she was angry, but she isn't so really. I think she kind of envies you to be honest. I think a lot of people do. It's like you're having a go, having a second chance.'

Jackie shrugged. He sipped his beer and stepped aside as a smoker passed through.

'She doesn't get a lot of luck your mum, does she?'

Luke shrugged too. 'She tries hard, but she seems to hang out a lot with women. Most of the people she knows are women. She's in a lot of women's groups.'

Jackie nodded. He patted his pockets, looking for his hip flasks. It was probably time for a sip.

'You're too wise for your years, Luke.'

After a time they drifted apart, and Luke went back to mingle with his guests.

But Dawn approached him with an alarming glint in her eye.

'I think I've pulled,' she said.

CHAPTER TEN

Emily moved into a hotel just outside Queensbridge and they met more frequently.

The dynamics had altered slightly, inevitably; because this was a very hard time. She was leaving her life, her child, her husband. She was relying a lot on the support of Jackie; and he was doing his best to provide it. Love isn't everything. It can supply a lot of things. But sometimes you need even more. She started looking for work. She encouraged him with his writing. He started a new book titled 'Death of a Swan'. He was looking for characters.

One night, lying in his arms, in a bed in a hotel, the doubts seemed stronger than ever.

'Do you think we're doing the right thing?' she said. 'Am I doing the right thing?'

Jackie stared at a hotel ceiling, by the light of a hotel lamp. He thought and thought, but he didn't have an answer. He pulled her close to him, and buried his face in her neck. 'I think we are,' he said.

CHAPTER ELEVEN

After a week they went searching for a flat. Hobbling for a flat. Limping and looking around. 'It would be better if it didn't have stairs,' he said.

'Oh shut up. You're not an old man.'

They went upstairs. It was an apartment by the quay. It looked across the river. There was a room in it that would make a perfect study; a desk in the window bay, looking over the water. 'I'll never write if I'm looking at the river.'

'Of course you will. You can write anywhere. Write for me, Jackie. Write for me.'

And they bought it. Just like that. He couldn't believe it: it was surprisingly quick. They walked round the rooms, looked out of the windows; and there it was. They were going over forms and signing a contract.

They owned a place. A place of their own. A home. Where the hell did that come from? They were up there, at the top of a flight of stairs. Fuck it. You'd limp on both legs for a view like that.

CHAPTER TWELVE

Everything moved quickly after that. Emily fitted the apartment with blinds. You could pull them up, roll them down. Everything to watch the river from different angles. She bought candles. Lots of candles. Jackie couldn't stand the smell of the candles, but by golly he was happy they were there.

'It's not everything,' she said, seriously, one day. 'But it's a start. You have to write a book, I have to get a job.' He nodded. 'We have to make a life. This is our chance, Jackie. We have to make a life. This is our second chance.'

He went with her to the house in Gloucester to collect the rest of her things. Robert had taken the boy to a local theme park for the day. She drove the black SUV that had hit him a year ago. The damaged panels had been replaced.

He didn't follow her upstairs; he stayed in the hallway. When his leg started aching he sat on the stairs.

When she came down she'd been crying. She was cradling a small cuddly bear of Jason's.

'Are you sure about this?' he said.

She nodded.

CHAPTER THIRTEEN

Life went on, in other directions, in other departments. The biggest development was that Mike had a date. That caused both Jackie and Dawn to pause and stare at him.

'What site did you find her on?' said Jackie. '*Fancy a fat bloke?*'

'Shut up. Don't start. You've got a part to play.' As things transpired, as Mike explained them, to Jackie's increasing horror, he had a date – but he couldn't get away from the bar; so they were going to have the date in the bar. Which was fair enough. That made sense. But – (and this was a big 'but' from Jackie's point of view) – Mike was nervous. *Oh for chrissake.* And he wanted Jackie to come in as back-up and chaperone.

'What?'

'It's just for one night. You owe me fucking hundreds for the whisky.'

'Yes but – this is a *date*, Mike. You're supposed to be having a date.'

Mike shook his head and slapped his tea towel down on the bar top. 'I know but – '

'Oh for fuck's sake.'

'Can you be here at seven?'

CHAPTER FOURTEEN

So it was that at seven o'clock Jackie found himself in his booth – which Mike had reserved for him because it was likely to get busy in the evening - in his best bib and tucker waiting to act as gooseberry for Mike's potentially, imminently, possibly, theoretically, maybe one day, perhaps today, hot date.

It was no wonder he was drunk.

Emily had gone to visit her mother to explain why she had entirely sacrificed, destroyed and thrown away her life (from her mother's point of view) for some aged lothario who couldn't even walk straight; and she wouldn't be back 'til tomorrow.

So that was convenient. That was an act of God. Though Jackie would much rather have had Emily with him in the bar.

Mike came over, with his date. He was wearing a blue sports jacket and an open-necked shirt. His dandruff seemed to have cleared up and it looked like there was some kind of product on his hair which gave it a lustrous sheen.

'This is Jackie. I owe my entire existence to him and the money he spends at the bar.'

'He tried to have me banned,' said Jackie, 'because somebody threw a punch at me.'

'Jackie tells stories for a living.'

Catherine, Mike's date, had made a terrific effort. She wasn't a slim woman, but she'd done her best to disguise it. Her make-up, hair style, clothing and accessories would have taken at least three hours to put on, gather, and otherwise assemble. He hoped Mike was going to be worth it.

She had three grown-up children.

They talked of this and that and that and this, and Jackie kept looking across at Mike thinking – *why the hell am I here?* But Mike kept pouring drinks and one or other of the bar staff kept bringing them.

Jackie didn't know either of them. Dawn didn't work evenings. There was a young man and a young woman who seemed pleasant enough but – Jackie felt a little out of his depth. It didn't take much to put Jackie out of his depth.

Catherine asked how his current book was going. What was it about?

'Erm – '

So far he'd only got as far as the title.

'It's about a swan.'

'Oh. That sounds interesting.'

'Yes, it's – ' he swallowed a glass of whisky so fast he almost choked on it. 'It's an interesting swan.'

Eventually, thankfully, the bar quietened down sufficiently that Mike felt emboldened and encouraged enough to take Catherine upstairs to his 'on the premises' apartment.

Jackie hoped they would have a good evening.

Shortly afterwards he passed out in a corner of the booth and the bar staff put him in a taxi and sent him home.

CHAPTER FIFTEEN

Two days later Jackie asked Mike how it was going with Catherine.

'She's got bad breath,' he said.

That was the end of that.

CHAPTER SIXTEEN

He loved Emily so much it hurt. He had a feeling that tragedy was in the air somewhere, but he didn't know where, and he thought maybe they could avoid it. You got older, you started worrying about things; you saw problems everywhere. Tragedy didn't always have to happen. It wasn't inevitable. It could be averted. All you needed was to have faith. He could have faith: he'd had faith before. Tragedy didn't have to happen. Nothing was inevitable. Death and taxes. Even taxes could be avoided.

But he knew there was something in his life with Emily that was going to go wrong. He couldn't put his finger on it, but he sensed it was coming. It was a looming shadow in the gloom behind the brightness. Maybe he was just being cautious.

One day he saw her son. She brought him over. They took him to the park.

He had never seen her so happy. She was so happy her radiance increased fourfold. She laughed, she smiled, she ran and chased. He had never seen anyone so happy.

In that moment he realised completely the sacrifice she had made to be with him.

One day she said to him, 'I'm pregnant.'

CHAPTER SEVENTEEN

Pregnant.

That was a thing.

Of all the things he'd thought were never going to happen again in his life, that would be high amongst them.

Pregnant. With the most beautiful woman he'd ever seen.

Pregnant with –

He couldn't even look at her.

'Are you okay?'

'Yeah.' He nodded. Blinked his eyes. He looked everywhere but straight at her.

'It's a baby.'

'I know,' he said. 'That's why I'm thinking about it.'

'It's a good thing, yes?'

'Oh God yes. It's the best thing ever.'

He hugged her so hard that eventually both of them almost passed out from lack of oxygen.

'It's probably best not to suffocate the child.'

'Yes. That would be a bad thing.'

He broke off the hug, and they sat on the sofa, looking out at the river and the rowing boats having their phoney races. And they laughed for about an hour.

Then they went to bed; and they kept on laughing.

Then they had sex again.

CHAPTER EIGHTEEN

Dawn's new boyfriend came in to the bar, and Mike and Jackie stared at him suspiciously.

He seemed all right. He looked fairly normal. Though Jackie didn't much like his tee-shirt.

He exchanged a non-committal glance with Mike and they arched their eyebrows and turned away.

Their little girl was leaving the nest.

Ten minutes later Mike said, 'She's come back again.'

'Who has?'

'Catherine. She asked me what the problem was and why we couldn't see each other any more and in the end I cracked and said – it's halitosis.'

'Shit.'

'Yeah, that's what I thought. I thought she'd go crazy and bawl me out and – ' Mike looked away, then picked up the whisky bottle and poured out two more measures. 'But she was – ' He shook his head again. 'She understood it. She said it was a problem she'd had for years. Something to do with sulphur in the mouth.'

'Jesus.'

'Yeah. She's been having dental treatment. There's a new thing. I didn't understand the mechanism but it's something to do with anti-sulphuric implants between the teeth.'

'Jesus.'

'Yeah. It's not cheap. Hundred pounds a session and she's having them every couple of weeks.'

'Jesus.'

'Yeah. She said she's doing it for me.'

Mike stared at his glass, swallowed its contents quickly and poured another.

'What am I supposed to do, mate?'

Jackie didn't know. He thought about it and shrugged.

'How much do you like her?'

'Quite a lot actually. Quite a lot. The more I think about it – the more I like her.'

'Well I think you've got your answer then.'

'I thought you'd put up more of a fight.'

'No, I'm pretty much going it with these days. I've lost control of the rational stuff. We just have to go with it, Mike.'

'We're doomed then.'

'Pretty much so.'

They looked across the bar to Dawn.

'She's all right though.'

CHAPTER NINETEEN

He was in the bar pretending to work on his novel, but in reality he was staring out of the window with his thoughts at the lower end of 'occupied'. If they'd been any less occupied he would have fallen asleep.

It was quite draining being an author.

'How's the swan going?'

'Fucking nowhere. It's paddling like fuck on the spot.'

Mike put a glass down and filled it with whisky.

'She's got her interview this afternoon?'

'Yeah. I'm trying not to think about it, I'll only get tense. I should have gone with her maybe, do you think?'

'No. Emily's a big girl. She can sort this out fine without you.'

'Yeah. You worry so much about stuff, you know? Stuff you can't control, stuff you have no influence over. It fills your mind, takes up so much space. If you could just keep your mind open for the good stuff, the important stuff, it would probably be a lot better, a lot easier, you know? You could get on with stuff.'

'Yeah.' Mike nodded and turned away. 'Your tab's due.'

CHAPTER TWENTY

Emily had several failed interviews, and it was starting to get her down. Even the little jobs she couldn't get, and she couldn't understand why. She did everything right. She tried so hard. Emily would bleed to make this relationship work and to have their child and to make a life that would be as good as it could be and better than it should be and everything encompassed in the life she wanted, the life they wanted, and the life of their child, and everything perfect for ever and ever. If only she could get it right.

It shamed Jackie that she worked so hard for them; tried so hard; worked tirelessly. While he drank and stared out of windows and talked about swans. She said, 'That's not it, Jackie. That's not what counts. Sometimes you simply love someone. It's in the beat of your heart, it's in every second. You love a person without knowing why. And I loved you, from the first time I saw you, sitting alone in that bar. Everything about you. The expression on your face. The way you looked uncomfortable. The way you tried not to make it hurt so much. Everything about you. Every little move. Every gesture, every comment, every smile, every grimace. You were like a man battling demons, and you never held it against me, even though I'd almost ruined your life. You're a good man, Jackie. A few drinks don't undermine that. I love you when you're drunk and I love you when you're sober. At least I presume I shall if I ever get to see it.' They laughed. Then they paused, then laughed some more. Then they went for a walk by the river. There were places to go and places to be; and this was their favourite of all.

'I think I'll just start,' he said, while they were walking with their arms intertwined behind their backs. 'With the book. I'll just start and see where it takes me; I'm not good at planning anyway.'

Her face broke into a thousand smiles which somehow became compressed into one. The tip of her tongue showed between her teeth. She looked like a child, a woman, a creature of happiness; and his heart filled with the very presence of her.

He put his arms around her and they tumbled, laughing, into a bank of bracken and foxgloves.

Two metres away an adder uncoiled itself and slid away. And a few grasshoppers lived to see another day.

CHAPTER TWENTY-ONE

He met her at *The Grapes* one Thursday afternoon. John, the landlord, wasn't there. In his place was a red-haired woman in a green dress with a cleavage you could drop a brick down. She had a smile like a mother. She'd warm the heart of any man. 'What can I get you love?' she said.

Emily favoured places other than *The Golden Lion*. She viewed that as Jackie's territory and never felt entirely comfortable there. She would rather shuffle onto a seat at somewhere like *The Grapes,* where you couldn't even be sure what the stains were.

Emily was avoiding alcohol because of the pregnancy, but Jackie compensated by drinking for both of them. He liked to think he was making a contribution. 'How did it go?' he said.

She took a deep breath and sipped from the glass of tonic water he'd brought her. 'It was okay,' she said. 'I got it. I got the job. I start next Tuesday, start of the month.'

'That's fantastic! Well done, lover!'

'Yes.' She smiled almost ruefully, and gave a shrug which seemed unconscious but somehow managed to incorporate every area of her body. 'I don't know whether I'm cheating them by not telling them that I'm having a baby. What do you think? I'm very nervous.'

'Er – ' That caused a pause. Morality came into it; ethics. But sometimes ethics seemed to be a one way street: they took from you and they didn't seem to give much in return. At the same time. It was ethics. And morality. And what you believed in. 'I think,' he said. Then paused again. 'I think that can happen to anyone at any point. Men not so much, obviously. But any of the women could fall pregnant tomorrow. The important things is whether you want the job, whether you'll be happy in it, and whether you can contribute sufficiently that you'll continue being happy in it. Personally I think they'll be lucky to have you.'

Emily nodded. That kind of made sense in a man's kind of way. But men weren't always wrong. So she took the job. Emily became a health care professional; which she had done in earlier years, before she married and started her family. She was to go into people's homes – usually older people – to assess their needs and capacities; as part of a larger team. 'You'll be terrific at it,' he said. 'You have a lot of care inside you.'

'I hope so,' she said. 'I hope so.'

CHAPTER TWENTY-TWO

Mike said, 'I had sex last night.'

'Yeah? How did that go?'

'Okay. I used those Viagra tablets you were looking for. I might have used too many, I'm still – 'you know' – today. It's a bit painful to be honest.' He wiped Jackie's table with a damp cloth, and sprayed a bit of stuff on it.

'How was the sex?'

'That was okay. I did better than I thought I might. We came to a sort of agreement beforehand, because of the 'bad breath' thing. She's still having those implants between her teeth. So we just looked in opposite directions.'

Jackie nodded, as though that was normal.

'So there wasn't any kissing then?'

'Er – ' Mike looked out of the window to the bottom end of the High Street where, any day now, work was going to start on the pedestrianisation scheme. It would make a big difference, he thought; it would make it better. 'We didn't kiss in the traditional sense,' he said. 'I kissed my hand and patted her on the cheek.'

CHAPTER TWENTY-THREE

They refurbished their apartment from top to bottom. A team of people of varying ages, expertise and appearance came in to strip the walls, rub the paintwork, tear out the skirting, rip out the wiring, slam in the plumbing, lever up the floorboards, pull down the ceilings. They threw a toilet out of the window. In the space of two days their lovely apartment was turned into a bomb site.

Emily and Jackie decided to move into a hotel for two weeks while the work continued.

'The place wasn't that bad,' Jackie said as they walked away.

CHAPTER TWENTY-FOUR

In the hotel room they played games on the bed. Cluedo. Backgammon. Poker. Flick-football. It was like being a child again: hotels take away all the responsibility. They ate sandwiches and spilled coffee and nobody cared because somebody else was being paid to clean it.

On the days she was working they met for lunch at a cafeteria in the indoor plaza known as *The Boulevard*. He thought lunchtimes might be tricky with a job like that, but it seemed everybody simply clocked off. They all disappeared for an hour.

It didn't bother Jackie. He was just happy to see her and hold her hand.

'The baby will love it,' she said; because part of the planning was a nursery. It wasn't going to be blue or pink, it was going to be yellow. Or orange. Or something in-between. Maybe blue. A different shade of blue. A blue they hadn't found yet. 'I think she'll be a scientist.'

'How do you know it's going to be a girl?' said Jackie. 'It could be a footballer called Tommy.'

'It's not a footballer,' she said scornfully. 'You've obviously never been pregnant.' He couldn't argue against that one.

They held hands and looked out of the window of the café in *The Boulevard*. It wasn't as good as going to the river, but they didn't have time for that; an hour only goes so far. Even if you milk it.

'It will be a good child, Jackie,' she said. 'It will be the best child.'

'I know,' he said.

It would be. It would be the best child ever.

He sipped his Jack Daniels and coke and knew that.

The best child ever. Ever in the world.

CHAPTER TWENTY-FIVE

Following the workmen, decorators moved in. In the space of a few days, and despite occasional minor altercations and differences of opinion, everything became immaculate. It was so good they could only stand blinking at it.

'Bloody hell,' said Jackie.

Jackie's desk was put into its final position; side-on to the window, with his chair backed up to a wall. The door of the room was to his right. He couldn't work with his back to a door.

The room immediately and for ever more became known as his study: though they both spent a lot of time in it, sitting on a sofa of ochre material, looking out at the view and counting the boats and the swans on the river. At one point they saw a merganser, although it appeared a little lost and seemed as puzzled as a bird can ever look. Apart from parrots, which always look lost.

One day when they were comfortably entwined on the ochre sofa, curled up like hamsters with no cares in the world, him drinking vodka and her drinking fruit juice, she said, 'How are we going to get the push-chair up and down the stairs?'

'We'll have to carry it. I told you not to get a place with stairs.'

'Shut up.'

She grinned. He grinned. Getting a pram up and down the stairs. Like there were worse problems in the world.

Out on the river, the slow-moving river, a cormorant dived after fish. A pair of rowing sculls raced past, going hell for leather as if whoever lost would have to buy the drinks for ever more. And a pair of swans surged regally against the flow; going to a place that only swans can know.

CHAPTER TWENTY-SIX

He tried talking to his agent again. Well he did talk to her, but she was busy and not really listening.

'Yes, what? You've got a new book?'

'Something like that. I've got the start of a book. I've got the title.'

'The title.'

'Yes. But it's a good one.'

'I hope it's not about another fucking duck.'

'No, it's a swan. They're entirely different creatures.'

'Don't waste my time, Jackie.'

CHAPTER TWENTY-SEVEN

So he went to London. Pushed out the boat and invited his agent for lunch. He travelled by train, took both his hip flasks, and leaned on his stick like a veteran.

He had booked a table at an Italian/French bistro-style trattoria in a street leading off the north side of the Strand.

He used to like going to London. It used to give him a buzz. The bustle, the movement, the taste, the smell. There were more people in a single moment than you could meet in a month of trawling, crawling and gallivanting the streets of Queensbridge; even at the height of the busy season.

But this time was different. He didn't like it at all. Everything appeared shoddy and grubby and half-built or half-demolished and even some of the stations were lacking wall tiles. It looked like a practice run for coming decay whilst at the same time embracing the glamour and glory of an onrushing future where everything would be perfect and wrapped in the cushioning of an ever-improving nirvana; as long as you could keep paying for the advertisements.

He was glad to sit down. He'd reached the restaurant early because he knew she'd be late, and it gave him time to get in a few drinks.

Forty minutes passed.

A lot of drinks can be consumed in forty minutes; and Jackie was certainly game to have a try.

He'd almost forgotten what he'd come for when his agent walked in.

Golly. It had been a while, but – he struggled to recognise her. He knew she'd been ill, but he didn't know she'd look that bad. He knew alcoholics who looked better.

'What?' she said, as she sat down.

'Nothing.'

'Are you looking at my hair?'

'No.' *Only a bit. Quite a bit. It does – it's hard not to look at it. But I'm trying.*

'It's chemical. The medication I'm on. Don't look at it. Don't make a thing of it. And pretend you haven't noticed.'

'Okay.'

They ordered two bottles of wine to help with the choosing of food. As Jackie didn't drink wine, they ended up at one side of the table. But Jackie's by-now-trained lackey kept bringing him Jack Daniels and coke. 'Do you want something to eat?' he said.

'I'm not fucking bothered really.'

'We've got to eat something – I've come all the way from Queensbridge.'

His agent stared out of a window that wasn't actually there; but if one had been there she would have been staring out of it. 'Okay.' She emitted a sigh that could have inflated a dirigible. 'Something with clams then. Anything from off the sea bed. I don't trust anything from higher up – it's all polluted with plastic.'

'What about cheese?'

'I don't like that either.'

They ordered various options, waited for the food to arrive, and continued drinking. Which was the only point of contact between them at the moment; and possibly ever was.

'I've got a great title. Do you want to hear it?'

'Not particularly.' She gave another sigh sufficient to inflate a second dirigible and make a start on its sibling. 'What is it?'

'Death of a Swan.'

A cold wind swept through a desolate landscape and circled the planet once or twice before settling on a rock like an emaciated vulture and peering gloomily at the prospect before it. If it could have summoned a cough, the vulture would have coughed. But it didn't even have the energy for that.

After the wind came a silence; where all the dreams and hopes of humankind were sucked into an impenetrable void so deep that a pebble dropped today would still not have landed by the end of the world.

The agent took a long, solid drink. She was a woman who appreciated wine.

'Is that it?' she said. 'That is the title?'

'More or less. It's a title in progress.'

'It had better be.'

They pondered on breadsticks and chewed on alcohol and Jackie found himself picking up grains of Parmesan cheese with the moistened tip of the uncertain little finger of his uncertain left hand. And wondering how long they'd been scattered there.

'Have you got anything at all?'

'That's the interesting part,' he said.

'You haven't, have you?' This time his agent's sigh went directly into the void, echoed around for a while, bouncing off the walls and the windows, before eventually re-emerging in the depths of her throat. Where even then it lingered for a while. 'Jackie,' she said, 'I can't sell a dream. I can't sell something on the basis of a title. Especially a shitty little title like that one.'

'I've done it before,' he said.

'Before was before. We're in a different world now – different age, different days. I'm going to need a lot more than a title and a promise. Your personality only gets you so far, Jackie. You need something on a page. A lot of pages. When you've got 400 pages then we've got something we can start talking about – do you know what I mean?'

Jackie nodded. 'I'll get something down,' he said. He picked at his pasta, which had much of the charm of a regurgitated octopus but with less personality.

'I'm going to be a father again,' he said.

'That's wonderful news, Jackie. Congratulations.'

'This is why I could do with selling something; to get some money, for the future. For the child.'

'I understand that, Jackie. But we need something more than wishful hoping.'

'I know,' he said. 'I'll get something down.'

On his way along the Strand, heading towards Charing Cross Station, Jackie saw someone he thought he recognised and trotted to catch up with him, wielding his walking stick like the vane of a crazed skeletal windmill.

But it was mistaken identity. The man looked at him as though he was an idiot, and vocally snorted at him.

CHAPTER TWENTY-EIGHT

One day Emily said to him, 'Do you really need that stick?'

So he stopped using it. It actually improved his posture to be without it. He should have done it long ago.

'Where's your stick, Jack?'

'I've given up on it.'

'I liked that stick.'

Dawn poured the pint, then reached for the whisky.

'You know he's thinking of getting married.'

'Who?'

'Mike,' she said. Nodding, gesturing with her eyebrows to the far end of the bar where Mike was discussing the provision of crisps and other savoury products with a rep who looked like he'd eaten far too many of them himself. 'Yeah. Married. Him and that woman.'

'Catherine?'

'That's what she calls herself.' Dawn took a swig of Jackie's whisky herself, and reached back to pour another one. 'Bit of a floozy if you ask me. She's got children, you know.'

'Yeah, but I think they're grown up and have jobs.'

'So she says.' Without thinking, Dawn had poured a second pint; so Jackie had to stand at the bar and drink it. 'Have you seen the way she walks?'

Jackie shook his head.

'She's got a funny arse.'

'I'll keep that in mind.'

CHAPTER TWENTY-NINE

It came more rapidly than anyone was expecting.

Late July, in the grounds of the crematorium, which did special cheap rates for weddings on weekdays, Michael and Catherine were wed. It was a glorious day. The weather was fantastic. 24 degrees. Or, as Mike preferred to say, 83. There were twenty-eight people present.

Dawn said, 'I wanted to wear a fascinator. But it looked stupid. So I got this big hat. Does it look stupid?'

'You look fantastic, Dawn.'

Jackie could not have been more honest. Dawn looked amazing. She had on an orange and russet floral dress which dropped to mid-calf. Strappy high-heeled sandals which came halfway up from the other direction. And a broad-brimmed hat that women in Italy would have killed their husbands for.

'You look amazing.'

She actually blushed as she hugged Jackie.

'This is my boyfriend, Sebastian.'

'We've met,' said Jackie. 'Well we haven't personally met – I've seen you across a room.' He shook Sebastian's hand, and gave him a smile which underneath seemed to suggest that 'if you ever mess with this young woman I shall fucking kill you twice', and Sebastian appeared to understand that.

'It's a pleasure, Mister Conor. I've started one of your books. It's very interesting, in a banal kind of way.'

Emily and Laura faced each other in a masterclass of frostiness, and their politeness was so excrutiating it made birds fly away. Laura was accompanied by her beau; a man of surprising appearance and little personality, who was clearly out of his depth when having to meet people and clung to Laura's hand like a whelk to a liferaft. His name was Lawrence, and he described himself as an 'architectural consultant'.

Jackie thought he looked like an idiot. Not only did he look like an idiot, Jackie was pretty sure he was one. Any man who sported a moustache that would embarrass a walrus was always going to struggle in Jackie's mind.

When he caught Laura on her own, Jackie said, 'So where did you meet him?'

'At a wellness clinic for reforming lonely people.'

'You met him online.'

'Yes.'

The bride wore turquoise and the groom wore blue, and looked outstanding in his double-breasted suit.

Other guests were friends and family of the happy couple; and Jackie had an overwhelming desire not to meet them.

The ceremony went well, and briefly, which suited all concerned. Especially as a funeral was booked for ten minutes later and a coffin was being wheeled in.

Photographs were taken in the crematorium gardens, which were extensive, attractive and filled with ashes which nobody cared about treading on. The dead are dead and the living get married, and it is an ideal way for the world to exist.

'Fucking hell,' said Jackie, as he tripped over a limestone urn. 'What bloody idiot put that there?'

CHAPTER THIRTY

The wedding party adjourned to a cordoned off section of *The Golden Lion*, where Mike had laid on a spread of unprecedented proportions. He had brought in outside caterers, who had decorated the area with a style and panache which caused everyone who walked in to pause for a moment.

'Where's the fucking pub?' said Jackie.

But it was there, underneath it all. *The Golden Lion* reigned supreme and its spirit lived on through all that the caterers and suppliers could fling at it.

'Fucking ace, isn't it?' said Mike.

As indeed it was. Drifts of chiffon and taffeta billowed from the ceiling, stirred by a slowly circling ceiling fan. It was like being brushed by the wings of courting flamingos. There were vases filled with flowers of such depth of colour and grandeur it seemed impossible that nature alone could have produced them. A concealed device was wafting out fragrance which was mildly coloured and changed every twenty minutes, so that it seemed like people were travelling through a mist which shifted through their hands so elusively they could never quite grasp it.

Posh food had been provided. Avocados with smoked salmon and soft cheese, imported from a small region of central France where the locals weren't particularly keen on it. There were quiches and flans in every colour of the rainbow. Vegetables so tiny they needed to be approached with tweezers. Baby quails so fresh they were still running about. The centrepiece was a suckling pig which was later revealed to be composed largely of braised tofu, because Catherine had vegetarian leanings.

'Toffee?' said Dawn.

'No, it's tofu – it's tofu. It's – yeah, actually it is toffee.' Jackie smiled happily and Dawn smiled back. Sometimes the simplest explanations are the best.

The hired help behind the bar poured drinks with gay abandon, and the guests were not averse to consuming it.

Bottles of champagne were produced and Jackie commenced to drink straight out of one. Which is harder than it looks when attempted one-handed. Most of it seemed to come back down his nose. Something that even Emily thought wasn't entirely seemly.

A banjo band was in attendance and a couple of the boys from it clashed empty metal kegs in the manner of all well-planned banjo bands. There was a female magician performing feats of magic that even the sober couldn't fathom. Laura, in particular, became enamoured of the young woman and spent a long time staring blearily at her, muttering, 'That is fucking impossible. I fucking dare you to do that again.'

Mike's carefree and spirited cousin Jolida was there. Jolida's party piece was to remove her bra without taking her dress off; and she did not fail to deliver. When she attempted to remove the rest of her underwear, that was the moment she fell over. But not before she had flung her bra into the crowd in the manner of a bride's bouquet. It hit an old man in the face and he was never seen again.

Jackie was pleased to notice that at one point Emily and Laura were chatting and giggling and touching each other on the arm. It was only later he discovered that they were laughing about him, which rather took the sheen off things.

Late on in the evening Mike's elder brother, Leonard, owner of a plumbing company and a man of wholly cheerful demeanour and a persistently ruddy face, clambered onto a chair to propose a toast. But when he fell off the chair that idea was abandoned; and it looked like he'd damaged an ankle. 'Oh fuck,' he said, as he rolled on the floor. But his spirits remained undimmed and he grinned as widely as ever as he gestured and waved; mostly in the direction of the bar staff who hurried to fetch him fresh drinks.

'Fucking good wedding, Mike.'

'Thanks Jackie. I paid for it with your bar tabs; I've been saving them up for a while.'

Emily and Jackie danced. Dancing was seldom one of Jackie's finer attributes, and even Emily – whose movements were as delicate and precise as those of a damselfly – struggled to coax anything out of him beyond spasmodic jerking and dangerous arm gestures. In the end Mike took pity on her and eased her away for a proper dance while Jackie continued to dance alone in front of a mirror, and impressed himself with some of his moves. Most of which, he thought, were highly original, and he was surprised they weren't more popular. 'You're a very good dancer, Jackie.'

'Thank you, Jolida. You're a pretty fine mover yourself.'

'All I'm doing is swaying, because I can't feel my feet. I've got a terrible feeling I might have wet myself. Or I might have just spilled a drink down my leg.'

'Do you want me to taste it?'

'Yeah, go on then.'

Jackie got down on his knees.

'What the hell are you doing now?'

'I'm tasting Jolida's leg.'

'You're a fucking pervert,' said Laura, as she turned and walked away.

Dawn's boyfriend, Sebastian, collapsed and brought down a lot of taffeta. Dawn didn't notice because she was asleep under a table, still clutching a half-empty bottle of champagne.

'Yeah, bloody good party, Mike. We should do this more often.' Even the banjo band passed out.

CHAPTER THIRTY-ONE

Emily was ambivalent about her new job. She said she'd known worse, but was never filled with hope and anticipation when she journeyed towards it. Her satchel bag never swung jauntily from her shoulder.

'There are too many people with too many views, and none of them making much sense. They are all competing and jostling and juggling with onions, and I wonder how anything ever gets accomplished. You know at home, when we look out of the window at the ducks and the swans? They seem to have an organisation to them – as if they know exactly what they are doing and where they are going and why they are going, and what they will do when they get there. But they're only little birds. How are they able to organise themselves when the people I work with couldn't find their way out a room with three open doors? It's exasperating, Jackie. It makes me sad.'

Emily was suffering badly from morning sickness; and Jackie wondered if this was having an impact on her mood and views. He suspected it must, but, like many men, Jackie had a rudimentary knowledge of certain terminology and conditions, whilst possessing no true understanding of the actual state. Mostly, his response was to squint and ty to imagine; but he wasn't sure that he always got close. He understood the principles of vomiting; but not the repeated and regular sickness of Emily. Apart from the realisation that it would never be pleasant. It had to be draining. And in all likelihood it hurt.

Emily sighed and pushed strands of hair from her face. She had let it grow long but was thinking of wearing it shorter again. Long hair can be so time-consuming.

'I'm just so tired,' she said, resting her head on his shoulder. 'We don't ask for much, do we? But we can't seem to get it. I think I'm at a low ebb.' Jackie thought things seemed just fine; but recognised that that itself was a problem.

Perhaps he needed to work harder on his book.

'Maybe we should go away for a couple of days,' he said. 'Take Jason. Go to the seaside.'

Emily nodded.

'I'd like that,' she said. 'This is a very hard situation.'

Jackie wrapped his arms around her and pulled her closer on the sofa.

He kissed her on top of her head.

It will be fine, he thought. 'It will be fine,' he said. 'We will make everything fine.'

CHAPTER THIRTY-TWO

A point had been reached, though, he knew that now. For a long, long time there had been a question hanging in the air; and he had been carefully trying to steer his thoughts around it. He had always assumed there would come a day of reckoning; but he hoped it would somehow delay. Because when it came it would bring horsemen of chaos, confusion, disruption and intrusion, and things would be dismantled.

At one point during the evening of Mike's wedding, when everyone was becoming embroiled in the festivities and Jolida was about to perform her party piece and fall over, Laura had said – 'What about her other child?'

That was the one. That was the question. That was the gigantic elephant that everyone kept walking into. The question they were thinking was, 'How can a mother leave her child?' Not why. But how.

He had asked Emily himself, at a moment one evening when his own spirits were at a low ebb.

And she had said – 'I don't know.'

And that was as far as it got.

CHAPTER THIRTY-THREE

'Mike.'

'Yeah. How's it going?'

Mike poured the pint. Dawn bent over her eternal crossword. Pretty much life was as normal.

'I haven't seen my son for a while. I think he has a problem with Emily.'

Mike poured out two whiskies. He thought about matters for a moment, then poured a third one for himself. But almost immediately he changed his mind, gave it to Jackie, turned and poured himself a straight glass of vodka.

'Have you talked to him about it?'

'No, I don't want to provoke things. It took me long enough to get back to him; I don't want to cock it up now.'

'It's never easy Jackie. Not with kids. My daughter in Australia? Last I heard she'd roped a kangaroo, jumped on its back and was hopping away across the desert.'

Jackie laughed.

'Fuck off.'

Mike topped up Jackie's beer.

'You know what I mean, though. Kids. They're never going to do what we want them to do, are they? And we're always going to want them to do something. We're stuffed.' Mike threw down the vodka and poured another. 'We hope they don't hate us but they don't have to love us. I don't think that's in the arrangement.'

Jackie grunted, and sipped his beer.

'You're a bit bloody cheerful today.'

'What can I say? I'm a cheerful man.' Mike looked around, gestured with his head, said, 'Come down here,' and moved along the bar.

Jackie picked up his beer and followed him.

'You know when I go. If I go soon – in the next few years – I'm leaving the bar to Dawn. She's a good girl and she deserves it.'

Jackie looked across to her. She was a study in concentration. Her hair hung about her face and her pencil hovered in midair. It was obviously a crucial stage in the crossword process.

'What about your children?'

Mike waved a hand dismissively. 'I've left provision for them. They don't want to run a bar. Stacey's in Australia – she doesn't want to come over here to look after this place.'

Jackie nodded. Bars were tricky things. You could try to sell them but you knew you were going to get ripped off. All that good booze, going to waste.

Nevertheless.

'What about Catherine?'

'I'm not going to leave it so her children can benefit. Did you see them at the wedding? I don't even like their names.'

Mike leaned in closer; he and Jackie were practically brushing foreheads.

'Dawn's a smart girl. You and I both know she's a lot smarter than most people think. She'll know exactly what to do. She can run it, or sell it, or hive the place out.'

Mike leaned back.

'Don't tell her that for chrissake, she'll do even less work.'

Mike shifted his gaze to the left.

'Got customers, Jackie.'

'Okay.'

Jackie took his drinks to his booth. Now that he no longer used his stick he could manage them in one trip. He pretended not to notice the peanut that bounced off the side of his head; and Dawn pretended not to have thrown it.

He looked from his window. The pedestrianisation process was either in full swing, had ground to a halt, or was almost finished. It was hard to tell from the level of activity and the cones and tapes that were cordoning the area.

Someone was staring at the work with great intensity and Jackie recognised him from the days when he had tried to perform some civic or social duty and had worked as a volunteer at a day-care support centre for the homeless.

The last clear recollection Jackie had was that the man had pinched his cigarettes and run away laughing.

He seemed to be doing okay now.

He leaned back in his seat. Jackie's little safety zone. Nothing could bother him in the bar.

Everyone should have a booth in a bar, he thought. God didn't invent them for nothing.

Laura entered the bar. She didn't stride through in her normal fashion, rather she slouched in, slumped in, threw herself down on the seat opposite, dropped her bag, waved her arm in the air, and Mike started getting the drinks together.

She looked flustered. Her face was hot and her hair was sticking to it, and her eyes had a slightly out-of-control look.

'My pelvic floor has collapsed,' she said.

'Bloody hell. Is that upstairs?'

'It's not in the bloody house, Jackie – it's not the fucking staircase. It's a woman's thing, you know? Jesus.'

Mike came running across with a large glass of wine and a whisky for Jackie.

'You're a fucking idiot. Not you, Mike – him.'

Mike nodded. He'd always known it.

Laura put her face in her hands and gave a sigh to match one of Jackie's finest. She looked a figure of despondency. 'I only swear around you, you know. Every time I'm with you I say fuck.'

She removed her hands, sat back in her seat, inhaled deeply through her nostrils, and took a large gulp of wine.

'I might need an operation.'

She raised her hand and Dawn came running with another glass of wine. Not for the first time Jackie marvelled at Laura's facility for making people run around after her.

'You know how I feel about things like that. I'm not good with hospitals. I'm not good with anything.'

Jackie said, 'It's all right. We'll help. We can keep an eye on you.'

'Even Emily?'

Jackie nodded. 'Of course. She's a good woman, Laura.'

'I know,' she said. 'That's the terrible thing. She's actually rather lovely.' She shook her head, then made serious inroads into her second glass of wine. 'Bitch.'

CHAPTER THIRTY-FOUR

They took Jason away for a long weekend.

Robert drove him across; with his clothing and toiletries in a purple backpack; and a plastic football. Emily provided suntan lotion. Enough to cover an elephant and its calf. Jackie provided a 'Jason Rocks' baseball cap, which Jason immediately and irrevocably despised. And the interchange went surprisingly smoothly.

Robert had accepted Emily's pregnancy with, what seemed to Jackie, remarkable passivity. Perhaps there is something about pregnancy that makes people kinder. Maybe he'd adapted to her loss more quickly than he'd anticipated. Or maybe he'd found another woman. He was a handsome man; it wouldn't be hard. He and Jackie shook hands when they met. 'How's your leg?'

'Amazingly good,' said Jackie, 'to be honest. I thought I'd be hobbling for ever more but the surgeons did a good job. The main problem's giving up the painkillers; I think I've become addicted to them.'

'Unlike the alcohol.'

'Exactly.' They actually shared a laugh.

After Robert left, with little fuss, they loaded the gear into the black SUV. They weren't going to the seaside: that appeared too crowded and lacking in suitable accommodation at the short notice they had provided. Instead they were going to a lakeside resort twenty miles away. It had wooden chalets, some entertainment, tennis and pony trekking, a cheerful family restaurant and a bar. The bar provided a singer and a small band on Fridays and Saturdays.

Jackie was not averse to belting out a song or two himself: but his singing was worse than his dancing.

They were booked in for three days and three nights. They had decided to eat in the restaurant on the first evening; but had taken provisions for the other days as Emily wanted to feed Jason herself. Jackie suspected, from Jason's manner, that his father had given him strict instructions to be polite to Jackie, but under no circumstances was he to like him. Jason was taking this directive very seriously.

Jackie had to concede that the Friday fell on the awkward side of easy. Nobody was quite sure what to do, where to go, what to say, or how to behave. It was a relief to them all when they went to bed.

CHAPTER THIRTY-FIVE

The next day, the Saturday, Jackie and Emily adopted a far more positive attitude. They were up at the relative crack of dawn of nine o'clock. They hauled Jason out of his bed, out of his jimjams, into his shorts, and made him trot round the lake with them (part of it at least). Jason clearly viewed this as being pretty much on a par with having to participate in an East German building programme in the final days of the country's death throes. 'Can't we go home?'

'Yes. After we've enjoyed ourselves.'

Afterwards they ate scrambled eggs, mushrooms, grilled tomatoes, lean bacon, sausages, hash browns, more mushrooms (Emily had bought a lot) baked beans, something that Jackie couldn't even identify (samphire) and toast.

At the end of the meal Jackie and Jason exchanged a look. That was probably the start of their relationship. If Jason had been older, Jackie would probably have introduced him to alcohol at that point.

'I'm going to take Jason for a walk.'

'Okay.'

It wasn't a bad morning. The weather was peaceful and warm.

The chalet was situated only ten yards from the lake, and its veranda overlooked it. There was generous spacing between the chalets on the site; and the noise of other people was muted.

They set off to the left, heading towards the camp store. Jason was wearing shorts and flip-flops. Jackie was in his customary holiday attire of jeans and Timberland boots. His limp was barely noticeable.

He struggled for something to say. For a man of words, such as an author, he was proving to be something of a failure in that area. Every comment, question or observation he came up with seemed embarrassingly and unbelievably trite. So he settled for saying nothing. Which appeared to suit Jason ideally.

They walked in a companionable silence.

At the store they found there was fishing tackle for hire. So they splashed out big time, hired a rod, an assortment of tackle, and a loaf of bread for bait. They also bought some biscuits, because they suspected Emily hadn't brought any. Jackie further invested in a straw hat.

Back at the chalet they discovered a utility shed at the rear of the building, from which they extracted two folding chairs and a low picnic table. All of this was carefully positioned, organised, repositioned and reorganised at the edge of the lake.

Emily produced a jug of water with slices of lime and cucumber in (Jackie never understood why) and a bottle of squash. Jackie himself supplied a bottle of Jack and a few cans of coke.

After a short period of faffing about and sorting out the fishing tackle, they began fishing. In earnest.

All eyes were focused on an orange-tipped float that was bobbing languidly on the water and upon which, periodically, a dragonfly landed.

Some time passed.

After a while Emily brought out a striped towel and a cushion and lay down on the grass. She was wearing a pair of sunglasses that divas would have fought wars over.

Jackie's attention had drifted away a long time ago. So he decided to be more jovial.

'I understand you're very good at football, Jason.'

Jason, who was still politely wearing his 'Jason Rocks' baseball cap, appeared to be somewhat less certain.

'Our coach has told the other players not to pass the ball to me because I fall over it; but he has worked out what he calls a team plan. Sometimes, during a game, he gives me a signal and I have to run as fast as I can from our half of the pitch, right up the wing into the other half. Then the other team think that something is going to happen and they all run after me, then the rest of our team can run up the middle and try to score a goal.'

'Does that work?'

'Sometimes, said Jason. 'The bad part is that when the other team catch up with me they trip me up and kick me. It's a very painful tactic. I get kicked more than anybody else.'

Jackie nodded.

'I might have a word with your coach,' he said.

The afternoon progressed amicably. Catchable fish were notable by their absence, but a mallard turned up with a flotilla of youngsters, and they were incredibly interested in the bread-bait. So that kept things ticking along.

Emily said, 'Why don't you put a worm on the hook?' Both Jackie and Jason were a bit squeamish about that. 'Or a piece of sausage.'

'That might work,' said Jackie.

So they changed the bait, threw the last of the bread to the ducks, and settled down for a final intense fishing session; where everything was concentrated on the float.

'What's that stuff you keep drinking?' said Jason.

'This is from my friend Jack. 'Mister Daniels' to you. It's kind of a herbal remedy and you will absolutely hate it so never try it. It tastes disgusting; that's why I have to put coke with it, to make it more palatable. It's like medicine for old people. It's foul.'

'You're older than my grandad.'

'Am I?'

'Yes.' Jason nodded gravely. 'He drinks medicine too. But not as much as you.'

'He's probably not as sick as me.'

Out of the blue they caught a fish. They didn't know what it was, but it was big and it flapped and Jackie wanted to kill it and cook it: but Emily said, 'No, it's disgusting, throw it back,' then went inside to open a pack of salmon.

Which they ate on the veranda in the evening; still bathed in sunlight, watching birds show off over the water; particularly swifts, which performed miracles of manoeuvre and looked like they'd never stop flying 'til they died.

After the meal they played Scrabble which, strangely, was Jason's choice of game. Emily gave Jackie a very severe look. 'Don't put any fancy words down,' she said, gesturing with her head towards Jason. So he put down words like snot and bum and got into even more trouble. But it did make Jason nearly wet himself.

CHAPTER THIRTY-SIX

Sunday came, and breakfast was the same as before, with the addition of smoked salmon and slices of avocado and beetroot. Breakfast was becoming the most feared meal of the day.

Then came the first qualifying game of the Conor/Marchant Footballing World Cup, which took place in front of a surprisingly unappreciative crowd on the chalet's veranda (there was nobody there) and a few ducks on the lake which still hoped for more bread.

It kicked off at 10.30 am.

The match involved a lot of running and grunting. The other two provided most of the running, and Jackie supplied the grunts.

'This bloody game's fixed,' he said after he'd fallen over for the third time.

In truth, football probably wasn't the ideal game for Jackie, with his advanced years and cyborgian leg.

Sadly the ruthless opposition had no sympathy for his plight and took full advantage of his weakness. Their attacking play was merciless. Emily was remarkably nippy on her feet and Jason truly was a human whippet.

Twice the ball ended up in the lake, and each time Jackie was elected to wade out in his jeans to retrieve it.

He was glad when it reached half time.

At that point the score stood at Emily and Jason 48: Jackie 4. He thought they only gave him them out of pity.

They flopped on the grass. Three of them, exhausted, lying beneath an exorbitant sun, with the blood coursing merrily through their veins.

Emily reached out her hand and took hold of Jackie's.

It was the best moment he'd had in the last five years.

CHAPTER THIRTY-SEVEN

That evening they dined on a feast of pizza and ice cream. Everybody agreed that knickerbocker glory pizza was the best they had ever tasted. And who knew you could get crumpets in ice cream?

Afterwards they played a game of 'Mousetrap' which they found in a cupboard, and was almost complete. Intellectually it was a little beyond Jackie and he was still frowning by the end of it and completely uncertain as to who, if anyone, had won.

'Where's the bloody mouse?' he said.

'We haven't got one. That's why we used the radish.'

Stupid fucking game.

As the day progressed beyond twilight, Jason settled down and sprawled out on the sofa under a light duvet, and was allowed to watch TV until he fell asleep; and Jackie and Emily took their alcoholic/non-alcoholic drinks out onto the veranda to enjoy the last evening at the lake. They had placed insect-repellent candles about the area, but the insects rather seemed to like them; so that exercise wasn't an unqualified success. But they tried their best to ignore them.

They spent some time gazing at a grasshopper which landed on the table and was about the size of a small crocodile, and seemed entirely content to stare back at them. They were holding hands again, loosely, beneath the table; and listening to the sounds of people playing in the distance; and something that could have been an owl or was maybe a vulture. The sound of the TV was a quiet drone behind them.

Emily said, 'You asked me a little while ago how I could leave Jason behind. I imagine everyone we know asks the same question. I would ask it, too; a thousand times. And I wonder if anyone could answer it.' She breathed deeply; stared out across the lake. Their hands hung passively, fingertips intertwined. Somebody on the TV laughed, and Jason laughed in response. 'Sometimes,' she said, 'life goes wrong.' She paused.

'That isn't it,' she said. 'Sometimes you don't even know that life is going wrong: you discover it later when it's already happened. And it's not the big things that cause it, it's the constant drip drip of little things, like a leaking tap. And one day the tap overflows, the sink overflows, and it forms a pool on the floor. And then a rivulet starts running away from it and you follow it – and you end up in a cul de sac. You don't even know whether you created it or not. Or whether somebody else made it. But you're there – staring at a brick wall. And you think – this isn't how I thought it would be.'

She leaned across, lifted Jackie's glass from his hand and took a sip.

'One sip won't harm us,' she said.

'But everything then becomes questioned,' she went on. 'Your career, your prospects, your marriage, your future. The home that you live in; the streets that you walk along. Even the rugs on the floor and the tiles on the bathroom floor. Everything begins to feel wrong somehow. I suppose it's a kind of depression. One day you find yourself arriving at a point where you're thinking, if I'm not happy, how on earth on God's earth can I make Jason happy? How can I even start to give him a good life when I'm not even happy in my own? I'd drag him down with me, into the quagmire. And the terrible thing is I didn't even know why. I didn't know what was going wrong.'

She took another sip from Jackie's glass.

'It's a short step then to thinking he'd be better off without me.'

Jackie stared at the grasshopper. It had listened intently to every word. It hadn't moved: hadn't blinked. But suddenly it took off, crashed around the veranda like a maniac, then flew off into the night. Damn thing nearly gave him a heart attack. 'Are you happy now?' he asked.

'Oh yes, I'm happy now.' She squeezed his hand. 'I'm actually very happy, despite my ups and downs. I know my moods are capricious and erratic, but they're only moods: they're not a reflection of me. In truth I think I needed more football in my life. And a window that looks out onto a river. I like the swans and the ducks.'

Jackie looked hard at her. Her grip was still tight on his hand. He looked at her eyes, sparkling in the candlelight. 'Are you crying?' he said.

'No. It's an allergic reaction to darkness.'

Emily laughed, sniffed, wiped her eyes on the back of her hand. Then wiped her nose on her wrist.

'It's the balancing of it all, isn't it?' she said. 'That's what damages us: trying to clutch everything that we want inside two tiny hands. Holding the world in our fingers.' She wiped her nose on her wrist again. 'In the strangest of ways, hitting you with the car brought me back to life. I felt so ineffectual before.'

Jackie understood this. He felt it himself. He'd been treading water for a long time before Emily contrived to crash into his life. Given the right day and circumstance, pain and discomfort can produce unexpected benefits. Direction can come out of nowhere.

He even, vaguely, remembered her fainting: and that might have been the moment he was first drawn to her. A woman elegantly fainting does call some attention and linger in the mind.

'Jason loves you,' he said. 'I can see it in every move and gesture he makes. The way he talks, the way he laughs. He loves it when you grab him and tickle him. He loves you like a son and views you as his mother: I don't think you need to worry on that score.' He poured another measure into his glass; topped it up with coke. 'I also think you can admit him into your life. Into our life. I don't think he's ever likely to take to me – he still calls me Mister Conor. But it may be time to talk to Robert about spending more time with him; sharing the time. He can come and stay with us – we've got that extra room that one day might be filled with friends we haven't met yet, but at the moment it's going spare and Jason could have it. We kind of decorated it with him half in mind. He could put up posters or dartboards or whatever he likes. We can knock a hole through the wall so he can look out at the river. Get him a catapult, get him a boomerang: whatever he wants. Moving out is not the same thing as moving away. Jason can come with you.'

Emily nodded.

'I shall have a word with Robert. And with Jason too, of course; to see what he wants. Often it seems as if he's overlooked.'

There was more laughter from the TV, but Jason didn't respond. The boy had fallen asleep.

'Have you told him that he's going to have a sibling?'

Emily nodded again.

'He'd rather have a guinea pig.'

CHAPTER THIRTY-EIGHT

Two days later Jackie was back in *The Golden Lion*. It was busier than usual. He was pretty much certain that he was going to be bushwhacked this time. But he wasn't. At least not in the first minute. So he headed for the bar. For some reason his leg was troubling him a bit, and he was hobbling slightly as he progressed. He thought he might perhaps have overdone it playing football. His last despairing attempt to keep out the 48th goal had been a wholehearted full-length dive to his left; and the whole lake shuddered when he landed.

'I think I broke my fucking leg,' he said. Mike grunted. He didn't look overly sympathetic as he poured the beer. 'I don't think I'm as young as I used to be.'

'You were never as young as you thought you were.'

Both of them glanced along the bar to Jackie's left, where a young woman who sparkled so much she made Jackie's eyes hurt was serving customers with wine and foaming beers. This was Anastasia. She was standing in for Dawn who had gone on holiday to Benidorm, with her boyfriend. Both Mike and Jackie hoped Benidorm was ready for her. 'How's she working out?' said Jackie.

'She's a bit fucking lively,' said Mike. 'I got her through an agency. She's doing my head in to be honest.'

They stared at Anastasia for a few moments longer. She was indeed an active and participant worker. They weren't used to this in *The Golden Lion*. She was never going to get the job full time.

Jackie took his drinks to his booth. But there were two people already sitting in it; a man and a woman of indeterminate age and appeal. Jackie took an immediate dislike to them.

He stood at the end of the table for a time staring at them, but they refused to respond or even acknowledge him. In the end he had to move to the next booth.

This booth only had half a window to stare out of, and was wholly and utterly unsuitable for a man of Jackie's requirements. He had to sit at the opposite side of the table to get any kind of view at all. His hatred of the couple in his usual booth brewed at a level few people have experienced.

He had a large notebook with him. He didn't know whether this was an affectation or he was making a serious attempt to make progress on his novel. But he put it on the table to the right of the glasses, and put a pen on top of it. There wasn't much in the book. In fact, if he'd troubled to open it he would have found there was nothing at all. But every great work starts somewhere.

When the activity at the bar ceased, Mike came across with a bottle of whisky and two glasses. He was pushing the boat out: it was a bottle of 30 year-old malt. 'Somebody left it at the wedding,' he said. He poured two measures and they studied them for a while, inhaled of them, cradled the glasses. Sipped and sipped and sipped again. 'Not all it's cracked up to be, is it?'

'No; a bit smoky for my taste.'

Mike poured two more.

'I wonder if I'm up to it, Mike.'

'What – the whisky?'

'No, the baby. Having another baby. I don't know whether I'll be any good.'

'You probably won't, but at least you'll have a go. Do you think you were up to it the first time?'

'It's twenty-two years later. I'm still not up to it.'

'There's your answer then.'

The whisky went down more smoothly the second time. The third one went down even better.

Jackie rubbed his eyes with the heels of his hands. He was tired. He'd been tired a lot lately.

'It's such a big responsibility, isn't it? Your life gets settled; then one day it isn't.' He stopped rubbing his eyes and leaned back in his seat. 'Did you ever think of having more kids?'

'Not really,' said Mike. 'I had the snip a long while back. Did it myself, in the kitchen.'

'Did you? Fuck!'

Mike laughed. 'No, I'm just kidding. After Bridget, three seemed enough; so I had it done.'

'Did you ever regret it?'

'No, not really. It wasn't long before me and Margot split up anyway. It was never much of a problem after that.'

Mike looked down at Jackie's notebook.

'Is that your book?'

'Yeah.'

'How's it going?'

'It will be a lot easier when I get the first page down.'

CHAPTER THIRTY-NINE

'Does it hurt?'

Laura shrugged; shook her head. 'No, not really. It's more of an ache than anything. I've had it for a long time, but it's been a lot worse lately. I worry that I'm starting to smell. I leak a lot. It needs to be tackled.'

She waved her arm in the air. From across the bar Anastasia looked at her blankly.

'Who's that idiot?'

'Anastasia. She's Dawn's stand-in. Dawn's gone on holiday to Benidorm.'

Laura waved her arm more frantically and gestured at the table. Anastasia continued to stare at her.

'She's just fucking looking at me.'

'I'll get you a drink.'

Jackie fetched a large glass of wine for Laura and a pair of whiskies for himself. He was still limping slightly. Whatever he had done to his leg was sufficiently jarring that it gave both the hip and the knee, and the area in-between, the opportunity to reassert their former eminence and remind him of exactly how important they were in his day to day life, and he would neglect them at his peril.

'Are you all right? You're limping a lot.'

'It's okay,' he said, in the tone of a martyr. 'It's not as bad as what you're having. Ceilings collapsing.'

Laura pulled a face. 'Tell me.' She swallowed most of the wine. Fortunately Mike had returned to the bar and, recognising the signs, was already hurrying across with another glass. He also left half a bottle of it on the table.

They chewed their drinks for a while and stared from the window. Two people who knew each other well: who had been together for a long time, and now were apart. But still knew each other well. 'How's it going with the moustache guy?'

'Pff.' Laura snorted. 'I gave him the elbow. Turned out he had a lot of mother issues.'

'I don't think that's uncommon,' said Jackie, 'with some men. They get to a certain age; a certain predisposition. It's hard for them, you know, to move on.'

'Pff,' Laura said again. 'Except I was the one he wanted to be his mother. Like I'm going to smack his big fat arse for him.'

She attacked her wine again with gusto. The way things were going Jackie's bar tab would be heading through the roof.

'Bloody ridiculous,' she said. She shook her head, drank some wine, shook her head again, then ruffled her hair. 'I've joined a new dating agency. Well it's not like a normal website – they come to the house to talk to you. This woman talked to me for about three hours. I did fucking A levels that were easier. And then they draw up a profile – using their highly state of the art computers – and they use logarithms to hook you up.'

Jackie nodded. This was surprisingly interesting; and he wished he'd got a couple more whiskies in.

'So the first guy they send me – details, you know, on the computer – he looks like Humpty Dumpty.' She drank more wine. 'I paid a lot of money for this. I showed his picture to Colleen, you know? And she just burst out laughing. 'Don't crack him on the head,' she said.'

Jackie managed to catch Mike's eye, and Mike appeared with two glasses of whisky and a small bottle of ginger ale, on a silver tray.

Jackie was beginning to think that Mike might be starting to take the piss.

'So that didn't work out so good. I said I'm not fucking meeting that: I don't care if it's Brad Pitt in disguise. So then they send details of another one. The second one: this guy – he doesn't even show his face. He says he's an airline pilot, an astronaut, and a championship winning jockey. I thought fuck my bloody arse he is. So I get on the phone to them. This woman I'm talking to – my 'liaison' – she sounds about eighteen. Kerry. *Kerry!* I said listen Kerry, I paid a lot of money for this, and all you've sent me so far is a faceless man and a big egg. 'They fit your profile,' she said. What sort of profile have they got if they're sending me bald fat idiots who tell lies? I would have been better off staying with you. And you were a bastard.'

'I'm not a bald fat idiot.'

'I know, babe.' She leaned across the table to give his hand a squeeze. 'But you were a bastard.'

Laura gnawed the nail of one thumb, and stared through the window to a place that wasn't in the bar, and possibly not even on the planet. But it engrossed her for a time.

'Am I unattractive?' she said.

'Of course not. You're scary; but everyone's entitled to something.'

'You got someone. You got Emily. How did that happen?'

'She ran me over – remember?'

'Oh yes. I forgot about that.'

CHAPTER FORTY

Emily's spirits rose as her episodes of morning sickness subsided. No longer were her place of work and her colleagues things to be derided, scorned, hated, feared and despised: it transpired that, in reality, some of them were quite nice. She no longer gagged when she spoke of them.

The uplift in Emily's spirits had a corresponding knock-on effect on Jackie's own aspect, and he began to exhibit a more positive attitude with regard to his fabled novel 'Death of a Swan', of which, as yet, not a single word had been written.

He put together old ideas, short ideas, long ideas and new ideas, and began to approach a point at which he might, God willing, with the wind in the right direction, the tide running true and the outriders flying, be able to formulate a plot.

At this juncture any plot would be good. Any plot was better than nothing. A single word was better than silence. He took the thoughts with him wherever he went.

One downside of the apartment they had bought was that it lacked a proper garden; or much of any outside space at all. In the absence of such they had taken to visiting a riverside café a short distance away. There they could sit and look out on the river and the life that chugged about on it and listen to the sounds of life going on around them, without having to be directly participant in it.

The place had outside tables, a white picket fence and there were tubs of geraniums and petunias generously dotted about. Dogs weren't allowed in, but occasionally would be seen tethered outside. That situation suited Jackie ideally.

As he once explained to Emily he had something of a problem with nature; particularly those creatures of nature that liked to show you their arse. Domestic cats topped that list: closely followed by several varieties of dog, most types of monkey, and he wasn't even sure about geese. He was of the opinion that this furry creature aversion stemmed from his childhood, when his family had a dog. 'It bloody hated me that thing. I could see it on its face.'

In his memory, he spent most of his early years walking backwards, because he feared that if he turned away from it the dog would attack him from behind. (It would, in effect, 'bushwhack' him.) 'What sort of dog was it?' Emily had said.

'A poodle. One of the evil kind. A right bastard. Never made eye contact – always looked at you out of the corners of its eyes. Waiting for you to drop your guard.'

As was his custom Jackie had a favourite table at the café; off to the side, almost in a corner, shaded by the branches of a walnut tree. He was sitting at it now, waiting for Emily, who often would take her lunch break there.

Jackie stood up as she approached. She was wearing a swishy swinging calf-length blue dress with blue patterning which Jackie thought might be butterflies, or might be abstract.

He held her chair as she slid onto it. Just because they lived together didn't mean he had to forget the basics.

He had already provided a herbal tea and a slab of sponge cake the size of Madeira.

'How's it going today?'

Emily waved her hand. She had already bitten off a huge chunk of the cake. It looked far too big to fit in her mouth.

'Okay,' she said. 'People whining, people moaning. At least two of the younger people crying. And then we got to the coffee break. How about you?'

'I've actually made some progress,' he said. 'I know what it's about.'

'Yes?' Emily's face lit up like the sun had come out. 'Look at you – the author who remembers how to write. Come on then – you have an expectant audience of thousands; although I'm the only one who has turned up so far. What's it about?'

'I think it's a thriller. Well it is a thriller. A crime thriller. I think this guy – ' he emphasised it with a karate-like chop of his hand – 'has to deliver a body.' He paused for a moment to think about it a little more. 'See – I think he had it in the boot of his car.' He shook his head. 'Well he wouldn't have it on the front seat, obviously. He had it in the boot. And it's really hot – the weather. So the body has started to go off.'

'It's not a swan?'

'No, that's just a metaphor really. It's a human body. Or – 'a' body – depending on whether you're still human after you die. So anyway – ' he gestured with his hand again, this time a horizontal karate chop. 'He's been driving around. Because the guys he was supposed to rendezvous with didn't show up. I think they're dead; I'm not sure yet. But he has to park up in a multi-storey car park – because he needs something to eat and wants to use the bathroom. And when he gets back later, there's a group of people around his car. Because the woman who was parked in the space next to him had a dog. And the dog started whining at the back of *his* car, and when the woman looked more closely there was 'fluid' dripping out of the boot, onto the floor. And the dog quite fancied it.'

He paused for breath. The café didn't serve decent alcohol, but Jackie, being a resourceful man, always went with his two hip flasks. With the discreteness of an alligator tiptoeing across a tablecloth he tipped one of them into his empty teacup.

'And there was a smell. So the woman contacted the car park attendant, and he had a look and a sniff, and they both agreed that this was quite uncommon. So they called the police. And the police were there when my guy got back.'

He leaned back from the table, then took a sip from his delicate china cup full of vodka.

'That's just the beginning, of course.'

CHAPTER FORTY-ONE

After Emily returned to work, Jackie walked through town to
The Golden Lion. Thankfully, for the state of the nation and Jackie's
well-being, Dawn had returned from Benidorm; and she had colour
on her face and arms to prove it. Plus she was wearing a straw hat.

She was already pouring his beer as he approached the bar.

'Hello Jack.'

'How was Benidorm?' he said.

'It's a bit crappy if I'm honest. But bloody great. You can get
a bucket of cocktail for the price of a chicken. I nearly drowned my
head in one. And they've got these little scooter things? Oh God,
Jack, don't put me on one of them again. I ran into the back of so
many cars. The effin brakes are rubbish.'

She turned towards the whisky optics.

'How many do you want?'

'Er – three.'

She shook her head as she poured them.

'And the place at night. You wouldn't believe it. I thought
Torquay was bad. The noise, the smell. I lost my boyfriend for three
days, but luckily I found another one. He lives in – what's it called?
Not Jerusalem. *Jericho!* No not Jericho, he lives in Jersey, which is
in the Channel Islands. I'm going to visit him for a weekend. I have
to fly down there as well, in a little plane that's only about eight feet
long.' She sighed cheerfully, before shaking her head again. 'I'm
becoming quite cosmopolitan now.'

Jackie picked up his drinks and turned away.

'Hey Jack – before you go, give us this one.' She scooted
down the bar to her celebrity crossword magazine. 'Actor who
played Joey in Friends. Four and seven.'

Jackie pondered it for a while.

'Oily Portals,' he said.

Dawn's head moved slowly up and down as she pored over the magazine. 'Still doesn't fit.'

As he walked away she said, 'I know you take the piss. Every time I sneak a vodka I put it on your tab.'

Jackie was grinning as he settled into his booth.

Yes. He had to work harder on his book. He had to think of it, complete it, invent all the stuff that came in-between, and write it all down.

Piece of piss, he thought as he sipped at a whisky and stared from the window. *A child could do it.*

But he knew it was harder than that. It had been eleven years since he wrote a book; he was in genuine danger of fading away.

Emily had been so pleased and happy when he outlined the beginning of his book. She wanted so much for him to succeed. He wanted it too. He needed it. A man can drink for only so long.

He was thinking, as well, that perhaps he needed a new agent. He thought his current agent didn't trust him any more. Possibly didn't even like him.

A few years ago there had been an incident.

It took place at the launch party of another author. Jackie had been invited along. Jackie would go anywhere for free drinks.

The event took place in a stylishly minimal bar in a narrow street not far from Oxford Circus.

The party itself was okay; a lot of people pissed as rats was not unusual; and when the publisher foots the bill nobody turns down another one.

It was when he left the bar to catch the last train home that he found himself rolling across the bonnet of a slow-moving taxi and kicking a delivery driver off his moped.

Even that might have been smoothed over, had not members of the public become involved.

'Who the fucking fuck are you?' was a phrase he seemed to remember using. And some fisticuffs were involved. Most of Jackie's punches were wild swings that basically connected with thin air. Nevertheless he did end up standing on the bonnet of the taxi at one point shouting, 'Come and get me, you bastards!'

Amazingly he did manage to catch the last train home. Authors are made of sturdy stuff and seldom miss anything.

He fell asleep on the train, but still managed to wake up as it pulled into Queensbridge Station in the early hours of a drizzly Thursday morning.

His last recollection of the evening was of stepping from the train and falling flat on his face.

CHAPTER FORTY-TWO

So he sat at his desk in the study overlooking the river. There was a computer monitor staring back at him; but he didn't like that. Computers were for amateurs. Hemingway didn't write on a computer. No author of any great note, as far as Jackie could recall (he didn't mind listing himself amongst the greats) ever wrote directly onto a computer. Words came out of the hand. They were an organic thing: every word developed from the word that went before. Every sentence was a construct of the phrase which preceded it. Nothing was a result of the glaring vacuity of a blank computer screen.

So he cleared the desk.

He put the monitor and its associated cables and keyboard on the floor.

He wasn't approaching this position blindly. He had been to a stationer's and bought a stack of paper, pads, pencils, ink – a state of the art pencil sharpener that turned pencils into lethal weapons – and he had looked out his favourite fountain pen.

He found, as he started to use it, that the pen leaked. But no great work was ever accomplished without a little suffering.

Writing a book. Writing a book. Everything stemmed from self-confidence: the confidence to believe that what he was writing was sufficiently worthy that people would pay money to read it. He had read a lot of books that he regretted buying.

He pushed up his sleeves and got to work. It was a bright day outside and it was a Tuesday. The only thing he lacked was a cigarette. He opened a pad of blank white paper and stared at it for a time. Then stared at it a little while more. After an hour he went to get a drink. An hour after that he went to *The Golden Lion*. It didn't mean everything was lost.

CHAPTER FORTY-THREE

'How did it go today?'

'Good. Nobody cried. Nobody left. Nobody threw their knickers out of a window. Maybe I'm getting more relaxed. The mellow part of having a baby.'

They had decided to have their evening meal by the river, at the café which closed at 8.00 pm. The salmon was overcooked, the vegetables were limp, but it saved clearing dishes and washing up. And there was always activity on the river to watch.

He was still thinking about his book.

The police would take them away – the car and the body. That was okay; it was a pool car for the syndicate he worked for, and none of the pool cars were traceable.

He would probably be on several cameras in the area: even car parks had cameras these days. But that was all right: he could work around that.

Then they would probably take the body to a morgue.

The morgue. That was the place. He had to get the body out of a morgue.

He would need another vehicle; and possibly some assistance. But he didn't want to tell his bosses. He might have to get his wife involved. She wouldn't be thrilled about that.

After an hour it started getting chilly so he put Emily's jacket over her shoulders, wrapped an arm around her, and they walked slowly back to their apartment.

They didn't do much. Pottered about. Listened to music; watched some tv. They went to bed early, around 9.30, and lay propped up on pillows, looking through the window.

Their bedroom didn't directly overlook the river, but part of it was visible as a silver streak on the right-hand side. The bulk of the view was the tops of buildings on the edge of Queensbridge and the rural landscape beyond.

The square tower of a church in a village two miles away occupied centre stage.

'What's the name of your character?'

'I'm not sure yet. I think he's a middle age guy, at least in his forties. So he won't be greatly physically agile. And I think his wife's from Aberdeen.'

Emily nodded.

'I knew a woman from Aberdeen. She had problems with her feet.'

CHAPTER FORTY-FOUR

'I'm not carrying this body around all day.'

Jackie stared at the page. The wife was getting obstreperous.

'We don't need all of it. We just need the torso. We can cut the other bits off.'

'What?'

'The arms and the legs. We don't need them. And his head. We don't need that.'

'I'm not cutting his head off.'

'No, I'll do that. I'll cut his head off.'

'With what, Frank – a pair of scissors? We're in the middle of a car park.'

'I'll get a saw.'

'You're disgusting. I'm going back to stay with my sister if you're starting with these shenanigans again.'

Agnetha grunted as she helped heave the body into the boot of the hire car.

'My mother was right about you. You have some serious issues.'

Mike came across with the bottle of malt and two clean glasses.

'How's it going?'

'A bit weirdly at the moment.'

'Have you killed the swan yet?'

Jackie looked exasperated. 'There isn't a fucking swan in it, for chrissake. I keep telling people this. The swan is just a metaphor.'

'For what?'

That simple question caused Jackie to pause for a few moments. He stared at the page in front of him. Watched Mike pour the whiskies. Clinked his glass against Mike's and took a swallow. Took another; offered his glass for a top-up.

'Damned if I know.'

CHAPTER FORTY-FIVE

After three days of relatively intense writing activity Jackie's novel stalled and he experienced mild depression.

It was going to be a long haul.

CHAPTER FORTY-SIX

'I envy her you know, Emily.'

'Because she's living with me?'

'Because she's pregnant. I'd love another child.'

Jackie stared at the table. The great author, the man of words, knowing that something important was required, once again sat as numb as a statue and said nothing.

A thousand thoughts were swirling in his head, but none of them came to his lips. He didn't even pick up his whisky glass. This was one of the times that alcohol couldn't help. A second child had always been an issue between him and Laura.

He raised his head and gazed from the window. The pedestrianisation programme was almost complete. There were just a few cones and strands of orange plastic tape remaining.

A concrete flower trough had been installed and insanely red geraniums, courtesy of the Council, were poking their heads above the rim and blinking in a startled fashion at their new surroundings.

Already there was litter in it.

'It's too late now, isn't it? All kinds of things going wrong. Too old. No bloke anyway.'

Jackie glanced across to Mike. Mike started getting the drinks together.

'It's a decision I made a long time ago; and now I'm wondering whether I'm growing to regret it. Not Luke and Ali's baby – that's our grandson; that's different. But Emily. Emily having another baby.'

Mike arrived with drinks. For a large man he could move surprisingly swiftly at times.

'Going through it all. Doing it again. I wish – I wish I could have that chance. I'd like to do it, you know? The pain, the discomfort, the vomiting, the constipation. I'd do it all again in a heartbeat.'

She took a sip from the glass of wine Mike had brought her. 'I left it too late.'

Mike was still standing at the table. He didn't know what the conversation was about but it was clearly serious, so he had a grave expression on his face as he gazed at her.

After a minute Laura looked up at him and smiled. She squeezed his hand. 'It's all right, Mike.'

Mike smiled back. Then he looked at Jackie, and moved away. He had left enough drinks to last a while. Jackie's tab was going to hit a record.

It was Laura's turn to stare out of the window, while Jackie watched her, and didn't do much drinking, and wished he could do something to help her. Not for the first time in his life he regretted the absence of a magic wand.

'We didn't have a bad life, did we?' she said.

'Of course we didn't. We're still having it – we haven't abandoned each other. It's this medical problem you have – it's getting you down. That's all it is. It would get anyone down; it's understandable. Plus, the men you meet online and through your highly expensive dating agencies are, by and large, needy lying bastards who are not helping you in any way at all.'

Laura nodded. 'I can't deny that,' she said. 'If I'm not being somebody's mother I have to look at pictures of their genitals.' She sipped her wine. She was having a slow wine-drinking day today. The more she felt harassed and flustered the faster she drank it. Today was a slow day. 'Have you ever done that?'

'Sent pictures of my genitals?'

'Yes.'

'No.'

Laura pondered that for a moment.

'Shame,' she said. 'It might have given someone a laugh.'
She sighed deeply.

'It doesn't get any easier, does it? Getting older. You'd think that somehow it would. You'd think that you would avoid all the bad stuff and focus on the good; but it never seems to happen. Experience counts for nothing.'

'This is all because of your medical issue. You know that, don't you? It's dragging you down. All illness is debilitating; it's sucking your spirit out and leaving you low: it doesn't mean it's the end of the world.'

Laura shrugged. She fiddled with her wine glass, but didn't drink from it. After a few moments she gave another shrug and a nod. 'Sometimes the end of the world would be a relief,' she said.

Dawn appeared at the end of the table. 'Hello Laura.' She gave a smile. Dawn, like Mike, like Jackie, like anyone, could see the sadness in Laura's eyes. 'Mike sent me over with these.' She put down a large glass of vodka and a small bottle of tonic water. 'Don't be glum,' she said, after a pause. 'It will be all right.'

Laura smiled at her. 'Thanks sweetheart.'

Dawn then did what she tried to do best. She tried to lighten the mood.

'Has he told you about my boyfriend?' she said, and she jerked her head towards Jackie.

'No babe. What about him?'

'He's got a hang-glider.'

CHAPTER FORTY-SEVEN

It had been arranged that Jason would come over for regular visits. The first was at a weekend. They drove across to Gloucester on a Friday afternoon and picked him up after school. They would deliver him back to school on the Monday morning.

Jackie had seen a happier looking rhinoceros he thought as Jason climbed into the car.

How much luggage did one kid need for a weekend?

They glared at each other in sullen silence for most of the journey home. Alpha males, jockeying for position. A kid and an adult. With a mother and a lover in-between.

Jackie gave him a look which said, *I'm watching you, kid.* Jason gave him a look which said, *Kiss my arse old man* and showed him the finger.

I'll bloody have you.

Yeah, bring it on.

Emily chattered merrily all the way home.

They stopped at a convenience store to stock up on things that Jason might like.

Jackie decided to stock up on extra Jack Daniels. He had a feeling it was going to be a long night.

CHAPTER FORTY-EIGHT

On the first morning, the Saturday, Emily was still in bed. She had taken to staying in bed longer of late. Jackie didn't know if it was related to the pregnancy or for some other reasons. But he didn't like to disturb her.

So he and Jason sat staring at each other across the kitchen table. Jackie had thrown everything in the cupboard at him. Cheerios. Crumpets. Jam. Sausage rolls, Something that Jackie wasn't even sure of. A banana; a kiwi fruit; a melon, and a container of samosas.

'Do you want some porridge?'

'No.'

Fuck you then, thought Jackie.

The impasse continued for some time.

'Is there anything you'd like to do today?'

'Can we go swimming?'

'What – in the river?'

Jason nodded.

'Er – probably not. It's filled with sharks.'

'No it's not.'

'Alligators.'

Jason gave a snort of derision so strong it almost made paint peel off the walls.

'What can we do?

'We could hire a boat.'

'Can I drive it?'

'Can the Pope shit in the woods? Sorry, I shouldn't have said that.'

'Okay.'

That was decided with relative simplicity, and there were big thumbs-up all round. All they had to do was wait for Emily to get up.

When she did, two things got underway at high speed. Jackie had to find and book a motor boat. Emily and Jason had to organise, arrange, possibly purchase and otherwise put together a picnic. That they could have on a boat, on a river.

The stress of this was so great that Jackie started drinking earlier than usual, and a lot heavier than usual. By the time they got to the boat he was so drunk he nearly fell off the wharf.

'It's not very fucking big, is it?'

'Ssh.' Emily nodded at Jason.

'It's a bit – it's a bit – '

'Tiny,' said Jason.

'Possibly.'

They piled aboard.

The grizzled and somewhat dishevelled man who was hiring out the boat instructed them in its use. 'That's forward. That's backward. I don't know what that's for. If you get into trouble push the button.'

'What button?'

'It's under the seat.'

And off they went.

There was some initial squabbling between Jackie and Jason over who should have steering rights. The drunk and the small boy wrestled for control of the wheel. Eventually Jackie decided to be the bigger man, and let him have it. There is some nobility to be gained from an act of selfless sacrifice.

He was grinning as he sat down next to Emily at the stern.

'Feisty little bugger, isn't he?' he said.

'I worry about him,' she said in a low voice. 'He's so small and fragile. He seems so vulnerable.'

'I don't think he's fragile at all. If he wanted to arm wrestle me he'd keep going until his arm dropped off.'

He took a sip from one of his hip flasks.

'And he'd probably win.'

The little motorboat chugged steadily upstream for the best part of forty-five minutes.

They wanted to give it a name; they weren't happy with its designated title of 'Number7 Wilson Hire'. Jackie wanted to call it 'Heapacrap' but that was deemed unseemly by the mother on board, so eventually they called it 'Duckfart'. That, apparently, fell within the realm of acceptability. 'HMS Duckfart the Third'. God knew what happened to the other two, thought Jackie.

When a rickety wooden jetty appeared at the right-hand side of the river, Jason steered the boat towards it, and almost ruined everything by smashing into it. There were a few moments of slightly hysterical but reasonably contained pandemonium. Then the engine was turned off, everyone clambered ono the jetty, Duckfart was tethered to a piling, and the picnic basket and its associated accoutrements were retrieved. Then a certain peace descended.

'Well that wasn't so bad,' said Jackie, as he wiped the sweat from his eyes.

The jetty was a strange affair that seemed to serve no practical purpose, as there was no access to it from the landward side. But it was stable and steady and they had it to themselves, so in many ways it was considered perfection.

Emily started sorting out the food. Jason wandered off to explore a nearby drystone wall. Jackie stared at the boat, wondering why he hated it so much. When he couldn't decide, he ambled off after Jason.

It wasn't a bad bonding session for Jason and Jackie. They hunted for lizards; found a slow worm; and the biggest beetle they had ever seen.

'I think it's a stag beetle,' said Jason.

Jackie nodded. 'I think you're right. Put your finger there and see if it bites you.'

'You put your finger there.'

'I said it first.'

They used a twig, but the beetle wasn't interested. It existed on a higher plane.

They started throwing stones into the river.

When something began rustling in the grass behind them they decided to return to Emily. You couldn't trust anything in the undergrowth.

After they'd had their lunch, Jason wandered off again. Jackie and Emily sat on the edge of the jetty. She had her feet dangling in the water.

'Are you okay?' he said.

She looked pale; and there was a sheen of perspiration on her face.

She nodded. 'I've been getting a lot of stomach pain lately.'

Then Emily suddenly, unexpectedly, and violently, threw up into the river.

CHAPTER FORTY-NINE

On the Sunday morning Emily was sick again. Violently, repeatedly, noisily sick.

'What's wrong with her?' said Jason.

'You know she's having a baby?'

Jason nodded.

'This is one of the things that happen when women are having a baby. She was as sick as a dog when she had you.'

'Was she?'

'Yes. Doctors said they'd never seen anyone so sick. You owe her a lot.' Jason looked so crestfallen that Jackie immediately regretted saying it. 'I don't know,' he said. 'I just made that up. I don't know why I say things like that.'

'Is she going to be all right?'

'Yes. It's just a passing thing.' He put a hand on Jason's shoulder. 'Come on, let's leave her in peace and go and get some breakfast.'

They walked down to the café by the quay and had burgers, chips and so much ketchup that it showed up red on a satellite camera.

'I don't like her being sick.'

'It's okay. Even grown-ups throw up sometimes. I've thrown up.'

'When?'

'Last week. I fell over a hedge and landed awkwardly and the contents of my stomach decided to leave my body.'

'Are you taking your medicine?'

'Yes. I'd had quite a lot of it that day.'

There hadn't been time to fill up his hip flasks so Jackie had slipped a half bottle of brandy into his pocket. He poured some of it now into his coffee. Jason was having a milkshake.

'Do you want to go feed the ducks after this?'

'I like ducks.'

'So do I.'

They went to a store and bought the biggest loaf of bread they could find, then returned to the main jetty to feed the ducks, swans and ever-attendant gulls.

Jackie asked him how things were going. With his dad, with school, with life, with everything. Jason was fairly insouciant about it all. 'It's all right I suppose.'

Jackie looked at him. 'Is that it? The whole summary of your life at the moment is 'it's all right'?'

Jason shrugged. 'I suppose.'

'You've had it when you have to write an essay.' Jackie tossed a piece of bread into the air, where a seagull caught it on the wing. He was hoping that a black-backed gull didn't come down to snatch up a duckling; that happened all too frequently and passers-by and witnesses became very vocally and communally upset. Jackie rather liked the black-backed gulls; he thought they were handsome beasts. But the duckling eating thing was a problem. 'Do you know what the secret to life is?'

'No, what?'

'There isn't one. We all just do our best and keep running as fast as we can. It's when you stop running that you get into trouble. Just keep running. Don't look back. Don't turn around. Keep on going. That's what life is about.' Jackie nodded at his own sage advice.

'You're a strange man,' said Jason.

'You're a weird kid.'

CHAPTER FIFTY

A few days later Jackie entered *The Golden Lion*, checked for bushwhackers, then headed towards Dawn at the bar.

'Did you go hang-gliding then?'

'Oh God, Jack – it's a good job I went to the bathroom first. I screamed all the way through it. He said we were only up there for ten minutes – it seemed like a lifetime to me.'

She placed a pint of beer in front of Jackie, then turned to get the whiskies.

'He said he'd like to do it naked. I told him he could eff off with that idea. Jersey was nice though.'

Jackie sipped at his beer.

'Is Mike not around?'

'No. He went to that lunch thing he goes to sometimes. The business thing.'

'Chamber of Commerce.'

'Yeah. He had his suit on.'

Jackie took his drinks to his table.

He had brought his writing notebook with him.

Frank, his character, knew that there was something 'inside' the body. But nobody wanted to know what it was because to know what it was would be to put oneself in grave and possibly imminent danger. So you just had to deliver it. But he'd lost it. Now he'd recovered it; but he didn't know where to take it because the people he was supposed to take it to weren't answering their phone.

Frank had a feeling that the people he worked for, his own bosses, weren't going to be happy that he hadn't delivered the body on time. Even though it wasn't his fault that the meeting had gone wrong.

Agnetha had gone back to her sister in Aberdeen. This kind of thing happened about twice a year so he wasn't unduly concerned.

What he had to do was –

'Hello Dad.'

'Hello son.'

Jackie stood up and they exchanged an awkward handshake, then both of them sat down.

'Would you like something to drink? Coffee – beer?'

'No, I'd better not. Got to be back in work soon.' Luke had on a short-sleeved blue shirt with the top button unfastened and his tie loosely pulled down. 'How you keeping?' he said.

'Good. Good.' Jackie adjusted his drink glasses and closed his notebook. 'Life keeps going, you know. How about you?'

'I'm good. Knackered with the baby, you know. But yeah, it's good.' Luke then did what everybody did in Jackie's booth: he stared out of the window. Then he looked back and stared down at his hands. 'Mum said you think I've been avoiding you.'

Jackie exhaled slowly through his nostrils. For ever and always, there was something. 'There was a bit of a cold wind blowing from the east.'

Luke nodded. 'It's the drinking thing, you know? Around the baby. The smell of it and – '

Jackie nodded too, after a pause. 'I understand,' he said. 'I thought it was Emily. I thought maybe you had a problem with her.'

'No, Emily's fine. It's - the other stuff.'

'Okay.' Jackie put down his whisky glass. It didn't seem the appropriate time to be drinking it.

'Anyway.' Luke looked up and made the effort to be cheerful. 'Alison wondered if you'd like to come round on Saturday, for lunch. Both of you, obviously.'

'That would be great.'

They smiled. One was wanly, the other was forced. Moments between father and son can often be the worst.

'We'll see you then then,' said Jackie.

'About one o'clock.'

'Okay.'

Luke stood up, smiled more brightly, then moved away from the table.

Jackie stared after him as he left.

If it wasn't for the love between them he'd never go near the guy.

CHAPTER FIFTY-ONE

Frank could cut up the body with a saw, and put the torso into cold storage. Without the limbs and the head it would probably fit into a suitcase. Which could be frozen. Then he could dump the spare parts, randomly, about the place. Or better still, take them to a pig farm and throw them over the fence. That would be both efficient and environmentally friendly. And he could have a trip out to the countryside. Go to a pub

'What?' Emily looked up from a magazine.

'I'm just thinking. He could cut up the body and dispose of it. And just keep the torso. Then I think there might be a paper trail that he could follow so he could find out where it came from and what its significance might be.'

'That would be useful.'

'Yeah. It would.'

Emily flipped through a couple of pages of her magazine.

'Have you killed the swan yet?'

Jackie stared stoically straight ahead.

'I'm getting round to it,' he said.

CHAPTER FIFTY-TWO

Cometh the Saturday, cometh the man. Jackie and Emily arrived at Luke and Alison's house promptly at one o'clock; as spruced up as if they were going to meet the President of the World and his daughter.

Jackie had made a special effort and had only been drinking vodka and sucking mints. He was almost vertical as he pressed the buzzer at the side of Luke's door.

Sometimes he wondered why his drinking didn't appear to trouble Emily.

He had asked her once and she had said, 'You were drinking when I met you and I liked you then, so why try to change things?' Which was a simple and equanimous response.

When the door opened Alison was standing with the baby in her arms, beaming from head to foot.

She looked enthusiastically radiant. Her hair was a mess and her cheeks were fiery, but she appeared as happy a woman as Jackie could remember seeing in the last twenty-five years. If happiness was a state of being that could be measured, Alison had bought it by the mile.

They bundled inside. Hugs, gifts, all kinds of things were exchanged there in the hallway, before they got anywhere near the rest of the house; which smelled completely and utterly of 'baby'. A smell Jackie had all but forgotten.

They progressed to the dining room/kitchen area; which displayed the kind of chaos Jackie remembered from his own house when Luke was young.

For a very small child, Dominic required a lot of space. He didn't even require it: he demanded it. Every inch of space was devoted to his needs. It was if the Ambassador of Babies had walked in and said, 'This is wrong. Do it like this – ' And had rearranged the house around the occupants.

Yet amongst it all, somehow, Alison had arranged a lunch.

It was set outside, on a metal table, on the small patio area which fronted the small garden and was approached via a set of French doors. There was even a parasol.

As fate would have it: luck being a matter of where the cards fall: Luke wasn't present. Not as any form of deliberate slight, but because of pressure of work and covering for a sick colleague. A situation that Alison seemed less than impressed with.

'It's funny how they're always sick on a Saturday, after a Friday night out.'

Amidst all the movement and commotion Jackie found he was sitting on a red leather sofa cradling his grandson in his arms.

He looked down at him with a feeling he couldn't explain, and a warmth he'd never experienced. He barely noticed when the womenfolk wandered outside. They had so many words to exchange that the dining room wasn't big enough to contain them.

'You're an ugly little bugger – do you know that? And you're a bit like me. In fact you're a lot like me – highly dependent, prone to tears, and desperate for a woman's attention.' He smiled at the child. 'I've been rehearsing those lines for days. I wanted to impress you with my word skills.'

Alison brought him a plate of food: olives, quiche, green leaves tossed in balsamic vinegar, vine leaf wraps, and cherry tomatoes. There were no potatoes, meat pies, crisps, sausage rolls, or anything that might have been of interest to Jackie, but he gallantly munched his way through it. Whilst sipping from a glass of mineral water. 'This is what it's going to be like,' he said to Dominic. 'The stuff you want in life you never get enough of. Whether it's women, sleep, money or pasties. You never get enough of them. If the leaves don't get you the diet drinks will. And give up on the idea of smoking.' He looked more closely at Dominic. 'Are you listening to me?' The baby was asleep. Jackie smiled. There were worse ways to spend an afternoon.

Strands of conversation drifted in through the open French windows as Jackie sat rocking his grandson. Everything about it concerned children, related to children, or circled back to them. It was like being in a strange lifestyle magazine. It was incredibly soothing in a way that Jackie would not have expected. He began to wonder if he was losing his manliness.

Emily was saying, 'I have a son as well, of course. I miss him dreadfully. I'm hoping to spend more time with him. We have a spare room in the apartment which we decorated with him in mind – it's a kind of musky blue and cream. We tried to make it 'manly'.' She laughed. 'Though he isn't really a very manly boy: playing the cello and running very fast appear to be his main attributes. He's on the gentle side.'

'Good God, child, you stink. What have you just done?'

Jackie stared down at the baby in his arms with horror. He'd forgotten that aspect.

'What the hell do they feed you?'

A few minutes later Alison came in to check on the situation. 'Would you like a drink, Jackie?'

Jackie smiled ruefully. 'I'd better not. What with the baby and – '

'We've got some brandy.'

'Okay.'

CHAPTER FIFTY-THREE

'I've got a date for the operation. Four months' time. That's bloody great isn't it? They said try to rest, keep taking the painkillers, and avoid alcohol. Stuff that,' she said, a moment before she swallowed a glass of wine. 'The alcohol makes the pills work better.'

'I've noticed that.'

'I could be dead before I get there. Bloody bastards.' Laura made to raise her hand but Mike was already approaching with fresh drinks. 'I'm a bit tense, aren't I?'

Jackie shrugged. 'A bit maybe. It's not really noticeable.'

Laura sighed and stared out of the window. She shook her head. Ordinarily that would have made her hair shake and swing; but this day it hung lankly about her face.

'It's the pain thing.' She drank more wine. 'You know what I'm like with pain. Remember what it was like when Luke came out? I nearly threw him at the wall.'

'It's different these days,' said Jackie. 'They're a lot better at things. They'll give you drugs for the pain.'

Laura was still shaking her head. 'They won't give me enough drugs. There's never enough.' She looked at Jackie as though she'd suddenly become aware of his presence. 'How did you cope when you were in hospital?'

'I cried a lot when no one was looking.'

That caused Laura to blink a few times.

She raised her arm and Mike came with bags of crisps.

'Seriously?'

'Yes. Once or twice.'

'God.' Laura leaned back in the booth and sighed deeply through her nostrils. 'Why the hell didn't you tell anyone?'

Jackie shrugged.

He studied the bags of crisps that Mike had brought over and decided he didn't like any of them. He thought Mike was definitely taking the piss now.

He shrugged again.

They both stared out of the window.

The geraniums in the concrete trough were doing better.

CHAPTER FIFTY-FOUR

Two days later Jackie walked into the bar and Dawn said, 'How's your swan?'

'What?'

'Mike said you've got a swan now. I bet that makes a mess.'

Jackie blinked at her for a few moments.

'It bloody will when I shove it up his arse,' he muttered as he stared along the bar to Mike, who was steadfastly avoiding making eye contact.

'Sorry?'

'Nothing. I'm just thinking out loud.'

He took his drinks to the booth. There were some crumbs on the cushioned seat. He didn't like that at all. He brushed them off, and thought the place was going to the dogs. He might seriously consider going to *The Grapes*. The guy in *The Grapes* would kill anyone who left a crumb.

He sipped his beer and looked out of the window.

His phone rang. It was a call from Emily's office.

Emily had been taken to hospital.

CHAPTER FIFTY-FIVE

Occasionally there are things in life that are just a blur. For Jackie, a man who drank a lot, many things in his life were a blur. But this was different. He pounded along the High Street towards the hospital, and Mike was running right at his side. The pair of them were grunting like buffalo. They ran through the side streets. Vaulted over (climbed over) chains strung between bollards. Ran down the middle of the road when they should have been on the pavement. Mike was falling behind, but he kept going. When somebody's car horn honked Mike gave the driver the finger. He hadn't sweated this much since he last had sex.

They burst through, crashed through, stumbled through and fell through the main doors of the hospital.

Then they stopped. Jackie didn't know where to go.

They went, politely, to a reception desk and waited their turn behind a woman who had a child in her arms and was protesting that somehow the hospital had managed to lose her father. And he was there yesterday.

That took a while.

Finally Jackie was able to say, 'I'm looking for my partner, Emily Marchant. She was brought in with, I'm assuming, pregnancy complications.'

The woman at the reception desk, who had her hair pinned back with kirby grips, nodded and typed onto a keypad.

'Yes. Here she is. Emily Marchant. She's in the Labour Ward. End of the corridor, turn left. Follow the green line.'

The green line took several twists and turns. It was like a maze in Alice in Wonderland. But eventually they found themselves in an open area where nobody seemed to be doing anything. There was a lot of space, and chairs, and posters on the walls, but nobody was actually about.

It was the ultimate conundrum. Which door do you crash through first?

So they stood doing nothing. There is an inherent politeness in people which can be hard to overcome.

After a time (a very short time) a man in a hospital-green outfit appeared, walking through the area with an important-looking pad in his hands. He was maybe thirty-two.

Jackie stopped him. 'Emily Marchant?'

The man blinked at him.

'Are you a relative?'

'I'm her partner. I'm the father.'

That elicited a nod and a pause.

'Okay. Someone will come and have a word with you shortly. If you'd like to take a seat - '

He gestured to the seventeen empty chairs.

'Is she all right?'

'Someone will talk to you.'

And he was gone. Just like that. As if he were a chimera.

Jackie and Mike looked at each other. Then they took a seat. More correctly, Jackie took a seat while Mike remained standing. For a centre of drama and emergency, they had never been in a place so silent. The clock on the wall was thunderous, although it didn't make a sound.

But it kept on ticking. The second hand moved remorselessly across its face.

After a time Mike, with his hands in the pockets of his trousers, wandered across to the window. After another length of time he said, 'There's a good view from here.'

Jackie nodded. 'Yeah. I've been here before; when I had follow-ups after my operation.'

'I'd forgotten about that.'

They both looked round as a door opened and a man in blue surgical scrubs and round glasses appeared. 'Mister Conor?'

'That's me.' Jackie stood up.

The man smiled. 'I'm John O'Connell, the duty Registrar.' He extended his hand. 'I'm attending to Mrs Marchant.'

'How is she?'

'She's stabilising now. But we are looking at a serious situation here, and you need to be aware of that.'

He gestured to a seat, and took one himself. Mike stayed by the window.

Registrar O'Connell pulled the surgical cap from his head, which made him look a lot older. He had less hair than Jackie was expecting.

'Emily, your partner, has experienced what is known as placental abruption. What this means is that the baby has basically shifted position, and taken the placenta with it – so much of the placenta has pulled away from the wall of the uterus.'

Jackie nodded. He was sitting with his elbows on his knees and his hands wrapped together. His gaze was fixed firmly on the floor. None of this sounded good.

'This is not a fatal situation,' said O'Connell, 'but there has been considerable blood loss. It was this blood loss, and subsequent drop in blood pressure, which caused Emily to collapse at work. The blood flow appears to have ceased through the normal clotting process. But Emily is very weak, and we are introducing blood into her system because it is essential to keep the levels up. The baby's heartbeat is weak and we need to monitor that closely. But at the moment things are settling down.'

Jackie nodded.

'Is she going to be okay? Will the baby be all right?'

'At the moment, yes. And I'm assuming that everything will continue that way. But it is, as I've said, a serious situation. We need to keep monitoring Emily. And she needs a lot of rest. And any stress or anxiety has to be minimised as much as possible.'

Jackie nodded again.

'Can I go and see her?'

Mister O'Connell took his chance to nod. 'Yes, there's no reason not to. But don't stay too long because we want her to rest. And try to be as calm and positive as possible.'

Both of them stood, and Jackie shook the man's hand again.

'Thank you, doctor.'

'This can be resolved.'

Jackie glanced across to Mike, who nodded.

Mike was going to wait.

CHAPTER FIFTY-SIX

Jackie was taken aback by the amount of equipment involved in Emily's treatment.

He had expected to walk into the room to find her propped up in bed looking a bit pale and tired. But there was all kinds of stuff. There was a blood drip going into her right arm, a clear drip going into her left arm, a blood pressure cuff was fastened around her upper left arm, hooked up to a monitor, and across and around her abdomen was a CTG strap to monitor the baby's heart rate. This, too, was connected to a unit which gave a constant readout.

It was hard to find Emily amongst it all.

She was loosely wrapped in a light hospital gown. Her face was completely devoid of colour; she was sweating quite heavily, and her damp hair was stuck to her skin.

Jackie brushed some of it away as he bent over her.

'Hello babe. How are you doing?'

Emily gave him a smile. 'We're still here,' she said. She folded her fingers around his hand and gripped it as convincingly as she could. 'We're still here.'

Jackie looked about for a chair, but there wasn't one. There was nothing that might get in the way of urgent medical attention.

'It's all a bit of a shock, hey?'

She smiled again. 'Not as much as it was for the people at work. Apparently I collapsed over my desk as if I'd been shot. A bit of a drama queen.'

Jackie brushed some more hair from her face.

'It gives them something to talk about,' he said.

'Two of the women brought me in, because they thought it would be quicker. I'm afraid I leaked all over Christine's car seat. It wasn't very dignified.'

'It's all right. We'll sort it out.'

'She needs a new car seat.'

'I'll sort it out.'

'Then they wheeled me in in a wheelchair.'

'They sound like good women.'

'They are. I thought I didn't like them, but – they were very good to me.'

Emily started to cry.

'They were very good to me,' she said.

CHAPTER FIFTY-SEVEN

Mike was still staring out of the window when Jackie returned from the ward. He looked grave but managed to raise his eyebrows in a query.

'They've basically sent me away,' said Jackie, 'because they want her to rest. I think I was getting in the way. They're going to keep her in overnight to monitor things – and they said come back again about seven. If anything happens in the meantime they'll let me know.'

Mike glanced at his watch as he moved away from the window. It was two o'clock.

'How was she looking? Does she seem okay?'

'Very tired. She's lost a lot of blood and they've put a tube in her arm to replace it; and there's some other stuff going on. It seems that two of her colleagues drove her in, and she bled all over the front seat. That was very noble of them. I'm going to have to thank them.'

'And buy them a new car.'

'Yeah, something like that.' Jackie raised his gaze from the invisible point in space that he was looking at. 'It's the blood, Mike, isn't it? Losing that much blood. Nobody wants to hear about blood.'

'They know what they're doing though, don't they?' said Mike. He ran his hands through his hair as he tried to produce some positives from the situation. 'If they're letting her out tomorrow – it doesn't seem too bad.'

'I guess.'

Jackie blinked a few times, then looked away.

'What do you want to do now? Do you want to wait here?'

'No. I'm a bit superfluous at the moment. I think, in all honesty, they don't want me here. The best I can be is a distraction.'

So they followed the green line back through the hospital, and stepped out into a day which was blissfully oblivious to the traumas within and was amusing itself with scudding clouds and circling birds, and a breeze that was, strangely, a little on the cool side.

They walked back through the streets they had run along earlier. Climbed over the chains. Kept to the pavements. Showed no one the finger. Didn't grunt like buffalo.

But it was a sombre walk.

'This is bloody hell,' said Jackie after a while.

'I know, mate. If you come back to the bar I'll get the new chef to cook you a decent meal. You need to – I don't know – start looking after yourself. You basically live off crap.'

'Is this the German guy?' said Jackie.

'I don't know what nationality he is to be honest. He could be Peruvian. He keeps shouting at me. He's a right angry bastard.'

In the event they didn't return to the bar, they stopped at a cafeteria instead. *The Steaming Kettle*. Wedgewood blue and plastic tablecloths. They ate scrambled egg baps and drank mugs of tea. Jackie liked mashed-up food where it seemed as though half the chewing had already been done for you.

As he started eating raspberry jam-topped sponge and custard, Jackie said, 'My leg's hurting again. I think it's psychological. I think I feel guilty for not going through the same thing as Emily. I'm getting it too easy.'

'You're going through it, mate. Just in a different way.'

Jackie ate solidly; and was so tempted he almost had another portion. He wished he had his hip flasks with him.

'We have it easy, don't we?' he said. 'Women have it rough all their lives.'

'And then they get us.' They both snorted.

'I'd better phone Robert, let him know what's going on. He ought to know, he's still her husband.'

CHAPTER FIFTY-EIGHT

He went back in the evening.

Emily was still attached to all her devices; but she was looking brighter. Some colour had returned to her cheeks; there was less nursing activity going on around her.

'You're looking better,' he said.

'You look terrible,' she said.

'I know. Mike forced me to eat a scrambled egg bap.'

He looked around. This time there was a chair. He hooked it over with his foot.

She held one of his hands in both of hers and looked straight into his eyes.

'They want to take the baby out. They think it will fare better in an incubator.'

'Right.'

Jackie had responded fairly quickly; but there was a long, interminable silence going on inside him. Words that he hadn't even thought of yet were still failing to appear in his mind.

'Er – '

They clutched their hands so tightly together that a lever couldn't have separated them.

'It's er – '

'I told them no.'

'Okay,' he said, after a moment.

'I'm the baby's mother. I don't think there is any better place for the baby to be than with me. I give it the strength and the love; I protect it, I will look after it.'

Jackie nodded.

'But they said I have to discuss it with you. Actually it's not even a 'they' it's just a 'he' – Mister O'Connell. He said we need to talk about it. We have to make a decision.'

Jackie again peered into the void that had suddenly started appearing in his life. Nothing was straightforward any more. Nothing was easy. Everything seemed to demand a consideration and a wisdom that he wasn't sure he possessed.

'Did he say anything else?' he said.

'He said if I continue with the pregnancy it may have an adverse effect on me and maybe even impact on the baby.'

Jackie continued staring. The void was vast, and did not give up its answers readily. It was a place of darkness and confusion.

'He said they've detected a heart murmur in me.'

'Right.'

CHAPTER FIFTY-NINE

The following morning Mister O'Connell showed up with reinforcements in the form of his immediate superior the Senior Obstetrician, who gloried in the name Christopher Lee.

Christopher Lee was a pleasant man in his late fifties who would have looked equally at home managing a white grape vineyard in France.

After the introductions he said, 'I believe my colleague has already explained to you what we would like to do, and the reasons for doing so. I would highly recommend this course of action. At this stage in your pregnancy – almost twenty-two weeks – the baby will be perfectly safe in an incubator, and will go on to prosper and thrive. There is nothing – I repeat, nothing – of any danger in this procedure. And it will be better for both of you.'

Emily, who had Jackie standing at her side holding her hand said, 'I want to keep the child as long as possible. Until the last possible moment.'

'We are trying to look at the bigger picture, Mrs Marchant. This is a very emotional time. You and Mister Conor need to think seriously about it.'

'We have.'

Jackie and Emily had never wanted to know the sex of the baby, but now Emily said, 'It's a boy, isn't it?'

Christopher Lee nodded.

'Yes it is.'

'I have a son already,' said Emily. 'He can appear quite fragile and delicate at times, but he's here. He's strong, he's a fighter. This child will fight too.'

'This situation may not have the same outcome, Mrs Marchant. I wish I could tell you otherwise, but this is my best and sincerest recommendation.'

'The answer is still no,' she said.

CHAPTER SIXTY

Then there was a quiet time.

The situation subsided. After several days at home resting and recovering Emily returned to work. Her hours were shortened and, though they never told her directly, her colleagues discretely reduced her workload.

Jackie did what he did best; which was to murmur words of encouragement and tidy up as much as he could. He took to making her lunches. He threw in every healthy ingredient he could think of. Colleagues in Emily's office began gathering around her desk, wishing they could have a lunch like that. Some of them secretly began to despise their partners.

Life slipped back to a slightly tense normality, where every day breathed a silent prayer that nothing more would go wrong.

'How's your duck?'

'It's a swan.'

'Oh yeah.' Dawn wiped Jackie's table with a damp cloth. 'Is it still making a mess?'

Jackie had given up even trying to explain things now, so simply said, 'It's not too bad.'

'Can you house-train them?'

'I got a dvd for it to watch but it won't look at it.'

'They're stubborn things, birds.' Dawn sat down for a minute on the seat opposite. 'We had a budgie when I was young and I spent ages trying to teach it to say my name. But the only thing it ever came out with was a noise like a fart, 'cause my dad used to fart a lot. God he was awful. He said it was because he had a hernia but I think he just liked farting.' She continued absently wiping the table with the cloth, then took a few peanuts from the packet in Jackie's hand. 'He was a swine. Anyway. What I wanted to say is – this baby of yours, he will be all right you know. I trust in God. I don't believe in Him, but I trust in Him.' She turned her head so she could look from the window to where somebody in the street was selling balloons, and making a reasonably good job of it. 'That sounds odd doesn't it?'

Jackie shook his head. 'Not really. I think a lot of people feel like that.'

'Do you think?'

'Yeah. He stands for hope, and that's what we hope for. That everything will turn out well in the end. Otherwise – '

'We wouldn't get through the day,' she said.

'Exactly. We wouldn't get through the day.'

Jackie sipped at his final glass of whisky, then changed the subject.

'How's your Jersey boy thing going?'

'Okay,' she said cheerfully. 'He wants to get engaged. I said we hardly know each other, we've only met about four times.'

'It's not much. So what are you going to do – are you getting engaged?'

'Obvs.' She gave a shrug. 'You've got to do something, haven't you?'

'Any man who gets you, Dawn, will be the luckiest man in the world.'

'That's what I told him.'

CHAPTER SIXTY-ONE

'She's not moving to Jersey is she?'

'Oh Christ, I hope not.' It was Mike's turn to have a damp cloth in his hand, and he was wiping the top of the bar with it. He plonked a whisky in front of Jackie without seemingly even pouring it. 'It's giving me sleepless nights.'

They both looked at her, poring over her crossword.

'They grow up,' said Jackie. 'They leave the nest.'

'I know,' said Mike, still wiping the bar with his cloth. 'It just happens faster than you hope. Somehow you hope it will always be longer. That they'll let us be selfish a little while longer. Let us – I don't know – '

'Bask in their radiance.'

'I can tell you're a fucking writer.'

Jackie took his drinks to his table.

Everything changes, he thought as he sat down. You think you live a quiet life, but everything changes, all the time. Even the simple things. The thing that worked yesterday can't be guaranteed to work today. It's all a consistent, low-level, under the radar, everyday adjustment to – whatever you thought yesterday. Life was never the same. It always altered. Even if you didn't want it to. Even if you did want it to.

The phone in his pocket buzzed.

He pulled it out. It was Robert, Emily's husband. He wanted to meet. But not in the *Lion*. He was in *The Grapes*. Jackie said he would be there in ten minutes. And he was.

The fearsome barowner wasn't there. The buxom cheerful red-haired goddess was – standing behind the bar in all her glory. Still with a cleavage that a man could drop a laptop down. She looked like the kind of woman who, no matter what you told her, would already have heard it.

'What can I get you, sweetheart?'

'Er – '

Jackie looked across the bar to where Robert was sitting at a table on his own, staring rather vacantly into space.

'What's he drinking?'

'Mineral water. He's driving.'

'Okay. I'll have a pint of Dragonpiss and two whiskies. Small bottle of ginger ale. No ice.'

The barmaid nodded.

'Do you want doubles?'

'Not yet.'

Jackie took the drinks to Robert's table, sat down, looked him in the eye, shrugged in a non-committal way, and said – 'Hi.'

Robert nodded. He had probably looked happier in his life, but he didn't look entirely worse.

'At least you can have a drink,' he said. 'I shouldn't have moved bloody towns.'

'How is the town?'

Robert shrugged. 'It's a town, you know. You think it will make a difference, but it's just a town at the end of the day. People you don't like. People you do like. It's – I don't know.'

'Yeah.' Jackie understood that. He understood all of it. He'd been there for most of his life. 'Nothing's ever easy.'

'No.'

Robert looked down at the table, frowned, shook his head. He pushed some crumbs around between the glasses. Jackie was shocked to notice them: the landlord's standards were slipping.

'I don't hate Emily. I still love her. I don't even hate you. I'll never view you as a lifelong friend, but – it is what it is.' Robert sipped at his mineral water and looked like he desperately wanted a proper drink. 'I don't want anything to happen to her.' He looked up; looked Jackie straight in the eyes. 'And she is Jason's mother. He needs his mother in his life. You know?'

Jackie nodded. 'I know.'

Robert looked down again. Looked down at the table.

'What you've said. What you told me.' He shook his head again. God, he wanted a drink. 'She had problems with the first pregnancy, you know?'

Jackie shook his head. He had a feeling inside that he couldn't identify; he couldn't put his finger on.

'She's never said anything.'

'It was okay in the end, but – ' Robert sighed deeply.

At that moment the most fascinating things in the universe were his own hands. He was fixated on their fiddling and twiddling and grasping each other under the table.

'What I'm trying to say is – you don't stop loving someone because you're not together. I have some money put aside. If you need it. Specialist treatment – private treatment. I don't know. Anything that might help.'

Jackie nodded. 'That's very generous, Robert.'

'She's always thinking that Jason is the fragile one, that he's the one who's delicate. But it's always been Emily. It's always been her. She's the one you need to protect.'

'I will protect her. She'll be safe.'

'Jason needs his mother.'

Robert sighed again.

Then he said, 'Oh fuck it,' and went to the bar for a beer. He also brought a whisky for Jackie.

'How is Jason?' said Jackie.

'Good; he's good. Turns out he's quite good at cricket now. He's signed up for a local club. It's this ability he has to run like a guided missile. He runs so fast you can't always see his legs; he's like a cartoon.'

Robert clinked his glass against Jackie's.

'He still calls you Mister Conor.'

CHAPTER SIXTY-TWO

Mike arrived at the table with the dwindling bottle of thirty year-old malt and the two clean glasses.

'How's it going?' he said.

Jackie pushed his notebook aside 'Good,' he said. 'Not too bad. No problems on the baby front and I'm making headway on my book. There have been worse times in my life. How's it going with you? How are things with Catherine?'

'Good. The pub hours are a problem, but in a way that's a good thing; it makes us like each other more when we're together. You appreciate your time more.'

Mike poured the drinks and they eased a couple down.

'I don't like her kids, though. Arrogant little twats. They obviously think a pub landlord is beneath them. But they don't mind coming in with their mates last thing at night expecting to get free drinks.' Mike threw his whisky back and poured another. 'Little tossers.'

'The thing about life though,' said Jackie, 'is – ' Then he paused.

'What?' said Mike, after a minute.

'I can't remember now. I'm a bit pissed.'

CHAPTER SIXTY-THREE

Jackie sat in his study pondering on life, the universe, the existence of existence, the nature of reality, the possibility of time travel, temporal lobe equations, and his novel.

Of all of them, his novel was proving the most difficult. Not for the first time he considered it to be the mental equivalent of thrashing his brain with a handful of nettles.

Then he started thinking about nettles.

He pushed his chair back; then walked across to the window with his hands in his pockets and an almost agonised look on his face. Looking out at the river was always calming, always soothing; and there was always something to watch.

Today it was simply sunlight reflecting off the small craft, reflecting off the water; and every drop of water had a tale to tell. It was easy to become absorbed by it. He had become lost more times than he cared to remember. There was a hypnotic quality to the river; its ripples and wavelets were mesmerising.

Books were so long; that was the problem. They demanded so many words. He was never sure that he had that many words in him.

The place he was in now – still in the 'notes' stage – had produced hardly any words on the page. There were many in his head – they were swirling all over the place. But they didn't want to bring themselves out into daylight.

He thought he might put some music on.

Even that was a challenge; background music is a difficulty in itself. It had to be something innocuous enough that he didn't have to pay close attention; but of sufficient quality that it could fill in the silence.

He had been known to spend two days sorting out the music. And even then he'd wind up changing his mind.

Plus, to get to the cds he would have to bend down, and he didn't really think he was possessed of the energy.

He wondered about vaping as a valid form of exercise, but couldn't see the point in aimlessly inhaling steam. If he was to try vaping he would want tobacco flavoured 'vape stuff'. It made sense simply to have the cigarettes. Even to look at one would be a relief.

No, that would be too tempting.

He wandered back to his desk.

Kill the swan, kill the swan. What fucking swan? People were starting to infect him with their own ideas.

Maybe he should put a swan in it.

What would you call a swan, if you had one?

Josephine. Josephine or – Jocasta.

His phone rang. The landline phone. Perhaps this was his agent: maybe she'd had second thoughts about his book. Maybe she thought there was some mileage and she would start spreading the word.

He picked it up.

Somebody wanted to sell him a boiler.

He put the phone down and went to the pub.

CHAPTER SIXTY-FOUR

In his booth Jackie spent some time inscribing the words Death of a Swan on the front of his notebook.

It was a good notebook. He'd paid good money for it. Sometimes he liked to sit just stroking the cover of it.

He realised that wasn't a very productive exercise.

He wondered if he was starting to drink too much.

He sipped a whisky while he pondered that.

It was a fickle friend, he knew that. It's a friend which can't be trusted. It smiles at you and beckons you and wraps its arms around you and gives you a lovely hug. But all the time it's reaching into your wallet and reaching down into your liver. It's murmuring things in your head that you really shouldn't hear.

'Have you got a picture of it?' said Dawn, nodding at the book.

'No, I might just sketch it. I thought you were in college today?'

'No, I couldn't be bothered. I don't really think I'm going to do well at business studies. I think I might do hairdressing.'

'My hair could do with a cut.'

'Your hair could do with a lot of things.'

Dawn removed the empty glasses and replaced them with fresh ones.

'Don't drink too much, Jack,' she said.

He turned back to the window. The balloon-seller had gone; there was nobody of any great interest out there. Sometimes a young woman with turquoise hair came selling toffee apples from a small wooden handcart.

She wasn't there today. He was surprised that toffee apples hadn't been banned. They seemed to cling to your teeth and try to rip them from your gums.

He didn't mind candy floss.

Maybe he was drinking too much. When he gave up smoking he used patches. They were really good. His doctor prescribed him three months' worth: a month on the strong, a month on the medium: by the middle of the third month he stopped using them altogether.

It had been Laura's suggestion to give up smoking. 'It will help us live longer,' she said. Jackie agreed. So he slapped the patches on. Laura gave up for about twenty minutes, then kept on smoking for another four years.

It was a pity they couldn't make alcohol patches. If there was a charity researching that he'd give it some money. Or at least take the staff for a drink.

Yeah: alcohol patches.

He'd put on about fifteen at a time. He'd probably end up sucking them.

He swallowed a whisky. Wondered how difficult it was to make toffee apples. Then he opened his notebook.

He felt, if he was being honest, a bit of a prat. Sitting there in a bar, a public place, trying to write a book, like a proper bloody author.

Jackie wasn't comfortable with some things. Some things he was. He didn't mind falling over a hedge and waking up with bruised knees. But writing in public: that didn't really work, did it?

He closed the notebook and slid his pen into the handy little loop: which was anything other than handy: it was a bugger to get the pen in. He'd have to do the writing in his head.

Maybe he could plunge straight in, with the bloke losing the body. Or starting with a phone call where the bloke says, 'I've lost the body'. Or – '

Some kind of prologue. Or a foreword. Or even a quote. If he could find a good quote about losing a body. Or losing anything. Losing his mind, losing his marbles. Losing the love of his life. Losing something. Just something to kick-start it. Something that didn't sound rubbish.

He'd already torn four pages out of the notebook. That, unfortunately, had the knock-on effect of making four other pages a bit loose; and that troubled him. He didn't want to have to buy another book.

He wished he'd been a filing clerk. It must be nice to do a simple job that you could do without demand and get paid for and go home at the end of the day – but enjoy it.

God, that would be good. A simple filing clerk. Why write books?

Why write books? That was a good question. It was kind of arrogant to think you could just put down words – write down your thoughts – and expect other people to pay money to look at them

Here's something I thought of. If you give me some money I'll show it to you.

He should write a book about writing a book.

'All right, Jack?'

'Yeah, fine.'

He looked round. Who the hell was that?

Emily came in, sat down next to him, put down her bag and said, 'Foof! That was a busy day.'

CHAPTER SIXTY-FIVE

They went to a restaurant at the top end of the town, far away from their usual haunts on the quay. It was one of those places that Jackie wasn't sure that he liked, but wasn't convinced that he actively disliked. It had music playing that he definitely disliked, but the place itself looked 'reasonable'. It was called *La Rumba*.

Emily looked lovely. She had on a yellow outfit. For some reason she always suited yellow. Jackie wasn't sure why; yellow was a colour he'd never truly noticed before.

She was looking better all the time. Colour had returned to her face and she was eating better.

Jackie had discovered some new 'pregnancy meals' which he assiduously prepared before she got home from work. He threw in the weekly restaurant visit as a bonus. She always ate fish; which he thought was good. You couldn't go wrong with oily fish. He still regretted not eating the carp he caught with Jason.

It dawned on him at some point in the evening that he was actually becoming domesticated.

Realities, too, were kicking in. Finance was high amongst them: how their finances would be when their son arrived.

This was the kind of grown-up talk that Jackie usually shied away from.

'I could get a job,' he said. 'If I haven't sold the book by then.'

'The kind of job that lets you drink at work?' Emily speared a piece of swordfish with a delicacy that Jackie could only marvel at.

'Obviously it will need a little thought. A gardener maybe. I could work as a gardener. They wouldn't know I was drunk.'

'You keep falling over bushes.'

'Apart from that.'

He tucked into his steak. It was all right. He'd had better, but he'd had worse.

'I could work from home. A job I could do at home. Perhaps I could be a writing advisor. A freelance editor. A writing consultant for wannabees – I've still got 'Avilon' on my cv. That still carries some weight. If you want to write about ducks I'm the man to talk to. I'm going to cut down on the drinking anyway; once I finish the book. I won't give it up entirely, because that would be silly. But I'd like to cut back. I shall cut back.' He cut off another chunk of steak and chewed it heartily. He looked round. 'Where's that bloody waiter with my flaming drink?'

Emily said, 'You realise the first word to come out of our child's mouth will be a swear word.'

'I hadn't thought about that. God, there's going to be so many challenges, so many responsibilities. Perhaps we should get a nanny in and I should stay in the study, swearing.'

'He'll hear you through the door.'

'I'll get a thicker door. You're looking well, though,' he said. 'The best you've looked since the hospital.'

'I feel well,' she said. 'I feel that everything is – 'going good' – as you fancy writers say.'

'It's the way what we write it. It's a gift that few people possess. I'm actually thinking of putting a swan in the book now, just to keep people happy. But I'll make it an ironic swan. It will have a knowing look in its eye.'

Pudding was always the deciding factor; that was the crucial element. Jackie did like pavlova. But he also liked crème brulee. This place had neither.

Jesus.

'They haven't even got rice pudding. You know – if you weren't so pregnant we could go home and have sex.'

'We could have sex anyway,' she said.

So they skipped dessert.

CHAPTER SIXTY-SIX

There were regular visits to the hospital now for check-ups and monitoring.

Everything was going well, although Jackie still detected an undercurrent which thought Emily should have listened to the advice that was offered, and had the baby removed.

Fuck them, he thought. Emily was the mother; she knew what was best. She could feel him inside her. She knew her own son.

'How did it go?' he said.

'Good. Usual. I wish they'd warm that gel up a bit though.'

'I don't suppose men ever have ultrasounds.'

'They're all right. They're not painful. They're just cold and sticky.'

'I had a thing years ago. I was very anaemic and they thought I was maybe losing blood. So they put a camera up my – 'thingy'.'

'Your backside.'

'Yes. They put a camera up. I'm not sure what they did first. Whether I had to swallow something. Barium maybe. But I ended up being strapped to a table, like I was being crucified. And they roll it around – rotate it, you know? The table. And you can see it on a screen. It wasn't painful or anything. But it certainly wasn't dignified. And afterwards I had to go to the bathroom. I was still wearing this hospital gown. Jesus Christ, you wouldn't want to be around that. It took me longer to clean up the bathroom than it did to have the procedure.'

Afterwards he walked Emily back to her office.

'What are you going to do now?' she said.

'I don't know. What's the time?' He looked at his watch. 'Half past eleven. I don't know whether to go to the pub or go home and do some work.'

'Why don't you go to that place on the quay?'

'The garden restaurant?'

'Yes, you like it there.'

'I could do that. Get something to eat.'

They kissed on the steps of the Social Services building and she walked inside.

Then he went to the pub.

CHAPTER SIXTY-SEVEN

But it wasn't the *Lion* he went to. It was *The Grapes*.

He leaned on the bar, chewing on whisky, talking to the buxom barmaid.

'Are you all right, lover? You look a bit morose.'

'Yeah. My partner's pregnant. It's – I don't know. A worrying thing when you get to my age.'

'You're not that old.'

'Feels it some days.' He swallowed his whisky, and she gave him another. 'Have you got kids?'

'Two. A boy and a girl. He's at college and she's at uni up in Newcastle. I don't know why she wanted to go up there.'

'Do you want a drink?'

'Yeah, I'll have a gin.'

She poured what looked like a healthy treble.

'Don't worry,' she said. 'I won't mark it up.'

'Are you married?' he said. 'Partner or anything?'

'I've been married twice,' she said. 'Both times to feckless bastards. Yes love – ' She moved away to serve another customer. Jackie stared into his whisky.

When she came back she gave him another one.

'You can have that,' she said.

'It's not easy, is it? The whole growing up, getting older – trying to pretend that you know what's going on kind of thing. It doesn't get any easier. You don't get any training.'

'If we got the training maybe we wouldn't do it.'

'Yep. Maybe.'

They drank their drinks in silence for a time.

'I'm Jackie,' he said.

'I'm Suzanne.'

CHAPTER SIXTY-EIGHT

Amazingly his agent did come back to him.

She said, 'That story you were talking about was rubbish. But I've been talking to one of the editors and they're thinking about doing a series of interlinked novels about a one-eyed detective who has a spaniel. He takes the dog along with him and it sniffs out clues. They're looking at a team of writers. What do you think?'

'Er – '

Jackie stared into space for a while. A one-eyed detective.

'What's the spaniel called?'

'I don't fucking know. Do you want to do it or not?'

'Yeah, put me down.'

'I'll email you the brief. They're going to need a synopsis and the first three chapters by the beginning of next month.'

'I can do that.'

'Get started then.' She put the phone down.

God, she was a brutal woman.

Jackie wandered into the kitchen with a glass of whisky in his hand, and looked in the fridge.

Jesus, everything looked so healthy. Why didn't they eat shit food any more? He'd murder some pizza.

He closed the fridge door and went back to his computer. The email had already come through. They were offering a four-and-a-half grand advance and six percent royalties.

That didn't seem a lot. What happened to the good old days?

He went to the window. It was money, though. He needed to earn some money. He had such responsibilities on the horizon. Even well short of the horizon; they'd already passed that point. They were rolling across the sea towards him, and it didn't look like they were planning on stopping.

He could do this, he knew he had it inside him.

A one-eyed spaniel, looking for clues.

CHAPTER SIXTY-NINE

Everything became rather frenetic in Jackie's head as he did, finally, try to make some effort. The offer of money was a strong incentive. He would pay good money to be offered some money.

He found himself pacing round the study in the night, when he should have been sleeping.

Then he had a brainwave. He could combine the two ideas that he currently had. The missing body, and the one-eyed detective with his trusty spaniel.

That would be good. If Jackie couldn't find it; maybe the spaniel would.

Yeah, he could go with that.

His mobile phone beeped.

'They've brought my operation forward. Apparently somebody cancelled.'

CHAPTER SEVENTY

'That's a good thing, right? You'll get it over sooner.'

Laura shrugged; twiddled with her glass.

'I suppose.'

She raised her hand and Mike came with another.

'I really don't want to do this, Jackie. I'm really scared of it.'

'Well you don't have to do it. The decision's up to you.'

'I wish we'd never split up,' she said. 'You are a prat, but at least you were my prat.'

The balloon guy was there again. Jackie looked at him for a while. Was that his proper job – was that what he did for a living? Maybe he was a student and he did it to supplement his student loan.

He looked a bit old to be a student.

He was dressed like a clown.

Jackie supposed you could rent that. Or maybe make it. Or have a boyfriend/girlfriend who would make it for you.

'Are you listening to me?'

'Yes. Every word. You wish you'd never left me because I'm so wonderful. That's just the fear of this operation talking.'

'You won't let me down, will you?' she said; and she looked him straight in the eye.

'What do you mean?'

'With what's going on. In the future. You won't forget me will you?'

'Of course not. Jesus, you're in a morbid mood today. Why don't we have a salad or something? Apparently his Peruvian chef's very good, but angry. We could have a nasty salad.'

'I'd rather have chips.'

'So would I.'

Jackie went to the bar to order the chips.

God. His leg was hurting, his head was hurting. He wished he'd never got up today.

He had to wait while other people were being served. God his life was difficult. People had no idea.

'Is Laura all right, Jack?'

'Yeah, she's good. Is your boyfriend coming over this weekend?'

'Yeah.' Dawn pulled Jackie a pint before she ordered his chips. 'We're going to the theatre.'

'What you going to see?'

'Lion King 2 or 3. I'm not sure which. It's got people in costumes.'

'Proper theatre then.'

'Yeah. Not that boring rubbish. I went to that once. I don't know who took me – it was when I was at school. Don't they go on?'

'Yeah. Fucking Shakespeare.'

'Fucking torture.'

It was the first time Dawn had actually come out with the F word. Jackie thought she should stop hanging around him so much.

He went back to the table. Laura was half way through her glass of wine.

'When we first got married we thought everything would go on for ever, just as it was then.'

'Like television.'

'Yeah,' she said. 'Then they invent new programmes. Dukes of Hazzard becomes Death Race Massacre on the M1.'

'And politics. Politics comes into it.'

'I never knew what politics was until I stopped going into dance clubs. Northern Soul – do you remember that?'

'I was more sort of head-banging, jumping about. Actually, sitting still, nodding my head.'

'And then we grow up.'

'And then we grow up.'

'And nothing ever seems quite the same.'

They sat in silence until Dawn appeared with buckets of chips on a tray, and a large bowl of mayonnaise to dip in then.

'All right, Laura?'

'Yeah, I'm good babe. You?'

'I'm good too. I'm going to train to be a hairdresser. I want to specialise in bleaching: I saw a programme about it. And merkins – do you know what they are? For people who've been in accidents, or had a bad burn. Or just want to fool about.'

'That's a – fine line of work,' said Laura.

'I think so. Do you want anything else?'

'No, we're good. Except fathead here probably wants another drink.'

'I'll get them.'

Laura started on the chips. She shoved the mayonnaise aside and opened a sachet of ketchup.

'How's it going?' she said. 'Is she okay now – stable?'

'Yeah. Everything's settled down. It's – working as it should.'

Jackie picked up a chip and dunked it in the mayonnaise. Oh salt – he'd forgotten the salt. He liked a lot of salt.

'Have you thought about names yet?'

'Not too much. We only found out recently that it's a boy. If it was up to me I'd probably call him Emmanuel Glycerine Napoleon the Third, or something like that. Fortunately Emily's there to keep me in check and make me relatively sane.'

'I've always liked the name Oliver.'

'So have I. I don't know why we called Luke Luke.'

That kept them going in thought for a while. You don't always have to say things out loud.

'It's funny,' Laura said. 'All this time, then suddenly you've got a grandson and you're going to have another son of your own. It's like a – I don't know: a second chance or something: a new start.'

'I hadn't really thought about it that way,' he said.

'You've got to be good, Jackie. You can't cock this up; you have a lot of people depending on you.'

He nodded, and ate another chip. Washed it down with whisky.

'It's a – '

He drank more whisky.

'Do you think I'm up to it?'

Laura shrugged, then ate more chips of her own. 'Probably.'

CHAPTER SEVENTY-ONE

Davenport. What the hell was that? Emily said she would like to get a davenport for the lounge. In orange.

Jackie had to get his phone out and google it. He wasn't even sure what it was then: it just looked like a sofa. Maybe it was a pregnancy thing; like wanting to eat coal.

He was in the garden cafeteria down by the quay, because it was a good day and he wasn't sure how many more good days there would be left this summer.

But this davenport thing was puzzling.

'Watchus up to?'

He looked up. It was Suzanne, the barmaid from *The Grapes*. She was wearing a peach-coloured trouser suit with a pastel tee-shirt beneath. Her brown leather handbag was on a long strap which angled across her chest.

'World of your own?'

'Pretty much,' he said, as he half stood up. 'I'm just pissing about really. Are you passing through, or have you got time for a coffee?'

'Yeah, I've got time.' She pulled out a chair, shrugged off her bag off and rested it on the ground.

'What's in your book?' she said, nodding at the notebook.

'Oh, it's just a notebook. I'm supposed to be working on something.'

'Like important government secrets.'

'Yeah. Something like that.'

He managed to catch the eye of a waitress and ordered a coffee for each of them. She didn't want cake or biscuits.

'What are you up to?' he said, while they waited for the waitress to return.

'I'm meeting a girlfriend in town later. I was just going to look through the shops.'

'Queensbridge's fine array of shops.'

'Yes; both of them.' She took a pack of cigarettes from her bag and lit one. Jesus, Jackie wanted one of them. A bloody Marlboro as well. 'Seriously though. What's in your notebook?'

Jackie looked diffident and vague and stumbling and clumsy and eventually managed to extricate one of his hip flasks from his jacket and pour some into an empty cup.

'I'm supposed to be an author,' he said. 'Well I used to be an author; and then I stopped writing books. So I suppose at that point I stopped being an author and became an ex-author. Or a defunct author. Or an author in abeyance. Basically – an author not in existence.'

'It must be hard not writing books,' she said. 'I didn't realise it was so difficult.'

'It's harder than you think.'

She drew on her cigarette and blew the smoke casually over her shoulder. 'So are you writing anything now?'

'Sort of,' he said. 'Yes and no. I'm supposed to be writing a book about a one-eyed detective with a spaniel.'

'What's the spaniel called?'

'I don't know. The detective's called Jack Rinkerman, or something like that. Some corporate name that a panel came up with.'

'Your name's Jack.'

'I suppose it is. I hadn't realised that.'

A young waitress came to the table and said, 'I'm sorry, there's no smoking in here. On the premises.'

'So I've heard,' said Suzanne. 'I'll give up after this one.'

The waitress smiled, blushed, almost curtsied, then went away.

'You've just got to stare them out, haven't you?' Suzanne crushed her cigarette out on a saucer.

Jackie wished Suzanne could be his agent.

CHAPTER SEVENTY-TWO

Laura's operation. By golly, they brought it forward a lot: she was in the hospital the following week. She was in for three days.

They didn't go to visit her there, but after she'd been at home for two days Jackie said, 'I think we ought to go to see her.'

Emily adopted the reluctant squint of someone who was not wholly certain that this was a good idea. 'I don't think she'll want to see me,' she said. 'I'm not sure I'm entirely appropriate.'

'Of course you are. You're my girl. My best babe. If I go anywhere, you should be there.'

So they went, on a Thursday, a little before 6.00 pm. The weather was starting to drizzle and there was humidity in the air. They took the predictable flowers and a basket of fruit. Jackie said they should have taken her a hamster.

'What on earth for?'

'I don't know. Just for the fun of it.'

Laura was in bed. Her sister had been going in at regular intervals to check on her. Jackie didn't mind her sister; but he didn't particularly like her. He was glad she wasn't in the room when they arrived.

Laura was not at the most radiant he had ever seen. It looked as though someone had thrown a bucket of weak tar over her hair.

Strangely, at least to Jackie, Laura seemed more pleased to see Emily than she was to see him. She almost immediately reached out a hand to grab hold of one of Emily's.

'Oh God, babe,' she said, 'don't ever have this done. If I'd had my legs cut off it couldn't be any worse.'

That was a conversation stopper as far as Jackie was concerned: so he tried to restart the discourse.

'I knew a bloke who had his leg cut off,' he said. 'I can't remember why now, but because he had a heart problem they couldn't give him a general anaesthetic, so he was awake while they were doing it. You wouldn't fucking like that, would you?'

'I don't fucking like you at the moment. Why don't you piss off and let me talk to Emily?'

'Er – okay.' It wasn't quite the reception that Jackie had been expecting, but –

He wished he hadn't brought the bloody fruit now.

The last thing he heard as he walked from the room was Laura saying, 'He's such a prat sometimes.'

Jackie continued to walk, along the hallway and into the lounge.

This was his old house: the house he and Laura had shared for many years.

It was a little different now; she'd changed a few things. But pretty much it was still the same. It didn't have a bad view from the position it was in, although the view was getting a bit obscured by encroaching trees. That was one of the problems with nature; it didn't know when to stop. *I should have a word with it* he thought.

Laura's sister came into the room. Maria. Who buzzed like a bee and seemed to be constantly irritating.

'Hello Maria.'

'Jackie.' She walked across the room to give him a hug. 'How are you doing?'

'Good, I'm good. How are you doing?'

'Well apart from Lester and his problems – you know.' She shrugged expansively. 'What can you do?'

Jackie nodded. Lester was Maria's husband. As far as Jackie was concerned Lester's main problem was that he was called Lester.

'We've been in Portugal, you know; we always go there. We've been thinking of buying a place over there. It's just Lester's knees.'

'Still playing up are they?'

'Oh, they're worse than ever.' Maria shook her head like a kingfisher killing a fish. 'They don't get any better. And he's not that old.'

'Yes, I know,' said Jackie.

'He's only 48. He looks older, but he always has. When you look at pictures of him as a child he looks like a little old man. A man's head stuck on a little boy's body. Anyway – ' she clapped her hands together. 'Can I get you something? Tea – coffee?'

'Brandy?'

'Okay. Do you know where it is?'

'Cupboard to the left, under the sink.'

'Okay.'

Jackie continued to stare from the window for a time at the slowly disappearing view; then he sat on the sofa.

Maria came back with a brandy and, strangely, had one herself. He thought she only drank alcohol every third year of the calendar.

She sat down opposite him, on an armchair that was beginning to fray at the edges but which was being cunningly disguised through the use of a fringed oriental throw which probably cost less than it looked. Laura got the house; but she also got the mortgage.

'Are you all right, Maria? You look a bit tired.'

'Well it's just – ' She gave another shrug. 'It's everything, isn't it? It gets a bit much sometimes. Coming here, going there. You wonder when it's going to ease off. Do you know what I mean?'

Jackie nodded. 'All the time, every day.'

Maria looked down, at the glass in her hand. There seemed to be a lot of wrinkles on her hands. She hadn't really noticed them before.

'I don't know that people were built to cope with this stuff.'

A silence descended. It wasn't uncomfortable, but it wasn't brilliant.

'I should be doing something,' said Maria. 'Get on, do some tidying up. She's been letting it slip lately.'

But she continued to sit on the armchair a while longer. Then she visibly gave herself a shake, drank the last of her brandy, then stood up.

'You take care, Maria.'

'You too, Jackie.'

As Jackie and Emily were heading home he said, 'Laura's language is quite foul really isn't it? I hope she doesn't talk like that around Dominic.'

CHAPTER SEVENTY-THREE

He went to *The Grapes* again, hoping the ferocious landlord wasn't there. Fortunately he wasn't. But, sadly, neither was Suzanne. There was a bloke he didn't like the look of at all behind the bar. Even his nose was tattooed. 'Suzanne not in?'

'She'll be in shortly. One of her friends has had a breakdown.' *Lucky bitch*, thought Jackie. *I'd like some drama like that in my life.* 'What can I get you, mate?'

'Pint of Dragonpiss – three whiskies.'

'Separate glasses?'

'Yeah.' Jackie looked round. He'd have to sit at a table in a corner, out of the way. He was in an out of the way mood. He carried his drinks across. His limp was getting better. He'd come to think that the state of his limp was directly related to the state of his mind. He wasn't sure what his mind was doing today.

In the absence of a window to look out of, Jackie stared at the table and pursued his thoughts as if they were elusive lemmings getting out of the way of an oncoming moose. He had a stack of thoughts so big that if he had to number them he would run out of numbers.

A shadow fell across the table. 'Are you hanging round me?' She was grinning at him.

'Not so you'd notice.'

'No. It was a subtle ploy, sitting in the corner.' She took her long-strapped handbag from her shoulder. 'I'll see you in a bit.'

He continued to stare at the table. What is it with life? Every time you think you've got it taped something else crops up. Like perfume. He didn't mind perfume. Emily used nice perfume. Laura always had good perfume. Now Suzanne had it too. He could smell it in the air around his table. He'd always thought he had a crap sense of smell. Maybe his senses were refining.

What the hell. He just kept breathing it in.

After a time, a relatively short time, Suzanne appeared behind the bar. The tattooed guy disappeared; presumably to pursue his own dreams of getting more tattoos. Jackie wondered if people had tattooed dicks. He wondered which would be worse: the person doing it, or the person getting it. He wasn't sure it would work; what with the constantly changing shape and size. Of the dick. It might be better just to paint it. Dick paint. He should invent it.

Suzanne looked across to him and gestured with her head. Did he want another whisky? Jackie nodded. He got up from the table and took his last remaining glass of whisky over to the bar. He eased himself onto a stool. Suzanne gave him a whisky and didn't put it through the till. 'You look like you've got the weight of the world on your shoulders.'

'I'm all right. It's just tiredness and confusion. I think you call it 'middle-age man syndrome'. I've known other men that it happened to and they all wound up as sad lonely bastards. I'm hoping and planning that I'll be able to buck the trend. I think that's where the alcohol comes in.'

Suzanne nodded, and opened a bottle of tonic water for herself. 'You could always come round to my place.'

'No, I'd better not. It will probably get out of hand.'

'It might not.'

'Yes it will. We both know that.'

Suzanne shrugged; then stroked his hair.

'Why are you here then?'

She had him with that one.

CHAPTER SEVENTY-FOUR

Jason came again for another weekend. This time he wanted to go bowling. *Oh for chrissake.* 'Where can we go bowling?' said Jackie.

'At the bowling alley.'

Fuck.

'All right. Can't we go to the pictures?'

'What are we going to see?'

'I don't know. Some crap that you'll like. Ninja mutant monster shit. Whatever you want.'

'There's an Italian film I'd like to see.'

Oh for chrissake.

'Okay, fine. We'll see that. What time's it on?'

'It's not out yet.'

For God's sake.

'Do you want something to eat?'

'Pizza.'

Thank Christ for something normal.

CHAPTER SEVENTY-FIVE

He had a burst of activity on the synopsis for the one-eyed detective novel. He was writing so well he had the equivalent of anal orgasms. Eighteen pages in a day. If he wrote any faster his hand would explode.

This process was so exhilarating that the next day he went to the quayside cafeteria and sat outside under the mulberry tree. He didn't want to be distracted by the pressures of the bars.

He ordered cake and coffee and then went mad and ordered a sandwich. He was becoming very cosmopolitan.

Somehow he knew she was coming even before she arrived.

This time she was dressed more casually. Boots, jeans, a striped shirt, denim jacket. Her bag was smaller, but still had a long strap.

'You going shopping again?'

'Just passing by.'

Life really was out to screw things up. Nothing happened for years on end then all of a sudden, in the space of six days, it kicked and lurched itself into action. It was like a shire horse that had been fast asleep, then somebody rammed it up the arse.

'I'm just sitting here musing.'

'I can see,' she said. She swung the bag off her shoulder, and took the seat opposite him. 'You got your hip flask?'

'Does the Pope crap in the woods?'

He passed it across to her and she took a sip. Then she took another. She looked around. She had very good hair, he thought. Good hair and good bone structure. The sun was shining on her face.

'Are we doing something or not?' she said.

That truly was a conversation stopper. Not that there had been much conversation up to that point.

He took the second hip flask out of his other pocket, and sipped from that.

He remembered Laura saying to him: 'Don't screw up your life, Jackie.'

'You must have someone already,' he said. 'Boyfriend. Partner.'

Suzanne shrugged. 'Boyfriends. What are they worth?'

Never having had one, Jackie didn't know. But having known men, he suspected not much.

CHAPTER SEVENTY-SIX

'Are you screwing things up, Jackie?'

'What?'

He was sitting with Laura, at her home. She looked as pained as all hell. The colour of her face was somewhere between grey, funereal, and dead. 'I've heard rumours.'

'What rumours?'

'You're not going to the *Lion* any more. You've shifted pubs.'

'That doesn't mean anything.'

'Doesn't it?' Laura leaned forward to grab a handful of shrivelling grapes from the fruit basket that Jackie and Emily had taken round. She winced so much it made Jackie clench his teeth. 'Does Emily know?'

'Know what?'

'That you're seeing another woman.'

'I'm not seeing another woman! For crying out loud.'

'What's her name?'

'Suzanne.'

CHAPTER SEVENTY-SEVEN

He took a trip on the final river cruise of the year. Emily had clients to see. It was just him and his notebook and the breeze. And his hip flasks. A group of elderly ladies was sitting nearby, chattering like a flock of linnets.

A man in a white panama hat was standing at the bow, with an expression of such gravity on his face it was as if he'd recently run over the bishop. He had his hands in the pockets of his baggy stone-coloured chinos; with the elasticated waistband.

It was as hard as shit being human. Hard as shit being a man.

One of the elderly ladies next to him nudged Jackie's arm gently and offered him a tiny fruit tart from a Tupperware box. He took one with a smile and thanked her.

'It's lovely on the river isn't it?'

'It is,' he said.

'I've been doing this for fifty-three years, ever since – I can't remember what it was now. But the last trip of the year – I'm always here.'

'It is nice.'

The lady smiled, then turned away.

Jackie ate his fruit tart.

The river's banks flowed by. Still lush, green, heavy with foliage, dense with reeds. It was a green screen that shielded the world from the ecstatic serenity of the river. It was no wonder ducks and swans liked it. He could live on it himself.

At the halfway point of its journey the boat steered alongside the bank, moored itself up, and everybody piled off into the garden of the pub that Jackie had been to with Emily a few months earlier.

The pub itself probably closed down in the winter.

But as it was still open Jackie bought a pint of Owl's Excrement and a large glass of whisky and made his way back to the jetty.

He leaned on the wooden rail, the way he had with Emily. He stared into the water, the way he had with Emily.

The smell of Suzanne's perfume approached. The woman herself appeared and leaned on the wooden rail next to him. Close enough to touch. Terrifying enough to reach.

There was silence for a time.

The river flowed by. The chatter of people in the garden behind him began to appear: somehow that sound had become cut off in the moment.

He didn't even have a piece of bread to throw to the ducks.

'Do you want to come back with me in the car? Or do you want to get back on the boat?'

Jackie stared at the water.

Fish had it easy. Everything but men had it easy. Even the newts had it easy.

You couldn't make it up, he thought.

He sipped at his whisky. He sipped at his beer. He pondered the water, and didn't risk looking up.

'I've got whisky at my house.'

That may have been the clincher: he was never going to know. But he did return to Queensbridge in the car. He felt bad every turn of the way.

CHAPTER SEVENTY-EIGHT

What can you do? A man is a creature of nature and as prone to his own weaknesses as he is to his strengths. What separates men from the beasts is that they don't have to worry about it. Guilt is a forbidden word in the kingdom of animals.

Jesus Christ. That was the best sex he had had in years. Possibly in his whole life.

He lay naked on his back on Suzanne's bed, in the posture of a crucified apostle.

They didn't make sex like that any more. They didn't make sex like that in his day. What the hell was he going to do?

She came back into the room, wearing nakedness as if it was the only way to be. Her hair was dishevelled, and its redness tumbled past her face, down to her shoulders and almost down to her breasts.

She wasn't a young woman; her body lacked the firmness of youth. But every inch of her was a depiction of womanhood in all its curving sculptured self-referring glory. He could have looked at that image for a while. A hundred years maybe.

She sat on the edge of the bed and put a glass of Jack Daniel's and coke into his hand. She was drinking one herself.

'It's shit isn't it, having good sex?'

He laughed against himself. Yes, it was shit.

He struggled up into a sitting position.

She stroked the scar on his leg.

'What happened there?' she said.

'I fell over a car. I wasn't particularly drunk, as it happened I was just walking, and a car came along. A big car. It didn't stop in time and I did some kind of pirouette.'

'It looks painful,' she said.

'It was at the time. It's not so bad now.'

She bent over and kissed his belly, and her hair fell across it.

'That's for luck,' she said.

'Are you working this evening?'

'Yes,' she said. 'John's still away and I said I'd do some extra shifts.'

'Who's the guy with the tattoos?'

'That's his son Marcus. He's a nice lad. He's studying engineering.'

'I bet he's in awe of you.'

'Who wouldn't be?' She finished her drink and said, 'Do you want another?'

He nodded.

The second glasses, which seemed to be considerably more full than the first, were drunk more thoughtfully.

After a while Jackie said, 'My partner's pregnant.'

'I know. You've mentioned it before.'

'I have to – ' He paused to take a sip from his glass. 'I have to think about things.'

'I know,' she said. She stroked his leg. The one without the scarring. 'You have responsibilities.'

'Yes,' he said, so softly it was almost inaudible. 'I have a share of responsibility.'

He stayed on her bed, sipping at his whiskey.

After a time she took the glass from his hand and moved across him, sliding her body over his.

Responsibilities, he thought. *I have responsibilities.*

CHAPTER SEVENTY-NINE

Emily was tired. Lugging a five-month old child around inside her was exhausting. Sometimes she looked so tired he wished he could pick her up and carry her.

He'd never manage that now though.

'Would you like something to eat?' he said.

'What do we have?'

'Anything you want.'

She sprawled on the sofa and shoved her shoes off with her feet. She was going to need bigger shoes soon.

'Oof. I'm absolutely exhausted. I feel like I could sleep for a month. But this little boy inside me won't let me, he keeps kicking me.'

Jackie smoothed her brow and stroked her hair back.

'Maybe you could take some time off work; spend more time at home.'

'We're hardly rolling in money, Jackie.'

'No; I know.'

It was always money. Money seemed to dictate so much of life. You couldn't live for thinking about money. If he'd worked harder. Written more books. Written his current book. Written the next one.

'It will be fine,' he said, as he continued stroking her hair. 'We haven't come this far for nothing.'

'I know,' she said; and she held his hand. 'Team Conor-Marchant keeps going.'

Team Conor-Marchant. He liked the sound of that.

He went to the kitchen to fetch her a drink. Pomegranate and mandarin was the favoured drink of the moment.

He pulled out a salad that he'd prepared earlier, and took out some fish to microwave. Trout.

Was it trout? He wasn't sure now. He bent over to look more closely. Yeah, trout.

Fish was good. Always fish was good.

He started preparing it on a tray. He was doing it for Emily. For Emily and himself. Emily and himself. Suzanne didn't come into it at all. Suzanne wasn't there. Not in his mind; not in his heart.

He kept preparing the tray.

Suzanne wasn't there. He kept repeating that to himself as he continued preparing.

CHAPTER EIGHTY

She sat astride him after they'd both climaxed. Her hair was damp and sticking to her shoulders. Her body was slick with perspiration.

'That wasn't so bad for a man with a gammy leg,' she said.

I fucking excelled myself, he thought. *I didn't think I'd last the course.*

She brushed her hair back with both hands. If he didn't know better he'd think she was trying to look gorgeous.

It was probably working. It would have worked without it.

'Oof.' She wiped herself down with a small white hand towel that somehow just happened to be there. She wiped it across Jackie's chest and put it into his hand.

'What do you want to do now? Do you want some scrambled eggs?'

Fucking hell. He couldn't even move the towel. Did he have to swallow?

'Yeah, I guess.'

She climbed off him and walked, naked, into the kitchen.

She came back a minute later and put a glass of Jack Daniel's and coke in his hand.

It was 10.00 am.

CHAPTER EIGHTY-ONE

You can't have it all. You can't have everything. You can't be the one who betrays. You cannot live like this, he thought.

He contemplated feeling sorry for himself and concluding that he wasn't good enough for either of them: but things don't work that way; there was no get out of jail card. Every man is as good as his word and as bad as his thoughts. He couldn't get better and he couldn't get worse. He was what he was what he was.

Except I could get worse, he thought.

He could leave Emily, abandon his child, and set up a new life with Suzanne. A new start, somewhere else. She was thinking of moving to Colchester: something to do with her older sister.

Colchester was in Essex. He'd never been to Essex. He assumed it was all right. They'd have ducks there, too. Everywhere had ducks. Ducks, swans, herons, lizards. Guilt and sex and thought and betrayal.

I like lizards, he thought. Harmless, docile attractive little creatures. Quick on their feet and nimble in their minds. You'd have to be quick to live off flies.

Right on cue a fly landed on his hand and he idly waved it away.

How many new starts could you have in life? he wondered.

He was sitting in the garden restaurant at the quayside with his hip flask in his hand when she came up behind him and put her hands over his eyes.

'Guess who?' she said.

CHAPTER EIGHTY-TWO

Two weeks passed. Three weeks. He was upholding his life at home, and had submitted his synopsis for the one-eyed detective and his ever eager spaniel.

'Don't get too excited,' his agent had said. 'They're starting to have second thoughts about it. Not about you – about the whole concept.'

Bloody great, he thought. This is all I need.

'I'm in trouble, Mike.'

'I know. I've heard.'

Jesus Christ, did everybody know?

'Even Dawn doesn't like you.'

Jackie looked across the bar, to where Dawn was looking at him with eyes that suggested it was her heart he'd betrayed.

'I couldn't help it.'

'Everyone can help it. You're only human, Jackie; but you need to be more than that. You're going to be a father.'

'I know.' Jackie nodded.

'Is it the woman in *The Grapes*?'

'Yes. Suzanne.'

'She's a fine looking woman. You'd be a fool to say no. And an even bigger fool to say yes. Do you know what I'm saying?'

'I know what you're saying.'

'Drink your drink and go and apologise to Dawn.'

CHAPTER EIGHTY-THREE

Why the hell did he have to apologise to Dawn?

Because she loved him and he loved her. He couldn't let her down. Guilt in his home and guilt in his heart were things he could handle, but he couldn't see sorrow in Dawn's eyes. If ever you needed a conscience, Dawn was the one to deliver it to you.

'I can't do this any more,' he said.

'I know,' she said, as she peeled off her top, then pushed him back on the bed. 'Neither of us can.'

She eased herself astride him with a dexterity that belied her years.

'This whole relationship is going to hell in a handcart.'

Then she fucked the brains out of him.

CHAPTER EIGHTY-FOUR

Colchester, Queensbridge. Suzanne, Emily. A son and a grandson – or a whole new start. No burdens, no responsibilities. Shrug it off like a snake sloughs its skin and move in a new direction. It was very tempting. This entire growing up business was hard.

'I am going,' she said. This time he was on top and he was going at it as if this might be the last time in his life he ever saw a woman, let alone had sex with one.

'I know,' he said. 'We're both going; but I think in different directions.'

'Oof.' She arched her neck and raised her body against him. 'Right there – like that – right now. Keep going.'

I'm trying, he thought. *God, don't let me finish too soon.*

'Like that – like that.'

Even her lips had sweat on them.

I'm trying, he thought. *Maybe we should –*

Out of the blue she slapped him across the face and said, 'Keep going.'

Bloody hell. This sex was getting better and better.

'Keep going – keep going.'

And, like a miracle of evolution, he did.

Don't stop, Jackie – keep going.

Keep going. Keep going.

Never stop, Jackie.

Going is your only chance.

CHAPTER EIGHTY-FIVE

Emily was taken to hospital again, this time with a 'funny heart'.

He was growing sick of that hospital. If it wasn't Emily it was somebody else. Where did all this hospital stuff come from all of a sudden? Ever since he'd been hit by Emily's car he'd seen an awful lot of hospitals. Why couldn't he spend more time at the fair?

The fair. There was a fair coming soon to the big field north of town. They could take Jason to that. Hook-a-duck. He'd like to hook a duck.

He'd like to go to the fair with Suzanne. He'd like to go with Emily and Jason. He'd like to be a multitude of people: each one separate and distinct.

Even his agent. He'd take his agent to the fair: if he didn't hate her so much.

'Mister Conor?'

'Yes.'

'She's fine. It's related to what we'd already discussed earlier. She just got a bit panicky, which is perfectly understandable. We've given her some medication and she's calmed down a lot. This can all be handled by her GP.'

'Good. Great. Can we go home now?'

'Yes, of course. She'll be with you shortly.'

Don't call me Shorty, he thought.

He put his hands in his pockets and stared through the window one last time.

CHAPTER EIGHTY-SIX

So a couple of weeks later they went to the fair.

Jason was 'quietly' enjoying it, whilst pretending not to. He had his 'Jason Rocks' baseball cap on.

They did everything you are expected to do at a fair; except go on rides. Jason went on rides; but the grown-ups leaned against each other and watched.

At one point they ended up at a shooting booth, where you could win a teddy bear. Jackie was finally able to reveal his true prowess: the special skill that he'd been hoarding for years.

'This gun's fucking rubbish,' he said after a while.

'Ssh.' Emily nodded at Jason.

'Well it fucking is. Here – you have a go.'

He passed the rifle to Jason who promptly shot five ducks.

'Fucking rubbish.'

They moved on. Nobody had the energy to throw darts at cards or balls at coconuts; and there was no hook-a-duck outfit. Which Jackie thought was ridiculous. Eventually they ended up near a candy floss stall. Jackie did like candy floss, so he went to buy a couple. When he turned back, Emily was lying on the ground. Full length. Completely gone.

She had on loose pale-coloured trousers, and a stain was spreading into them; seeping. It was the colour of blood. Jason was standing next to her, watching.

Jackie stepped forward as fast as he had ever moved in his life and put his hand on the side of Jason's face and turned it away, so he wasn't watching.

The stain on Emily's trousers got bigger. It was spreading down both legs.

CHAPTER EIGHTY-SEVEN

This time it was serious. Serious enough that nobody had the time to tell him what was happening.

He stood in a waiting room, holding Jason's hand. Jason was shaking like a leaf in a gale. He was so scared he couldn't even cry. But he was gulping with convulsive spasms, like hiccups.

Eventually Jackie found the wit to call Robert. 'You'd better come and collect him,' he said. 'This isn't a place for him to be.'

Robert was there in an hour. He must have come by plane. Jackie was sitting in the waiting room still holding Jason's hand. The boy had started to cry at some point, and Jackie couldn't stop him. In the end he just let him get on with it.

There was no news to pass on.

They exchanged a few words, shook hands, and even shared a hug. Then Robert took Jason home.

Silence descended on the waiting room. Yet, just out of sight behind closed doors, all kinds of commotion was taking place. It was a commotion that Jackie couldn't begin to penetrate. He couldn't have intervened even if he'd wanted to. His was a quiet voice; a whisper in the heart of a storm. All he could do was stand by a window that he had hoped never to have to stand by again: thinking thoughts that he couldn't even think: he didn't know what was going on his head.

The evening progressed, with occasional nods and smiles from passing nursing staff. Then ultimately he was told to go home again. Emily was being monitored. The baby's heartbeat was still a concern. There may have to be an intervention; but that was still undecided at this point.

Basically: Jackie was in the way. There was nothing he could achieve by being there. He was, in effect, a superfluous entity standing in a room at a hospital.

At 11.00 pm he found himself in the street outside begging a cigarette from a passing stranger.

11 o'clock at night. What the hell was he supposed to do?

CHAPTER EIGHTY-EIGHT

'It will be all right,' she said softly, as she stroked his hair and smoothed his face. 'She'll be all right. They'll both be all right.'

It was the best sex they'd ever had. It was ferocious, furious, deranged and often brutal. They fucked like angry wolves. He thought at one point the neighbours were likely to knock on the wall. They fucked so hard that they crawled away from it bruised; barely able to even stand. It was never like that in his younger years. 'Every time might be the last': he'd heard that said somewhere.

His wife was in hospital and Jackie was having sex with a snarling woman. He wondered how much more shame he could inflict upon himself in one day.

Then came the calm. Soft in her arms; being stroked with a hand like a whisper.

'It will be all right,' she said. 'It will always be all right.'

She said it so gently he almost believed her.

CHAPTER EIGHTY-NINE

At 2.00 am his phone rang. He was needed back at the hospital.

He started running, but managed to stop a taxi; and was there within fifteen minutes. Hair dishevelled; clothes awry. Probably stinking of another woman's sex.

They were going to remove the baby. Emily had finally consented to the caesarean section. Everything was set up ready. Straight from the womb, into the incubator. Everything would be fine: they kept telling him that. Everything, everything, everything would be fine.

He was still nodding as they started wheeling her away. Everything would be fine. He knew that; he trusted them. He trusted everything. Everything in the end would turn out well.

He went with her as far as the doors to the theatre, and they held hands all the way. They said he could come in. But he hesitated at that point. Jackie was very squeamish: anything that involved blood, pain, suffering or screaming – particularly if it was someone he knew and loved – that wasn't going to work very well. He'd faint before he got through the door.

So everything proceeded without him.

And he didn't know what to do.

He was suddenly abandoned in the middle of a hospital in the middle of the night.

After a while he found something.

'Do you keep booze in here?'

He had wandered into a kind of office/workstation for doctors and nurses. Desks, filing cabinets, and a big fridge in the corner.

'I've heard you keep alcohol for some patients. Bottle of Scotch or something.'

The male nurse, who was seated at a desk poring over paper records, pushed his glasses up his nose and squinted at him.

'Who are you?'

'Emily Marchant's partner. She's in the theatre or whatever it's called. I'm just a bit tense.'

'Do you know how many rules I'd be breaking if I were to do that?' said the nurse.

'Just a drop.'

The nurse stared at him a little while longer.

'It's over there in the cupboard. I'm not looking and you're not here.'

'Thanks.'

CHAPTER NINETY

At 5.00 am Jackie saw him from a distance. Through a window. From afar.

His own son. His second son. The child of his heart and his soul.

He was so tiny. Jackie had seen bigger field mice. It seemed impossible that he was there. So small, but complete. And already fighting to keep himself going.

God, he was strong: Jackie could see that. There was a kid who wasn't going to give in.

God: look at him. Tiniest thing in the history of the world, but already making a fight of it.

God.

Jackie started crying. Once he started crying he couldn't stop.

What was his son's name?

He couldn't recall now. He was sure they'd picked one out, but he couldn't remember it. It probably started with a J.

'Mister Conor? You can go and see Emily now.'

He was shown into the acute care ward. Emily looked as drained as if she'd just given birth to the Titanic.

'He's good isn't he?' she said. Then she started crying. 'We did it Jackie. We did it.'

'You did it,' he said. 'You're the bravest woman I've ever known. I love you so much.'

He was frightened to touch her in case he hurt her. But they touched and laughed and smiled and cried as much as they could for the next two hours. Then a nurse told him he had to leave because Emily needed to rest.

He nodded and stood up and backed towards the door. Then he stopped and said – 'What's his name again?'

CHAPTER NINETY-ONE

Christian. His son was going to be called Christian. Christian Conor-Marchant.

That had a kind of ring to it.

He said that as they sat in the booth at *The Golden Lion*; Jackie, Mike and Dawn.

It was supposed to be a celebration; but Dawn kept glaring at him.

'Have you finished with that woman yet?'

'Yes,' he lied.

'You effin better. I'll kill her myself with my own two hands. Anyway – ' she raised her glass of champagne. 'Here's to Christian,' she said.

'To Christian,' they all said.

And they drank the champagne, and it was better.

Christian Conor-Marchant was here. He was in the world.

'Well done, Jackie!' someone shouted from across the room.

Jackie looked round.

Who the bloody hell was that?

Christian was slightly more than three pounds thirteen ounces of humanity.

CHAPTER NINETY-TWO

'They liked your synopsis and the sample chapters. But they're dropping the project. But they want you to write another book.'

'Okay.'

'A hardcore thriller. Straight down the middle. Possibly incorporating that missing body of yours. Do you think you can do that?'

'Of course,' he said. 'I can do anything.'

'You're not going to get too drunk again?'

'Absolutely not.' He shook his head in the direction of the phone. 'I've reached a new level of responsibility.' As he spoke he poured another Jack Daniel's into his glass. 'I'm completely on top of things.'

'Good, because you're going to need to be. Put something down, send it to me, and I'll start drawing up a contract agreement. Those bastards aren't getting something for nothing.'

'What bastards?'

'The publishers.'

'Oh right.'

'Don't let me down. Don't let yourself down. Be a fucking hero, Jackie.'

'Okay.'

'Oh. And congratulations on the baby. I knew there was something else.'

'Thank you.'

CHAPTER NINETY-THREE

An incubator unit was a scary thing to look at.

Everything about it appeared so clinical, clean, professional and practical. Except for the little parcel of life within it. Jackie's son. Jackie's son Christian. It was hard to stop looking at him. If he put the gloves on he was allowed to reach in and touch him. Touch his baby's hand. His leg. His foot. It was – it was –

Every time the baby reacted. He knew Jackie was there. He didn't know who he was, but he recognised him as one of the good guys. Even though he kept trying to kick him away. But he tried to kick everything away. He clearly was going to be a footballer. Or a ballet dancer. Or something to do with legs.

He was so strong.

Tiny, tiny; but Jackie could feel it in him. He was a strong kid. Jackie was going to have his work cut out on the football pitch. He'd fallen over three times playing with Emily. And she was pregnant at the time.

'You're a good kid,' he said; and he couldn't keep the tears away. So he went back to Emily.

Emily still hadn't seen her baby: she was still being cared for on another ward.

She'd heard him cry, though. As the incubator was being wheeled away, she'd heard her baby cry.

That was the hardest part of all.

Every time Jackie went to see the baby and came back to her, she had tears in her eyes.

'How is he doing?' she said.

'As usual, he's fucking brilliant,' he said. 'He's still an ugly kid, but I think he'll grow out of it. I've only just noticed that he's got my physique – strong and lithe and muscular. And he's got your eyes and nose and beautiful looks. So I think, between us, he'll be all right. Except he seems to have a problem with wind.'

'So he is you then.'

'Well yes. But obviously not as accomplished at it as I am. But every time I see him he's grown bigger. That milk you're giving him – whatever is in it – is like rocket fuel. Booster fluid.'

'I don't know how long it goes on,' she said. 'How long I keep producing it.'

'If it runs out I'll give him a shot of Jack.'

Emily tried to smile. It was a very weak affair.

'Why can't I see him?' she said. 'Why do they keep me away?'

Jackie didn't understand that himself.

When could she go and see him?

He could carry her there himself.

CHAPTER NINETY-FOUR

'So it looks like they're going to take something, anyway. Something, even if I don't have to write it yet. Some kind of book or idea or – anything really. I'd just like to get some money.'

'Uh-huh.'

She was riding him rhythmically, as gentle as a pussycat; her sweat was dripping onto his shoulders. He hadn't noticed before that she had faint freckles on her arms and chest.

'When's she coming out of hospital?'

'This afternoon.'

'You'd better get cleaned up then.'

She rammed her crutch into him, then hammered it a few times more. Good God, that hurt. He was going to have a bruise for a week.

CHAPTER NINETY-FIVE

Mike took him, then drove them both home. There was no reason Jackie couldn't drive; apart from the obvious. He had a car somewhere, locked in a garage. He thought it was a Citroen.

They were only home for two hours to get cleaned up, then they were going back to the hospital. For now, their life was going to be spent at a hospital. Taking turns, looking after, looking over their baby. Getting in the way of the nursing staff and hoping they still remained pleasant. Trying not to get too emotional and wanting to break open the incubator. Trying to contain their own fear and delight. Terrified that something might yet go wrong; so joyous that their son was there.

'We'd better hurry up,' she said.

'Yes, I know.' He dropped everything and they went outside to where a taxi was waiting.

CHAPTER NINETY-SIX

There were eight incubators in the unit. Five of them were occupied. There was a tremendous amount of activity: babies are not peaceful animals. They want attention; constantly. The smaller they are the more they want. Christian Conor-Marchant seemed the most demanding of all. Jackie thought – *we've had it when he discovers caffeine.*

All the time he moved, cried, shifted, changed – did something with his lungs or body. He always gave the impression that he wanted to be somewhere else. Swimming or dancing or fighting with a fox. There had been concerns about his swallowing; but that appeared to be resolved now, and his heartbeat was getting stronger. There was little wrong with their child; except he was tiny. And even that wasn't lasting long; he was getting bigger every day. A fighting, punching, wrestling individual.

Sometimes they took him out for a short time and held him, rocked him, cradled him and murmured to him. Sometimes they just looked at him; gazing down at him in his little Perspex world, with his tubes and drips and bandages.

There were chairs which extended into beds, so they could spend the night alongside the incubator; with nurses carefully stepping over and around them. There was a communal room for parents. They could watch TV, make toast, cook ridiculously cheap microwave meals. Clean up, tidy up, make small talk, make big talk. Talk about the ups and downs of their children. Their progress; their setbacks. It was becoming a second home.

Periodically they took time off. Mostly, that was Jackie. Emily would go home long enough to shower, change, look out fresh clothes, fly briefly about the apartment; then she was back at the incubator.

Jackie didn't have her stamina.

Love could not be quantified; but the energy which went into it could. Women had more energy. That's how it seemed to Jackie when he looked round at the other parents. The women had more energy. The men got more emotional. It was always Jackie who wanted to lie down. Maybe it was his age.

CHAPTER NINETY-SEVEN

He held him in his arms; tubes and drips and everything. He was so light he was almost ethereal.

He was trying to look at him; the baby. Christian's eyes were trying to open and focus – to see this strange creature, the monster who held him. The man who breathed on him and touched him and stroked him. The man who rocked him.

If Jackie could write and sell his book he could provide for this child for ever. It would have to be a good book of course; the book of his life.

People had done that before; they'd written the book of their life. They'd run the race of their life. You only had to do it once. Twice would be nice but once would suffice.

Write the book. Write the book. The missing body; the headless swan. Whatever it was.

Write the book, Jackie. You can do this.

The baby started crying. Jackie bent over him and kissed him with lips of gossamer.

CHAPTER NINETY-EIGHT

'Some guy keeps shouting at me and I don't know who he is. Do you know who he is?'

'He's a fan,' said Dawn, as she focused on pulling him the perfect pint of ale. 'But he's too shy to speak to you.'

He can't be that shy if he shouts across a room.

'Do you think I should talk to him? Have a chat?'

Dawn turned towards the whiskies. 'I shouldn't bother. I think he just likes shouting at you. How many of these do you want?'

'Four for now.'

'You're drinking too much.'

'I know,' he said. 'It's the pressure of fatherhood.' He took his glasses to his table.

He was very very tired. He wasn't just tired, he was totally knackered. And his body was bruised from having sex with Suzanne, who grew more and more brutal in her approach. Yesterday she'd wanted to flog him with a badminton racquet.

He wasn't sure he was quite up to that yet.

Laura was supposed to do pelvic floor exercises.

He should introduce her to Suzanne. She had thighs and a pelvis like an Amazonian princess on a battlefield. She could crush a coconut with her crotch.

His phone buzzed with a call from his agent.

'Have you started it yet?'

'I've been in a bloody hospital!'

'Well you'd better get on with it, they're already waiting. Time and tide, Jackie; time and tide.' There was a pause. 'You're not in a bar, are you?'

'No!'

Jesus. Give me a break.

CHAPTER NINETY-NINE

He was laying on his back in a grassy field, in the last of the summer's warmth. Jason was sitting next to him, stripping increasing layers of protection from a long stalk of grass. 'Is the baby going to be all right?' he said.

'He'll be fine, Jason. He's going to be your brother. Your half-brother. That makes him even more important.'

'Mm. How does that work?'

'Because you get a choice in it.' Jackie heaved himself upright and took out a hip flask. 'Do you want to go see him?'

Jason continued tugging at the grass. 'No. Yes. Will it be scary?'

'No. Your mum will be with you. Or I'll be with you. You'll never be left on your own.' Jackie took a long sip from the flask. Then another. They should put bigger openings in those things. 'You can touch him if you like. Introduce yourself. Meet your baby brother.'

'What does he look like?'

'Pretty ugly if I'm honest. But he's got your mother's better features. Hopefully there won't be a lot of me in him.'

Jason ripped the last shreds from the stem of grass, then reached for another.

'You're all right.'

'I know,' said Jackie. 'But I'm not that great.'

CHAPTER ONE HUNDRED

Suzanne wiped herself down with a towel. The towels were getting bigger and bigger.

'I'm going to look at a flat next week. In Colchester. Would you like to come with me?'

He already knew the answer.

He wasn't going to go.

She knew it too.

'If it wasn't for the kid, would you have come?'

That was a much harder question to answer. His thoughts were as fickle as a polecat in a hen coop. He didn't know which piece of chicken to go for next.

It wasn't even worth talking about it, because they were both grown up and they both knew all the answers.

'Fuck again tomorrow?' she said, as she threw the towel at him. He nodded. They'd fuck again tomorrow.

Maybe this was what his life was becoming. Go to the hospital and look at his son. Leave there, and fuck himself senseless with Raksha. And in the middle of it all was Emily: a woman he genuinely, sincerely and honestly did love. An innocent butterfly caught in the maelstrom of his lust. *Vic is a sick prick Mick.*

'What?'

'Nothing. I'm just thinking out loud.'

CHAPTER ONE HUNDRED AND ONE

He sat somewhat forlornly in his booth at the bar. 'I think it's over,' he said.

Mike nodded.

'With Suzanne. I don't think I'm good enough. To be honest, I don't think I'm good enough for either of them.'

'I could have told you that,' Mike said, as he continued to wipe the table clean with a damp cloth. 'I'm not sure you're good enough to drink in here.'

'Have we finished the malt?'

'I'm afraid we have. I've got something else, though. A special batch of Caribbean rum. A hundred and forty percent proof. I'll bring it over in a bit. I spilled some on the carpet earlier and it burned a hole right through it. I think some bloke makes it in his garage.'

'That should be all right then.' Jackie leaned back in his seat. Jesus Christ – what was going on in the street now? It looked like a bloody carnival. 'Are we having a carnival?'

'What? No.'

'Who are those fuckers then?'

'There's a food fair passing through. They might have brought some street entertainment.'

'Suffering Christ.' Jackie was in a good mood today. However. He was beginning to think that he actually could get on top of all this. He could find a way through it. All it required was focus and determination. Two qualities that he mistakenly believed he possessed. Focus and hard liquor seldom make good bedfellows. On the other hand they could co-exist, if one was patient and thoughtful and – he forgot what he was thinking about. Bloody hell.

He looked at his empty glasses. There really were too many of them on the table. Dawn was right. He should listen to Dawn. She'd learned a lot from her celebrity magazines.

CHAPTER ONE HUNDRED AND TWO

'Do you think I drink too much?'

Suzanne exhaled strongly; puffing her cheeks out. That had been a strenuous effort. 'In what sense?' she said.

'Well – alcohol terms. Do I drink too much alcohol?'

'Obviously. But it's your nature: the nature of your beast. If it doesn't kill you you'll probably be all right.'

Jackie nodded; then entered a pensive mode.

'On a scale of one to ten, what do you think are the chances of it actually killing me?'

'Twelve.'

He nodded again. He could live with that. Anything below thirteen was good.

'Are you working today?'

'Yeah.' She looked across the room, to a clock. 'I have to go in a minute. You'll have to let yourself out.'

'Okay. I'm going up to the hospital shortly. Take over from Emily.'

Suzanne pulled on an emerald green top and a pair of matching briefs. 'Don't go too drunk. You should listen.'

'To what?'

She looked round for her jeans. 'To the people telling you how much you're drinking.'

CHAPTER ONE HUNDRED AND THREE

'What the hell are you reading?'

'It's a celebrity magazine. Dawn loaned it to me.'

'Bloody hell.' Mike shook his head, then walked away.

The crossword was surprisingly difficult. He'd never heard of any of these people. Some of them didn't even sound like people: it was like a combination of the name of a goat and a city in China. Who the hell were they? How did they exist? Did they make a living out of being in crosswords?

God.

He pushed the magazine aside.

Laura entered the bar unexpectedly; looking terrible.

'Good God,' he said, 'are you all right?' He stood up and helped her onto her seat. 'You look awful.'

'Thanks.' She slid her bag off and lay it on the seat next to her. She looked exhausted. Her hair looked like it had been in a fight. 'Phoof.'

'Do you want anything to drink?'

'I'm supposed to avoid alcohol so I'll just have wine.'

Jackie went to the bar and returned with a glass and half a bottle of Chardonnay.

'It's very – very – ' she gave a gasp – 'uncomfortable. Remember when you had that nightmare about having a hot poker shoved up your ass? It's worse than that.' She struggled a bit, and readjusted herself on the seat. 'Where's the fucking wine?'

'You've got it in your hand.'

'Oh yeah.' She treated herself – after all her exertions – to a generous slurp. 'Has Luke been in touch with you about your baby?'

'No. he's turned into a right little sod for some reason.'

'He always was a right little sod. I never liked him much either. Why didn't we get a sensible child? A fucking chartered surveyor. Jesus. I'm ashamed to tell people. 'What does your son do for a living?' Oh he's a – er – in architecture. Architraves – he does a lot with architraves. Why did we fucking get him? A frog would be more interesting.'

'So,' said Jackie, as he toyed with his umpteenth glass of whisky and thought – *I've really got to stop this.* 'All that aside. How's it going with your pelvic ceiling reconstruction or whatever it is? Is it all over now?'

Laura threw back the glass of wine and poured another. 'Yeah. I've just got to get through this stage and then it's all over. I'm never going to do it again.' She rooted through her handbag. 'I need some painkillers. Haven't you got some? You used to take loads of painkillers.'

'I don't need them any more.'

'Lucky fucking you. Oh – here they are. Fucking rubbish. They don't work. I need more. It says 'Don't take more than eight a day.' Fuck off – I take eight an hour. I'll tell you what I need.'

'You're a bit – '

'Sweary.'

'Yeah. That would be a word.'

'Fuck 'em. They haven't had it done to them. And I'm bitter.'

'About what?'

Everything. I'm bitter about everything. I think it's my age.'

CHAPTER ONE HUNDRED AND FOUR

'The people at work want to have some kind of celebration for Christian's birth. I thought perhaps we could have it at *The Golden Lion*. Maybe your friend Mike could arrange it? His wedding celebration was nice.'

'Er – '

Jackie looked up from his notebook; in which he'd written exactly nothing.

'That would be good. I'd like to meet your friends. And I'm sure they'd be delighted to meet me – the drunken idiot you hang around with.'

Emily smiled. 'That's what I was thinking.'

So Jackie spoke to Mike. Mike spoke to the unpredictable chef in the kitchen. They decided to go for a buffet. It was the only option. A mixture of hot and cold.

The angry chef waved a finger under Mike's nose and demanded extra money. Mike said, 'Yes, yes. Whatever you want, you insane cunt.'

And it was set for a Thursday.

Jackie made an extra special effort. He washed his hair and everything. He found his best shirt: which was a blue and white striped one. He washed and ironed it. And he wore his best jeans. Which were stylish once, but might come back into fashion.

On the day itself, the Thursday, many people spilled through the doors of *The Golden Lion*; and they all looked very happy. Jackie had never seen so many happy people. If he'd hallucinated he wouldn't have seen so many happy people. He began to wonder if he was at the wrong party.

Obviously Christian, for reasons that everyone was aware of, could not be in attendance. But somehow, miraculously, without Jackie even noticing, Emily had taken a hundred and forty thousand pictures of him; and these were distributed randomly about the roped-off area of the bar.

Dawn nodded at them and said – well she didn't say anything, she just nodded at them.

'I know,' he said. 'That's my boy. That's my son.'

'I'm so pleased for you, Jack.' And Dawn kissed him on the cheek. 'You look after him. He's the best thing you've got. Even better than me.'

And she walked away.

'Hi – I'm Eloisa, Emily's line manager.'

A strange woman in a dumpy dress was thrusting her hand towards him.

'Oh yes. Emily's said a lot about you.'

Who the fuck?

'I'm so pleased that everything is working out well. We were so worried about her. It's a very stressful time.'

It's getting more stressful now, love.

'It is. But Emily's a strong woman. And Christian is a proper little fighter. You can see it every time you look at him. You can see it all the time: he gets stronger, he gets healthier. He's going to be a big kid.'

'I'm so pleased.' The strange woman gave him a big hug.

Fucking hell. He started looking round. Where the hell was the bloke with the Jack Daniel's? 'Hi. I'm one of Emily's colleagues. Janice? I don't know if she's ever mentioned me?'

'Yes – she mentions you a lot. She's er – how's it going with you, Janice? Is it all – '

'Yes, I'm getting over that,' she said. *What the fuck?* 'It was hard for a while, but – you have to go on, don't you?'

'You do.' Jackie said. 'Can I get you a drink of something?'

'Oh I'd better not, I'm driving.'

'You could get a taxi.'

'Oh all right. I'll have a gin.'

And thus, in a thuswise fashion, the evening progressed. People came and people left. More people lingered than left. Mike knew how to lay on a spread.

At eleven o'clock, when the evening was drawing to a close, Suzanne walked through the doors of *The Golden Lion*. Jackie turned to look at her. Dawn turned to look at her. Mike turned to look at her. They all stared at her. She walked across the room and ordered a drink from the temporary barman.

It was all good. Life was going nowhere.

CHAPTER ONE HUNDRED AND FIVE

They sat in a small bistro-restaurant in a small town outside of the small town they lived in. Suzanne looked as stunning as he'd ever seen her. Her hair was a waterfall in shades of red that was tumbling into a vermillion ocean. Her top was a deep shade of apricot – not a colour that Jackie would personally have picked for a woman. But it did suit her complexion. And her eyes. He wasn't sure that he'd ever really noticed them before, but they had a green quality that was – well: if you took mother of pearl and scraped the green out of it, that's what it would look like. With added sparkle.

He tried not to look at them. It wouldn't do him any good.

He was eating mussels from just along the coast. Something called samphire, that he thought he'd once been forced to eat before; but wasn't as bad as it sounded. And beetroot. Who the hell likes beetroot? There was white wine on the table; but Jackie never trusted anything that was pale in colour. He was drinking Jack and coke. Quite a lot of it.

'We make a good team, Jackie. We're a good pair.' Jackie nodded. He couldn't deny that. 'We get on well together. We like each other. We like each other's company. And we're very compatible. Physically.' Jackie nodded again. He couldn't deny that either. If she didn't beat him to death during one of her increasingly frenzied assaults on him they would probably have a wonderful life together. Maybe that ferocious pattern was part of it; because they both knew this was a limited affair.

He sighed as he looked away, then sipped at his Jack and coke. The temptation to walk away and start again was always there. For everybody. At any point in their life. Such a long way to see. And so little you could do with it.

'We can have a good life, Jackie. We can start again. A fresh start. We're still young enough. We can have a good life.' Jackie toyed with his mussels and shoved them around the samphire. 'You can still see your son.'

They could have a hell of a life; he was sure of that.

But there were problems now.

'I have obligations,' he said. 'Mental obligations. Moral obligations. Obligations to me and – other people. I can't fuck it up again, Suzanne. I've fucked it up too many times.'

He sighed again; drained his glass of Jack and coke and signalled to a waitress to bring another.

Suzanne nodded, and sipped at her glass of wine. She too stared into the distance.

'When do you want to end it then?'

He didn't know; because he didn't want to end it.

'The last possible moment,' he said. 'An instant before the beginning of the end of the possible final moment.'

She nodded again, and sipped her wine. 'So we'll keep going,' she said.

CHAPTER ONE HUNDRED AND SIX

He walked into the bar the day after his lunch with Suzanne. Dawn was just finishing off with another customer. As soon as she could she got to him. 'Are we all good?' she said. 'Is everything cool?'

'Yes.'

'There's no dooby anywhere?' Jackie frowned at her.

'What?'

'You know. Dooby. Deep dooby.'

'It's called shit, Dawn. And no there's no dooby. It's not called dooby anyway – it's doody. Deep doody.' Dawn finished pulling his pint.

'You seem a bit tense,' she said.

'It's the whole dooby conversation; it's doing my head in. Where's Mike, anyway?'

'Last I heard he was in the kitchen having a fight with the chef. I think he actually hit him.'

'Who? Mike?'

'No, the chef. I think he hit him with a pan. How many of these do you want?' She stood in front of the optics with a glass in her hand.

'I'm changing my drinks. I'm going with Jack Daniel's now.'

'Aren't you the fancy one? You'll be eating pretzels next.'

He carried his drinks to his booth.

Someone else had been there and there were crumbs.

God. He couldn't live like this.

He went back to the bar and borrowed a cloth from Dawn. *People just don't care any more.*

Once he'd finished wiping, dusting, flicking and waving, he was able to sit down with his glasses.

It was getting hard just to drink in a pub these days. You had to do your own cleaning up.

After a minute a grim realisation crept up on him. Who the hell was he going to talk to? Dawn was busy. Mike was being beaten up in the kitchen. There was no one – as far as he could see – outside the window, who could be of any remote interest.

He didn't want to sit there with his own thoughts. That never worked out well for anyone.

Eventually Mike appeared at the bar, wandered across, and sat down opposite him.

'Fucking hell,' said Jackie. 'What happened to you?'

'It was an incident.'

'Did you bring that rum with you?'

'Jesus Christ.' Mike put his hands flat on the table and said, 'I've just been beaten up with a saucepan and you're asking me about the high-level knock-off rum?'

'I thought it might take your mind off it.'

'Fucking hell.'

Mike waved across the bar to Dawn.

'Bring the scary rum.'

CHAPTER ONE HUNDRED AND SEVEN

Two days later Jackie was back in the bar with Laura.

'What happened to Mike?' she said. 'He's got a big bruise on his face.'

'The chef hit him with a pan.'

Laura looked horrified, concerned, alarmed and sympathetic all in one expression.

'God. What did Mike do?'

'I haven't got the full story yet. But as far as I can gather from what Dawn told me, Mike fell over, then got up, and tried to strangle the chef.'

'God.' Laura was still horrified and bemused. 'Did he sack him?'

'No, he's quite a good cook. They're not easy to find. How's it going with you? How's your discomfiture?'

'Pff.' Laura waved a hand in the air, and Dawn and Mike immediately looked up. 'It's getting better, you know. It's not as bad.'

She looked down at the table. There weren't even any glasses on it yet. What the hell was the staff doing? It was all going to pot these days.

'I have something to ask you. And it may sound a bit weird. But I wondered if I could come and see Christian.'

'Er – '

'Not to touch him or anything. Just to look at him. See a little baby. Look at him and see all that life. You don't get many chances, you know? Not when you get older. I just wondered.'

Jackie nodded.

'I'll have a word with Emily.'

Laura waved her hand in the air again; and this time Dawn came sprinting across with a glass of white wine and a Jack Daniel's for his highness.

'I'm sorry, Laura,' she said.

'It's all right babe. I'm just having an – 'older woman' thing, you know?'

Dawn nodded earnestly. 'Yeah. My mum gets that.'

'You've only brought one Jack Daniel's.'

'For eff's sake, Jack. Give me a chance.'

CHAPTER ONE HUNDRED AND EIGHT

It was a strange thing to see in some ways, for Jackie, who was still struggling to sober up.

Emily and Laura had shared a long embrace and were now standing side by side, holding hands and looking at Christian who was pretty much doing nothing at all. Even by Christian's standards.

Jackie thought maybe he needed more to drink, and started looking round for an exit. He began patting his pockets, looking for his hip flasks. Oh – he already had one in his hand. That was good.

He sat down in a comfy chair. It was good that the NHS didn't waste all its money. If they put a cocktail bar in it would be brilliant. This was the day Jason was coming in. Emily was doing Laura, Jackie was doing Jason. Perfect distribution of labour. Thank God he was sober.

He came in at two o'clock. Robert brought him. Robert went in, briefly, to have a look at the baby. Then he went away. It was all down to Jackie now. He and Jason stood side by side, holding hands, looking at Christian. A long time passed in silence.

It was Jason who broke it first. 'He's not – he's not – '

'No he's not,' said Jackie. 'But he'll start to get better. His looks will improve. He'll get handsome like you. He might get more handsome than you. He might take after me.'

Jason snorted softly. 'Is that a joke?'

'Sort of.'

After another pause Jason said, 'I suppose he's all right. In an interesting way.'

Then he turned away.

'Where's mum?'

CHAPTER ONE HUNDRED AND NINE

Suzanne punched him in the face. Straight out; just punched him in the face. 'Will you stop fucking doing that? Jesus.' Jackie rubbed his jaw.

'Am I the best sex you've ever had?'

'Like I'm going to say no. You'd probably kill me with a meat cleaver.'

'Seriously though, Jackie.' Suzanne paused and rested with her hands on his chest. Sweat was streaming off her like it was a wet day in the rain forest. 'Why don't you come with me? Seriously. I know we've been through this before but this is it now. Last chance. I'm walking out of that door tomorrow with my bags.' Jackie turned his head away and stared at the wall. They knew the answer. Everyone in the world knew the answer. 'It's a one way street, Jackie.'

'I know.' She slapped him again. Lightly.

'Look at me,' she said. He turned his face to look at her. 'Tell me you don't love me.'

'I can't tell you – '

She slapped him again. 'Tell me.' She looked down at him with her eyes of iridescent green. They looked through him, into him, into his soul, into his heart, into his body, every area of his body, every corpuscle, every muscle, every sinew, every twitch, every thought and reflex that he hadn't even thought about possibly producing yet. 'Tell me.'

Jackie stared at her for a long time. This was one of those moments: a moment in his life: one of those moments that define everything: his past, his present, his future. Everything that he represented. His honesty, his judgement, his trust, the trust that he was offering. Everything was in there.

'I don't love you,' he said.

CHAPTER ONE HUNDRED AND TEN

Dawn and Mike had a falling out. 'Don't fucking look at me!' he said.

'Don't fucking look at me!' she said. It wasn't clear what they were arguing about.

Jackie wandered into the middle of it.

'Can I have a – '

'Fuck off.'

That seemed to come out of both of them at the same time.

'Right.'

Jackie wandered away. Fortunately he'd brought his hip flasks.

CHAPTER ONE HUNDRED AND ELEVEN

'Mike said he's going to give me the bar.'

Jackie nodded.

'How's that going to work out with your plans for moving to Jersey?'

'I'll tell him to eff off.'

'Who? Mike?'

'No, the lad in Jersey. It's too windy there anyway: the smell of the sea gets right up my nose. I don't want to live in the English Channel, they have submarines and everything going up and down. Apparently they were invaded by Germans in the world war. Bunch of cowards. I think they're half French; that probably accounts for it.'

Jackie simply stood watching her, with his mouth half open. He should be writing this down.

'Besides. I love it round here, Jack; I really do. I love living round here. Even with my mum. And my cousin Polly. Have you met her? God – ' Dawn rolled her eyes. 'She comes in at night sometimes with some shifty-looking type on her arm. You can't miss her, she looks like a goldfish. Too much fake tan. The last guy she had bred pigeons. 148 of them. I think that's how many he had. In a loft over Crompton way. Some of them are worth a lot of money. Effin pigeons, effin budgies. This town's going crazy. Never mind you and your swan.'

'Have you been taking something, Dawn?'

'Hey? What?' Dawn kept pouring drinks out somewhat randomly. It wasn't even clear who they were for. 'No it's just this bar business. Giving me the bar. It's got me a bit emotional, you know? He's a lovely man, isn't he, Jack? A lovely man.'

'He is.'

'I'm not giving you free drinks, though. You'd put me out of business in a week.'

Jackie took his glasses to his table. There were rather a lot of them today. He wasn't even sure what some of them were.

Laura came into his booth. She was looking slightly better; her hair appeared to have recovered from its fight with itself and was lying neatly on her head. Her face was a normal colour. Apart from her overuse of blusher.

She gestured at the table.

'What the hell's all this?'

'I don't know. Dawn kept pouring them, I kept collecting them. I think I'm going to have to remortgage the apartment.'

Laura frowned, then stared at the glasses for a long time. She took a pair of glasses of her own out of her bag.

'What's that one?'

'Dawn said it's an English version of a pina colada. Basically it's a pineapple chunk in a glass of vodka. If you pay extra you can have a cherry.'

Laura passed on the pina colada. She picked up another glass and said, 'What's this?'

'That's er – God knows. What does it smell like?'

Laura took a cautious sniff.

'Urine.'

'That might be Mike's sample. He's got a bladder infection.'

CHAPTER ONE HUNDRED AND TWELVE

The five of them sat in Jackie's booth in the bar. Emily, Laura, Mike, Dawn and Jackie. They were chewing the fat; arguing, debating, discussing and discoursing.

Periodically Dawn got up to serve a customer. But it was a quiet period of the day: there wasn't much going on.

They spent a long time discussing the 'living statue' who had taken the place of the balloon seller at the bottom of the High Street. The general consensus was that he was a prat; and one day Jackie was going to tell him that as he walked past, muttering. He might even throw an ice cream at him.

Emily was going to bring the baby home from the hospital tomorrow.

Life was good.

Everything was good.

Even for the drunks.

The last thing anyone outside would have heard was Jackie saying – 'I didn't fucking do it! Fuck off.'

And the sound of glasses being clinked.

Parts of this novel would not have been written as they are without the generous advice support and encouragement of Dr Bobby Barthakur.
Any errors in the medical treatments and procedures described are entirely the responsibility of the author.

Printed in Great Britain
by Amazon

37363172R00165